A COPPER-SKINNED MONSTER WAS RISING FROM THE GRASS...

The Indian raised a hand from which dripped something like water—it was the gleam of a long, curved hunting knife, at the center of the Indian's body.

Tanner let go with a shot. The Pawnee swerved to the side with a short, deep grunt, and then, recovering, bounded straight in.

Johnnie Tanner could see the contempt and rage in the glance with which the Indian measured him. He could see the frightful power of the naked, bulky arm, as it raised the knife a little higher, preparatory to springing in and finishing the fight with a single stroke.

That instant, Johnnie leaped, drove straight under the impending arm, and struck hard, upward, into the body of the man. At the same time a powerful blow flattened him to the ground. . . .

Books by Max Brand

Ambush at Torture Canyon
The Bandit of the Black Hills
The Bells of San Filipo
Black Jack
Blood on the Trail
The Blue Jay
The Border Kid
Danger Trail
Dead or Alive
Destry Rides Again
The False Rider
Fightin' Fool
Fightin' Four
Flaming Irons
Ghost Rider (Original title: Clung)
The Gun Tamer
Gunman's Reckoning
Harrigan
Hired Guns
Hunted Riders
The Jackson Trail
Larromee's Ranch
The Longhorn Feud
The Longhorn's Ranch
The Long, Long Trail
The Man from Mustang
On the Trail of Four

The Outlaw of Buffalo Flat
The Phantom Spy
Pillar Mountain
Pleasant Jim
The Reward
Ride the Wild Trail
Riders of the Plains
Rippon Rides Double
Rustlers of Beacon Creek
The Seven of Diamonds
Seven Trails
Shotgun Law
Silvertip's Search
Silvertip's Trap
Singing Guns
Steve Train's Ordeal
The Stingaree
The Stolen Stallion
The Streak
The Tenderfoot
Thunder Moon
Tragedy Trail
Trouble Kid
The Untamed
Valley of the Vanishing Men
Valley of Thieves
Vengeance Trail

Published by POCKET BOOKS

Max Brand

VENGEANCE TRAIL

PUBLISHED BY POCKET BOOKS NEW YORK

**POCKET BOOKS, a Simon & Schuster division of
GULF & WESTERN CORPORATION**
1230 Avenue of the Americas, New York, N.Y. 10020

ISBN: 0-671-83034-1

First Pocket Books printing January, 1954

10   9   8   7   6   5

Trademarks registered in the United States and other countries.

Printed in the U.S.A.

CONTENTS

1 A BOY'S DREAM 7

2 TANNER'S STORY 12

3 THE FENCE TALKER 16

4 THE INDIAN AUTHORITY 21

5 THE STOLEN PEARL 26

6 THE CHASE 31

7 NIGHTS OF TORTURE 36

8 KIND FOLKS 41

9 FOOD AND SLEEP 46

10 MORE WILD TALES 50

11 A FAREWELL 56

12 DOWN THE OHIO 61

13 THE CARD GAME 66

14 THE FIGHT 71

15 THE GENEROUS HUNTER 77

16 THE THREE PAWNEES 82

17 MORE HISTORY 87

18 THE THIEF AGAIN 92

19 JOHNNIE WRITES HOME 97

20 A RIDING LESSON 102

21 MIDNIGHT 107

22 BUFFALO 112

23 THE CHEYENNE 117

24 INDIAN GULLET 122

25 BROKEN KNIFE'S STORY 127

26 JOHNNIE FIGHTS ALONE 133

27 SPOILS TO THE VICTOR 138

28 THE WET SCALP 143

29 ON WITH THE DANCE 147

30 THE BLACKBIRD 155

31 THE HUNT 158

32 THE WHITE BUFFALO 163

33 STRIKING EAGLE 168

34 RANEY PHILOSOPHIZES 173

35 THE PAPOOSE 178

36 BIG CHIEF JOHNNIE 186

37 THE WONDER BOY 194

38 TO THE RESCUE 199

39 IN PAWNEE CAMP 203

40 HARRY, THE PAWNEE 207

41 UPSET 212

42 THE LOST PEARL 216

43 GOING HOME 221

1 · A BOY'S DREAM

JOHN had reached the princely age. He was fourteen.
Ordinarily, at this age, a boy has most of the powers of a
man and none of the responsibilities. But John Tanner
had had the responsibilities for several years. Since he
was eight, in fact, he had chopped kindling, washed and
dried dishes, helped with the laundry on Mondays,
scrubbed floors and windows. His aunt kept body and
soul together by running a boarding house and, if it had
not been for the help which she received from young
John, she would have had to employ an experienced
servant.

She used to make a point of telling him that he amply
earned his board and lodging and his schooling. He
took a stern pride in this knowledge, and the work made
him a little grimmer about the mouth and a little steadier
in the eyes than are most boys of that age. Only on Sunday afternoons and for a few hours on holidays could he
get out into the back yard and play Indian.

That was the passion of his heart. For in those days
stories of encounters with the plains Indians were coming
in from the West. Buffalo robes and beaver poured in
from the distant wilderness of the green, treeless sea. And
once, parading through the streets of New York to adver-
tise a show in which they appeared, he had seen four
plains Indians, garbed and painted as for war.

An indecent exhibition, Aunt Maggie had called it. But
it gave to the imagination of the boy the wings which
were sufficient to carry him into the land of his fondest
dreams, not only when he lay awake staring at the darkness of the night, but also during every still moment of
the day. If he paused in his dish-washing, if he leaned
for a moment on the handle of the spade with which
he dug up the soil of the back yard to make the truck
garden, in that instant there streamed inward upon his
soul a picture of the stretching plains, the dark and thundering buffalo herds and the wild red riders which raced
upon the stampeding flanks of the bison.

He thought of that far country not with an active hope,

but as a child might dream his way into the fairyland of the "Arabian Nights." Nevertheless, it was in his brain and in his blood.

The back yard of the house was deep. It stretched straight through the block, occupying the vacant lot on the next street. That would be built upon, one day, but now it was a tangle of shrubbery and young trees, and it made for John Tanner a very good imitation wilderness in which he pursued his games. A high board fence gave him reasonable security against observation on any side, except for the upper windows of the neighboring houses, and these were mostly shuttered during the greater part of his play-day.

His outfit was very simple. It consisted of a very old pair of overalls, which he himself had cut tight, so that his leg was fitted as with deerskin leggings, a pair of heavy socks with a leather sole sewed on, in lieu of moccasins, and a headdress made of some good-sized chicken feathers, stained yellow, red and purple, with ink. He had for weapons a bow and a number of home-fashioned arrows, constructed with infinite patience, a worn-out, dull hatchet for a tomahawk, a hickory joint and branch as the knobby war club and, above all, a discarded butcher knife, half of the blade of which had been broken away.

What remained, he had turned to a point on the grindstone and made it as keen as a razor. Since it was the best sort of Sheffield steel, it was a real weapon, and the heart of John Tanner used to leap when he so much as thought about it.

He spent a great part of his time with the knife, practicing throws, and growing in the course of years so expert that at twenty feet he could sink it almost without fail into a sapling not a span broad.

Of course, he delighted in his skill. He dared to tell himself that in accomplishing this feat, he proved himself to be a real plainsman or a mountain man.

As has been said, there was not a great deal of time for these sports, but he did trailing, imaginary and otherwise, in that vacant lot. He aimed his wooden rifle many a time and hurled his keen knife a thousand thousand times into the heart of brutal enemies. He took imaginary scalps, backed imaginary wild stallions, and conquered in a hundred wars.

Furthermore, and perhaps best of all, sometimes he would rest a moment during his play and then, perhaps, small sights and sounds of true wild life would come to him, and always out of the air. There would be the whir of wings and the whistle of birds, with the full song of the springtime. He used to go out and stalk the singer with such pains and secrecy, it might have been thought that he was striving to come at not only the singer but the joyousness of the song itself.

So for six years he had lived with Aunt Maggie. Then his father came home and all was changed.

He had not heard very much about his father. He only knew that his mother had died shortly after his birth and that when his father was mentioned a hard, bitter look appeared upon Aunt Maggie's face.

Then home came Gilbert Tanner from the East, where he had been traveler, adventurer, trader, during those ten years. He had sent home money now and again, but never very much, so that his appearance amazed both Aunt Maggie and the boy.

In looks he resembled his son. He was of middle height, strongly and yet actively made, with a good, gray-green eye and tawny hair. But he had been burned a sort of sallow brown in the Orient. And the marks of suffering were in his face.

It was not in his person, however, that he astonished the two at home. It was in his wealth!

He was dressed, in the first place, quietly, but like a gentleman of means. He carried a stick, and the manner in which he used it turned the cane almost into a scepter. His neck scarf, which fitted well up under his chin, seemed to add to the haughtiness of his manner.

He had six large trunks! They filled the whole attic of the boarding house. They crammed it from end to end, together with certain carryalls and numbers of bags which were also parts of his luggage.

He came in the evening. And they sat up till midnight.

"Maggie," he said to John's aunt, "you'll send your boarders away as soon as possible. Pay them back everything they've advanced for this month, and get them out. Then we'll furbish up the old house a bit. The hull seems to be sound, but the cabins ought to be rebuilt, I'd say, and the top-hamper should be replaced, too."

"Gilbert," said she, sitting up with her work-reddened hands gripped hard together in her lap, "will you tell me what it means? Are you rich, Gilbert?"

He looked thoughtfully at her, with the eye of one who computes.

"Yes," he said, "I'm rich. I think I can say that, as money goes in the world. There's to be no more work for you, my dear. You've done your share of it, both on your own account and for my boy."

"He's been no care. He's been a joy and a profit to me," said Aunt Maggie, with tears in her eyes.

Gilbert raised his hand and overawed her to silence. "I want you to try to forget these years," said he. "I'm going to try to give you happiness that will enable you to forget them. For my part, I shall always remember."

He turned to his son.

"You'll learn to forgive me, John," said he.

John Tanner turned crimson. It had never occurred to him that he had a right to make demands upon his father. He never would have dreamed of accusing him of anything whatever. So now he could only blush with violence and look miserably down to the floor.

But, the very next day, he had the first glimpse of heaven. He was taken downtown, he was clad from head to foot in the best of clothes.

"This stuff will do until the tailor can turn you out," said his father. "Now, you tell me what you're most interested in."

"Indians," said the boy, and then blushed once more, after he had blurted out the word.

His father looked sharply askance at him with an eye suddenly cold, keen, critical.

Then he said: "Well, you mean the redskins, by that, eh?"

"Yes," said John.

"You want to take scalps, I suppose, and have a herd of ponies?"

John looked at him wistfully. A boy's confidence may be won, but it cannot be forced.

"I used to want to do the same thing," said the father.

"You know," said John, "I just think about it a little."

"It's the shortest way through the winter evenings," rejoined Gilbert Tanner. "I suppose that you have a rifle, my boy?"

"Oh, no! Of course not."

"Never shot one?"

"Yes, quite a lot. Aunt Maggie gives me a little money for birthdays and Christmas, now and then. And I go down to the ranges and shoot at the targets."

"You like that?"

"More than anything, mostly."

"You shall have rifles," said the father. "Horses, too. Depend on that! Rifles, pistols, horses, and everything that you want. You might make a list. You're going to start a new life, Johnnie."

That new life began that very day; they returned to the house with a pair of small-caliber rifles and a pair of light pistols.

"They're for you to start with," said Gilbert Tanner. "Afterwards, you'll have something better."

Better? It was a paradise that the boy saw laid before his eyes upon the bed of his room, a shining metal paradise. He stroked those weapons. He loved them. And Gilbert Tanner looked on with a somewhat grim smile.

That evening, after dinner, Aunt Maggie went to bed with a headache. So much happiness had upset her terribly. She trembled, and laughed, giggled and almost cried through the whole course of the day.

And John Tanner sat on the edge of a chair and watched his father on the other side of the living room. His father was erect, not from nervous excitement, but as a cavalryman is erect, or one accustomed to wear an air of authority in the presence of other men. Those bright, gray-green eyes of his were rather hard for John Tanner to meet, but he managed the job, smiling a little from time to time. He wanted to find words to express his gratitude for that flood of presents, which was enough, as he felt, to crowd an entire life full of joy. But the words would not come. Something filled his throat.

"Rifles or pistols, which do you like the best?" asked the father.

"Pistols," said the boy, instantly.

His father raised his brows a trifle.

"I suppose I'm wrong," said the boy, penitently.

"Well," said Gilbert Tanner, "pistols are very good

things—if you're boarding a pirate junk, say; or holding up some wealthy fellow in the dark of the highroad. Pistols are very good for that, of course."

His smile was a mere shadow of mirth.

"Otherwise," he said, "I should think that a rifle would be a good deal more useful."

"I don't know much about it," said John. "But you know, if you had to charge through a lot of Indians, then a pair of pistols would be—"

He stopped himself, clapping his hand over his mouth, his eyes round and staring. He felt that he had made a fool of himself. But his father merely nodded.

"I understand, perfectly," said he. "The pistol's the thing for work at short range. But it's not equal to something else."

"To what?" asked the boy.

"To this," said his father.

And, from somewhere about his clothes, he produced what looked like a pistol, except that about the root of the barrel there was a heavy steel cylinder.

"This little Yankee trick will shoot six times without reloading. There's six dead Indians for you, John. Six of 'em dead all in a second or so. How's that?"

2 · TANNER'S STORY

JOHN was stunned with admiration. He could see that all of his favorite dreams would have to be refurnished, immediately, with new linings. Then he looked up suspiciously into the face of his father.

"You're not joking, father?" said he.

"Of course, I'm not," said the father. "I haven't cracked thirteen jokes in the last thirteen years. You see how the thing works? Samuel Colt is the inventor. And I suppose that he'll change the history of the world somewhat with this bit of a trick of his. This is the way it goes together."

He laid it out on the table. It seemed to fairly fall apart in his hands.

"You know it by heart!" cried the boy, in admiration.

"Well, Johnnie," said his father, "no man knows the thing that he can't make. And certainly no man knows what he can't put together. You'll learn this in a little while."

He explained with care; the attentive eyes of the boy drank in every detail.

"Six shots!" said he, and shook his head again.

Why, by such a shower of bullets, a whole crowd could be split and scattered. A whole crowd of charging, yelling, raving Indians, eager to rush in after the first shot was fired, amazed, confounded by the bullets that followed— how they would break to either side and scamper away from the miracle gun!

"Will they have them, now, out West?" he asked.

"Here and there, perhaps. I don't think in many places. Though I got this from a Yankee skipper in the South Seas!"

He chuckled softly as he spoke.

The boy, bright of eye, looked the question which he did not ask.

"No," said Gilbert Tanner. "I didn't buy it. Not a bit!"

"What could you have done for it?" said John.

His father stared straight at him. And again it was hard, as always, to meet the steady glance of those keen, gray-green eyes.

But he managed to endure the weight of them, the keen probe also, that seemed to reach to the very back of his brain.

"Now, then Johnnie," said he, "I think that you're man enough to keep secrets."

The eyes of John shone.

"You bet I am, sir!" said he.

"The skipper I took that gun from was a rival of mine," said the father.

"A business rival, sir?" queried John.

His father looked at the farthest corner of the ceiling.

"Yes, in a way. You could call him a business rival," said he. "And it was like this, John. I can't explain all of it to you. But some day I shall."

He paused, and added earnestly: "Some day, I want you to know the history of every day of my life. There were some black days in the list, some mighty black ones.

But now I'll tell you this in brief, because it was my red-letter day, and enabled me to come home again."

"Then it was the greatest day that ever happened for me!" said John, with emotion.

"It will be," said his father. "The time may come when you'll feel the benefits of it more than you do now. But, at any rate, you've a right to know about that day, since it brought me home and gave me this gun that you like so well."

John sat up farther on the edge of the chair. His eyes were stars.

"The main thing for you to understand," said Gilbert Tanner, "is that I had a smallish ship and this rival of mine, this other skipper, had a goodish big ship. And I had a small, handy crew, and he had a big gang aboard. Another thing. The cargo I had aboard, he wanted. He thought that he had a right to it. And, in a way, he did. And the cargo that he had aboard, I thought I had a right to. And, in a way, I did."

"I don't quite understand that," said John Tanner, biting his lip in anxious attention and perplexity.

"Some day I'll be able to go more deeply into it," said his father, with that same faint, ghostly smile.

"Thank you, sir," said the boy.

"Now, then, when I made out that craft of his, shouldering through the sea fog, I put about and ran straight before the wind. With the wind free, I logged very well; but when I looked astern I could see that the other fellow was logging still better. His bigger spread of canvas was helping him, and the air was very light."

He paused, considering.

"And then?" cried the boy.

"Then I saw that I couldn't get away. So I decided to make a fight of it. I saw by a flaw on the sea what I thought was a change of the wind, and I had my men stand by, ready to take advantage of it. The other chap was shooting over us by that time, giving us orders, by word of cannon, as you might say, to heave to.

"But just then the change of the wind came, and we were about with our little craft in no time and shot back alongside him. It took his breath, you might say. He was so much bigger that he expected to swallow us whole, without an effort. Or, you might say, he was so much

14

bigger that he didn't expect us to show any teeth at all. He expected to run us down and stamp us into the sea, like an elephant stamping down a cane thicket."

"But he didn't catch you!" cried the boy, striking his hands together in a fury of interest.

"Oh, he caught us all right. Or, rather, we caught him. For as we slipped along his port bow, we threw grapplings aboard, and all in a moment we were fast to him. My lads were ready, and his weren't. My boys went up the big wall of that trader like so many cats, and they dropped down into his decks with cutlasses already swinging, with pistols cracking, and those infernal Malay knives—I'll show you some samples later on—swinging and darting in and out."

"You beat them!" cried John Tanner.

"Well, it was a close thing. They hadn't expected us to come aboard in just that fashion and, when we put in our appearance, they scattered, and we got the front half of the ship for ourselves before they knew what was happening. But then the skipper rallied his officers and some of the best of the men and met us in the waist, and we had a few bad minutes.

"However, you'll always find, Johnnie, that the fellow who starts winning is apt to keep on winning. He had more men; his men were just as good as mine; he was just as good a leader as I, and just as good a fighter. But I had the impetus of the first rush. And his numbers crowded one another. They lacked elbowroom, and after a few minutes they broke and ran for it."

"Where did they run?" exclaimed John Tanner.

"Into the sea, most of them," said his father, calmly. "But the skipper and his mates didn't run. They had under their hatches what they were willing to die for. And that skipper made for me with this revolver spitting fire."

"That very one?" cried the boy.

"This very one. But he stepped on a slippery place on the deck."

"Blood?" gasped the boy.

"Well, I suppose it was blood. And he staggered and went down, and a pair of my boys nailed him flat."

"Killed him?"

"No, not killed him. Because, when he saw that the

finish was at hand, he bawled out to me that he would give me what was worth his life, and more than his life.

"Well, in his own fashion, and for his trade, he was what we called an honest man. I heard him and shouted to the lads who had him down. I sent some of them to call to the crew which was in the water that they were free to come back on board. And some more began to look after the cargo, because the part I wanted had to be transferred to my ship. As for me, I went into the cabin with the skipper and had a glass of wine with him."

"Were you friends so soon?" asked John, more and more amazed.

"The way of it was, Johnnie, that I held this very same gun of his, which I had picked off the deck, and I kept it pointed at his head.

" 'Now,' I said, 'what's the price that you'll pay?'

" 'You have it in your hand,' said he.

" 'You mean this gun?' said I, growing a little angry.

" 'Twist the dragon's head from right to left," said he, 'and then push it back.'

"You can see, Johnnie, this enameled dragon's head on the gun handles? I did as I was told, as I'm doing now, and this was what fell out into my hand."

As he spoke, Gilbert Tanner twisted the dragon's head, pulled it back, and into the hollow of his hand, before his son's eyes, there fell out a great pearl which glowed like a little moon in the middle of a dark, clear sky!

3 · THE FENCE TALKER

"THERE'S the half of the fortune that I've brought home," said Tanner. "It's not much to see or to hold, but it has a price on it. And it has a story behind it, too."

"It's beautiful," said John Tanner. "I never saw anything like it. You better take it back again, before I go and drop it."

"You won't drop it," said his father, with that same grim smile. "No one drops it, but a good many people have had it taken from them. That's made more talk and trouble than anything that I ever heard of in my life. But it's fairly safe here. I don't think that any one ever would look for it in the handle of this gun, do you?"

"No," said John. "I guess they never would. It's a fine place to hide it. But suppose you drop the gun?"

"Now that I'm back here in the middle of law and order, Johnnie," said his father, "I'm not going to take a chance of dropping that gun. Besides, concealed weapons cause trouble, sometimes. So I'll just put it away in a bureau drawer in my room, and there she can rest a while until I find a jeweler honest enough to make a fair price and rich enough to pay it. For quality, and all that, I should say that's the finest pearl in the world, Johnnie. The Hindus call it the Daughter of the Moon. Not a bad name at that, eh?"

"No, sir," said John.

He returned the pearl and stepped back a little, eying his father with a new and grave attention. Gilbert Tanner eyed him in return.

Then he pointed his finger straight at the boy, as if the finger were the barrel of a gun.

"You've learned a few things about me, to-night," said he. "There's a great deal more that you're going to learn later on, when I know you better and you know me better. You're going to learn everything that I can tell you—and some of the pages will be black. D'you understand?"

Johnnie Tanner thought of that bloodstained deck of the trader and the fighting swordsmen who had struggled on it.

He nodded.

"Yes," said he, "I guess that I understand a little."

"Run up to bed, then. You've had a long day. Remember one thing."

"Yes, sir," said Johnnie.

"We're friends to the finish, eh?"

Johnnie came back. A strong instinct drew him. He held out his hand and gripped his father's with all his might. He found that hand cool and hard as iron.

"Yes, sir," said Johnnie, "to the finish."

When he went up to bed, he felt as though something had been added to him, like a new life. His own personality had been enlarged. There was a trust, a grave affection, a sense of loyalty which breathed out from the very

17

manner and eye and voice of his father; and a response swelled up in him.

When he was in bed, he lay for a long time on his back, staring at the blackness of the night and seeing, not the darkness, but the former life and the deeds of Gilbert Tanner.

He had not heard a great deal, only enough to make him guess at prodigies. It was plain that his father had been an adventurer. Perhaps he had done much harm in his day. But also he must have done good, for good was in his direct, sincere nature. There had been crimes, perhaps, but not great crimes, the boy hoped. It must have been a life of violence, to judge by the single sample which he had heard, but there had been violence, too, in such a life as Drake's and among others of the great heroes whom the boy worshiped.

He fell asleep at last and drifted into happy dreams, from which he wakened with the sun high and bright.

He should have been up at break of day according to his old schedule, and now he bounded, in alarm, from his bed to the center of the room. He reached for his clothes, but as his eyes fell upon them he suddenly realized that they were new—and so was his life!

There was no more drudgery to be done in the kitchen or about the house. He was free! There was only school, and school would not begin until Monday. This whole day, he was master of his movements. So he dressed and went down to breakfast, not entirely able to escape from a sense of guilt.

His father did not remain in the house long after that meal was over. He had business which would take him downtown; Aunt Maggie also would be out until noon; and by nine Johnnie Tanner was alone in the back yard to amuse himself until luncheon time.

Free hours were golden to him. He wondered if he ever would grow accustomed to them? In the meantime, his mind had been filled with an ideal theme for day-dreaming. He would not be an Indian on this day. He would be a captain of a trader in the South Seas. He would command a crew of bold and desperate men, and he would first flee before an overpowering enemy, and then attack her by a sudden stratagem and master her!

It was a good day for such an affair. There was a stiff

18

wind blowing out of the northeast, so that the clouds kept scudding across the sky, and the sun was now fainter, now more brilliant.

The same wind made brush in the vacant lot shake and tremble and bowed the heads of the saplings. It was not hard to imagine that that row of young trees composed the masts of one vessel, driving before the wind, and yonder row was still another, much loftier, and a little to the rear and to the lee of the smaller group. In a moment he was in his glory.

How should the crew of a South Seas trader be accoutered?

His mind was a blank upon that point, so he put on the familiar Indian togs, instead. Still one thing was lacking to make the whole design sufficiently perfect and that was the revolver in his father's room.

When he thought of it, a shudder of excitement and of pleasure ran through his young body. Would it be wrong, would it be theft if he went up there and found the weapon and borrowed it for his morning's play?

He considered the thing carefully. He had been trained scrupulously in the ways of an exact honesty, but he felt now, that he would be easily forgiven by his father for such a small offense. He could not harm the weapon, and surely the weapon could not harm him! He had only to keep his forefinger off the trigger.

So he went up through the house to the room in which Gilbert Tanner had been lodged. The first thing his eyes fell upon was a curved scabbard hanging at the head of the bed, and from the upper end of the scabbard projected a jeweled hilt, with a small hand guard. He stared at it, fascinated. He was strangely tempted to draw out the weapon, but he remembered that it had not been showed to him by his father's free will. The revolver was quite another matter. Its mysteries had been explained to him freely.

He pulled open the top drawer of the bureau, and there was the thing immediately under his hand.

If there had been anything wrong in his procedure, surely luck would not have been so kind to him at once!

He took up the treasure.

Was the pearl still in it?

He turned the dragon's head and pushed it back and

the bright little treasure rolled out into his hand. It seemed to glimmer with far greater, creamier brightness, as it shone there in the shuttered dimness of the room. Suddenly he felt that he was alone, and that such a possession might be a danger.

Replacing the pearl in its hiding place, he shoved the dragon's head forward, twisted it into place and went down the stairs into the back yard.

It made all the difference, having the real weapon which gave point and truth to all of his play acting. With that revolver at his belt, he climbed into the swaying trees; swung, agile and light, from branch to branch. He knew those branches, the strength and the height of every one. He had spent many hours among them, by day and even on moonlit nights, and now he went his way with a feeling of security.

He was, as he told himself, near the top of the mainmast; he was about to sing out orders which would turn his ship in its course and drive it on a changing wind straight under the bows of the enemy; and at this moment he was hailed from the top of the board fence.

He looked down through the green branches and saw a long and lanky fellow, dangling his legs over the top, sitting there, as though he were in a chair. As a matter of fact, there was a flat board along the top of the fence which made the position tenable enough.

"Hello, stranger," said the man on the fence top.

"Hello," said the boy.

Said the other: "You one of them wanderin' Delawares or are you a Blackfoot, maybe, up in the Rockies?"

The boy was thrilled by these names. "Hey," he said, "d'you know those places?"

"You bet I do," said the man.

In five seconds young Tanner was on the ground before the fence, with his ships forgotten, and even the revolver that was stuck in his belt.

"Come on down!" said he.

The stranger shook his head.

"When I was a little youngster," he declared, "my ma, she used to say to me, 'Harry, don't you never go any place nor anywhere except the boss of the house has invited you.' And that's a thing that I never forgot. You know the way that things will stick in your head?"

He said it seriously, tapping his forehead as he spoke and winking and nodding at Johnnie as though to refresh the boy's memory of similar things. He was as lean and as light of body as a scarecrow. Apparently he was very poor, for his coat was of one cloth and his trousers were of another, and they were deeply frayed where they touched the tops of his heavy boots. The heels of those boots were worn far down on the outer side.

"My father's not home," said Johnnie, "but it's all right for you to come down."

"He ain't home, eh?" said Harry.

And his little eyes flashed as they looked toward the house. He gripped the edge of the fence and swayed forward as though he was about to jump down, but then something made him change his mind. He checked himself and settled in his former position.

"I'm pretty good up here," said he. "Talk like a preacher and can't tell a lie from a high place like this."

He grinned at the boy, and Johnnie grinned back. He never had seen a man like this before. The fellow looked all the part of a tramp. And Johnnie, had he been another boy, would have been afraid, perhaps. But he knew the strength of his hands and the strength of his wide young shoulders; if he should match himself against the lean chest of the stranger, he would not be the least bit frightened.

4 · THE INDIAN AUTHORITY

AFTER a moment John said: "What were you doing out there? What Indians have you seen?" The other closed one eye, as though this helped him to remember. "Well, sir," he said in a confidential manner, "I'll tell you how it was. I been a trader, a mule-skinner, and I've prodded oxen in the caravans. I've trapped a spell, and I've been trapped, too!"

He broke into high-pitched, harsh laughter.

"You've been trapped?" said Johnnie, amazed.

The other waved his hand to dismiss the subject.

"That'd be a long story to tell," he declared. "About

21

the Injuns that I've knowed—well, I've knowed 'em from the little bow-legged Assiniboins right down there to them horse-sealin' Comanches, drat their dirty hides! And to the Apaches, too. A sneakin', no-account lot those Apaches are!"

"I've heard about 'em. I've read a lot about 'em, I mean," said Johnnie Tanner. "I'd certainly like to know!"

"The best way," said Harry, "to know Apaches and Comanches is to ask Mexicans about 'em."

"Mexicans?" said Johnnie.

The other winked.

"Apaches and Comanches is a Mexican disease, a regular Mexican disease," he said.

"I don't know what you mean," said Johnnie.

"You would if you lived south'ards of the Rio Grande," said Harry. "And a good spell north of it, too. They do a lot of suffering from Apaches and Comanches. When the Mexican moon comes along, the greasers get chills and fever, I can tell you."

"What's the Mexican moon? I never heard of that."

"Why, the Mexican moon," said Harry, "is the moon that's shining when the Comanches and the Apaches hit the trail south."

"They go to war, you mean?"

"I mean they go horse stealin' and cattle lifting, and they fight aplenty, too, if they have to."

"They're good fighters, I guess," said Johnnie, with rounded eyes.

"You better believe they're good fighters," said Harry.

In the sincerity of his belief, he closed both eyes this time, and kept them closed while he nodded confirmation of his last statement.

"I guess they're pretty near as good fighters as white men, maybe?" said Johnnie.

The two little eyes opened with a start and stared at the boy, unwinking as the eyes of a bird.

"Now whatcha mean by that?" he demanded.

"Why, that they're nearly as good as white men, was what I asked."

Harry looked at the sky, then he looked back at the boy.

"I see whatcha mean," said he. "Ten thousand Injuns

and ten thousand drilled soldiers, all lined up on a fine level field and they charge, eh?"

"Well, I suppose so," said the boy.

"Well, it never happens that way. Never at all!" said Harry. "The thing of it is that Injuns is like the clouds in the sky. Sometimes they is, and sometimes they ain't. You go a-chasing after one Injun, and he turns into thirty and lifts your hair."

"That means, to take a scalp?" suggested the boy, proud of his knowledge.

"Yeah. You know something yourself," admitted Harry.

He went on: "I was saying that you chase one, and he turns into thirty. And suppose that there's thirty, and a whole troop of cavalry chases out after them; why, the thirty turns into one, and then the one, he raises a cloud of dust, and when the dust blows away there ain't any Injun left."

"Jiminy!" said Johnnie. "How do they do that?"

"Medicine," said Harry, gravely, almost hoarsely. "They make a medicine, and the medicine takes them away. They's hardly a thing that they can't do with their medicine, one kind or another."

"I've heard about making medicine," said Johnnie. "Some place I read where it said that medicine making was just a superstition."

He was rather proud of that word; he flushed a little after using it.

Harry stared at him in his unwinking way for a moment.

"Some calls it one thing, and some calls it another," said Harry. "But I call it vile luck to be on the wrong side of it. That's what I call it. But speaking of Injuns and white men, for every Injun that the soldiers and the mountain men and all the rest kill with guns, the Injuns kill a white man back. But rifles ain't the things that kill the reds. It's the whisky as does it."

"I've heard that, too," said Johnnie. "I guess whisky is a pretty terrible thing."

"You guess, but I know," said Harry. "I've been where the whisky is the whiskyest. And that's Santa Fé. And I tell you this. A rifle might kill at a half of a mile. But whisky will kill you when you're a month away!

23

"You gotta listen with your brains, as well as your ears," said Harry. "You gotta think. The ears, they're only the doors. It's what happens inside the house that counts and matters."

Johnnie nodded. He began to feel that he had met one of the most extraordinary men in the world.

"But, man for man," went on Harry, "an Injun on the plains is like a fish in the sea. And a white man, he ain't. He's gotta come up to breathe, now and then. Injuns, they don't!"

He tightly closed both of his eyes again, in the intensity of his conviction.

"I guess you're right," said the boy.

"You guess, and I know," replied Harry, sharply.

"And who are the greatest fighters?"

"You mean, what Injuns?"

"Yes."

"Tell me, do you mean what whole tribe?"

"Yes, what whole tribe, or anybody."

"Well, I'll tell you. You take and make it anybody, and I'd say that those Delawares that wander around and do guiding, mostly, they're the best hands. They got the best guns, for one thing, because they work for the whites. And they got the finest horses, because they pick 'em up here and there, the very best. And they got the brains, because they ain't got hunting grounds of their own, and because they're scattered, and because they're in between —they ain't whites, and they ain't reds, you might say."

"You mean, their skins?" asked the boy.

"No, but I mean their hearts and souls and gizzards inside of 'em. You can trust a Delaware as long as he can trust you."

"They must be pretty fine," said the boy, with enthusiasm.

"All Injuns is fine, compared with us," said Harry.

"Why," said Johnnie, "I thought that they did a lot of murdering, and such things, a lot of the time."

"They been taught," said Harry. "They been tricked and kicked and fooled and robbed until they're sick of it. They haven't got laws and lawyers and all such stuff. They only got their bows and arrows and their guns and their knives. You kick an Indian to-day, and he cuts your throat to-morrow, and everything is even, the way that I look at it."

"Oh," said Johnnie. "I never looked at it that way."

"Mostly folks don't," said the stranger.

"Were you going to tell me about the best fighting tribe, too?" asked Johnnie Tanner.

"Why, I can tell you the best fighting tribe, too. I can tell you with my eyes shut. If you mean who can put the most braves onto hosses, the most braves that are real men, and tough as rawhide and mean as turpentine, then it's the Dakotas."

"The which?" asked the boy.

"The Sioux. You've heard of 'em?"

"Oh, yes. Now I remember the other name, too."

"They're something to remember," said Harry. "They got clouds of horses. And they's clouds of men to put on 'em. And every man is a handmade and hand-shaped piece of dynamite, right off the old hearth, and you believe me when I tell you, too!"

"I believe you," said Johnnie, solemnly.

"But," said Harry, barking the word and raising one long, skinny finger to mark his exception, "if you mean the tribe that has the highest average, that a hundred of them could lick about any hundred of any other people, white or red or yellow or black, then there's only one tribe that you could pick, and that's the Cheyennes!"

"I don't think that I've heard of them," said the boy.

"Ain't you?" asked Harry, tilting his head critically to one side.

"No, I don't think that I have," said Johnnie Tanner. "What are they like?"

Harry squinted in thought. "Why, they're like greased lightning on a down grade. That's what they're like. And they're averaging something like six foot tall, and they got hair down to their heels, and pretty girls and hardworkin' squaws that only know how to look straight ahead, and the finest horses on the plains, and a lot of guns, and they ain't rolled much whisky over the backs of their tongues, up to now. So they ain't spoiled. But Old Man Whisky, he'll get 'em in the end, and rot 'em, the same as he rots all the people, one time or another. I been and rotted, myself. I was a man, once, but the whisky, it come, and it rotted me, like the mildew rots a rose."

He looked darkly at the ground, and Johnnie, with a pang of sympathy and of pity, cast about him for some subject which would take the mind of the poor fellow from himself.

"I've had three wives," said Harry, gloomily, "and fifty horses, and seven guns, and back-rests, and hatchets and knives, and a whole barrelful of beads, and the headmen of the tribe, they used to come and smoke in my tepee and ask my advice. 'Long Arrow,' they used to say —that was their name for me—'Long Arrow, we are in trouble, and we need a wise man's tongue to help us. So we have come to you.' That's the kind of a man that I've been, in my day, before the whisky come and rotted me. Now, look what's left!"

"Well," said Johnnie, "I'm mighty sorry to hear about your trouble. But when you were out there, I wanted to know if they had revolvers, too?"

"Revolvers?" said the other. "Wait a minute. Come to think of it, I've heard something about such things. Pistols that shoot six times, you mean? But I've never seen one."

"Well, there's one," said Johnnie.

And proudly he held up the revolver, smiling.

"Well—the old scratch!" said Harry, staring, and speaking under his breath.

He held out his hand.

"Lemme look at it?" said he.

5 · THE STOLEN PEARL

A CERTAIN compunction had seized upon young John Tanner. He looked at the gun, and then he looked up toward the face of the unknown man upon the fence. Harry had been among the Indians, and he had been "rotted" by whisky. In addition, he had at one time enjoyed the company of several wives, and something out of religious teaching told Johnnie Tanner that it is not well to have more than one wife at a time.

There was that celebrated Henry the Eighth who had had six wives. Or was it eight? But he had married them at intervals. He had even made sure of solitary wives by chopping off the head of the predecessor. Vaguely the boy realized that the stranger was not all that the law might require of an honest man, but he could not put his finger upon the differences, exactly.

"I don't know," said Johnnie Tanner. "You see, it doesn't belong to me."

"Well, you got it, ain't you?" demanded Harry, impatiently.

"Yes, but it isn't mine."

"Well," said Harry, "lemme look again. Aw, I see what it is. It's just a pistol with a knob at the base of the barrel. That's all it is."

"No, because that knob turns. You look here," said the boy.

He demonstrated the action of the gun, and the eyes of Harry swelled and burned in his head.

"I know," he ventured at last. "It's just one of those tricks. It don't amount to anything. It's just a trick!"

"It's a trick that'll kill six men," said Johnnie, savagely upon the defensive.

"Come on!" sneered Harry. "Whoever killed six men with one of those little things?"

"I dunno," said Johnnie. "But it can kill six men. There's six bullets in it. Every time you pull the trigger and fire it, the chamber turns, like this."

"I guess there ain't much in it," said Harry indifferently.

And he surveyed the lusty proportions of the boy and then glanced cautiously toward the house and over each shoulder.

"My father says that it'll shoot six times," said Johnnie, more excited than before. "There's the chambers that hold the bullets."

"I don't see them very good," said Harry, shaking his head. "I don't see them at all."

"Why, you ought to be able to see them," said John Tanner. "Look at here!"

He held the gun up closer.

"Not yet. I'm mighty short-sighted," said Harry.

John Tanner stood on tiptoe. He extended the revolver above his head to the fullest extent of his arm.

"There—you see?" said he.

"Wait a minute," said Harry.

He leaned far forward, squinting earnestly. Then his

27

long, lank arm darted forth and snatched the revolver away. "I'll just go home and look at it with my spectacles on," said he.

Johnnie Tanner, bewildered, aghast, saw the long legs of the vagabond whisked over the top of the fence, and Harry dropped from sight, laughing, on the farther side.

"You thief! You thief!" screamed John Tanner. And he threw himself at the fence as if, like a cat, he expected to climb up the sheer, steep wall.

He fell back from it once and again.

Then he ran to a sawbuck which stood in the yard, a buck on which he had sawed off many a length of wood to be chopped for the stoves. A sort of madness was in him. The revolver was enough, in itself, but there was far more concerned. His father had come back from his journeys a rich man, but one half of his wealth was inclosed within the handles of the gun.

He had seen the thing. It grew in his mind. It was called the Daughter of the Moon. It became to his imagination as big as the moon itself, the great, lonely moon, which puts out the stars and rides alone in the black part of the sky.

Strange things had been done for it, ventured for it. Now it was lost through the folly of a witless boy.

So he told himself, his face puckered, his mouth twisted to one side, while he dragged the sawbuck close to the fence.

Springing onto it, he remembered the face of his father, earnest, grave, the bright, gray-green eyes fixed upon his own—the expression of a man who looks for a companion and strives to find himself in his son, his own flesh and blood. That flesh and blood had betrayed him and thrown away, at a gesture, in a silly instant, half of all that the man had labored for, had endured privations and peril, for, during the many years.

He leaped onto the top of the sawbuck, jumped up and hooked his fingers over the top of the fence.

It was a precarious hold, because the breadth of the top crown board prevented him from curving the fingers around any solid substance. But those many hours in the branches of the trees, those many more hours handling ax or hatchet or saw, had given him almost a man's power in his arms and in his fingers.

Holding steadily, fearful of a slip, he muscled himself up and up, and with a final jerk threw himself across the top of the fence.

He looked wildly before him.

There down the street, already a block away, the tall form of Harry was striding rapidly, with a sort of rolling swing to his walk.

John Tanner cast himself flatly across the top of the fence and dropped light as a cat to the ground on the farther side. He rose and, in rising, he saw his quarry turn and look behind. The next instant Harry was sprinting at full speed, his legs bending outward oddly at the knees.

Johnnie put out after him with all the might of his strong young legs. He lost ground during the first block. He felt that he was holding his own in the next. And then, beyond a doubt, he was gaining.

The first hope sprang up in his heart. He only knew one thing—that he dared never return, that he dared never to look his father in the face unless the revolver were in his hands.

As he ran, his heart bursting with the effort, he visualized the scene when Gilbert Tanner returned to the house and found that his gun, his treasure and his son had disappeared.

He would brand his boy as a common thief—an uncommon thief, in that he would steal from his own father!

In the next block, he was sure that he was making headway, and once, twice, he saw the long face of Harry, contorted with effort, look over his shoulder. Johnnie thought he could see desperation in that face, and this gave him an added power. He wanted nothing but a chance to fight it out with the thief, hand to hand. Then let God decide the right! He had faith in God, had young Johnnie Tanner. Sunday-school lessons had stuck in his mind, on account of the poverty-stricken wretchedness which made him reach out toward some fuller hope of happiness. Now a prayer went wordlessly up from his throat, from his soul, as he struggled after Harry.

Harry swerved from the sidewalk. A buggy was passing slowly. Harry overtook it, leaped up, precariously, onto the step between the spinning wheels, and was seen to gesticulate wildly to the driver. The next instant room was made for him, and the buggy went on at a sharp trot,

The trot increased; Johnnie Tanner was jerked behind as though anchored to the ground. His lungs burned with a fire. A dark mist gathered before his eyes.

But then he saw, passing him in the opposite direction, the old mail carrier in his little Federal wagon, clucking to his horse and peacefully slapping it, now and again, on the back with the reins.

A feeble force was this, but better than nothing.

He darted across the street. His voice was a scream as he ran beside the wagon.

"Mr. Jenkins! Mr. Jenkins! A thief—"

Mr. Jenkins pulled up the horse and, as he did so, he opened his round blue eyes, and his mouth opened, also, and his silver mustache broadened amazingly.

"Mr. Jenkins! There's a thief in that buggy back there. He's stolen money from my father. Help me to catch him."

"A thief, eh?" said Mr. Jenkins, with a calm that seemed hideous to the boy. Then the mail carrier snapped, as he craned his head around the side of the closed wagon and spotted the fleeing rig: "Hop in here!"

Johnnie, in a flash, was inside the vehicle of the government. And the horse, stung by a sudden slash of the whip, was turning the wagon at a shortened, sprawling gallop.

"Dog-gone my spots, and keelhaul me for a lubber," said the silver-mustached Mr. Jenkins, through his teeth. "A thief, eh? Stole money from your pa, did he? We'll steal him. We'll teach him to steal! Trice him up and give him fifty strokes with the cat, say I! A thief, eh? And stealin' from the poor!"

Much of this language was lost upon Johnnie Tanner. He only knew that a fury had been roused in the driver of the mail wagon that reddened his face and splotched his cheeks with purple, forcing him to lay the lash cruelly upon the back of the horse.

"Lay out! Stretch out, Maizie!" cried the mail carrier. "Sheet home to topgallants, and let fly, all. Put on the royals. Set up the royals and the skysails. Lay out the water sails and all the studding sails. We'll have a look at the pirate. We'll have a sight of him, darn his rotten timbers. Look at that, boy. We're gaining, sure enough!"

They were gaining, to be sure.

For the poor mare, Maizie, was flying over the cruelly

hard cobblestones at a surprising rate, and the buggy before them drew back rapidly.

Then it turned a corner, whisking out of sight by magic.

"We got them!" cried Jenkins. "We got them, sure, son. They've turned straight down toward the river, and there ain't a chance for them to get away, unless they swim the whole river to New Jersey, which I reckon they ain't likely. We got them as good as in our pockets. We'll teach him to steal, the villain!"

He took a furious pleasure in this denunciation, and the heart of young Johnnie Tanner leaped high with a pleasurable excitement.

They turned the corner. Straight down the hill they looked out onto the dark sheen of the Hudson River. Just at the base of the slope of the street, there was a slip, and in the slip a ferryboat with two enormously high funnels, and from the funnels smoke was pouring.

"Blast me alow and aloft!" said the mail carrier through his teeth.

"What's the matter?" exclaimed Johnnie.

"He wants to make that ferryboat, and he's agoing to make it."

Straight before them they saw the buggy jerk to a stop at the base of the street and the long, gaunt form of Harry leaped out like a jumping-jack out of a toy. He raced for the gangplank of the ferry.

The last of the crowd was swarming aboard, herded along by sight of the boatman who carried the end of the long closing chain in his hand. He held out an arm to include the speeding Harry in the mob. Then he went on and hooked the chain over its rod, on the farther side. Further ingress to that boat was forbidden.

6 · THE CHASE

JENKINS, drawing up his wagon at the edge of the slip, shook his fist and the whip in it at the ferryboat.

"The rascal!" he exclaimed. "There he goes. But we'll send the police onto the next boat that—"

But most of his speech did not reach the ears it was

intended for. Johnnie Tanner, leaping to the ground even before the wagon was at a halt, sprinted straight down the boarding and toward the gangplank. The chain was drawn across to bar the end of the slip. The side wheels of the boat were beginning to turn, and thicker, blacker smoke poured out of the funnels. The ferry stirred, moved and passed under the overhanging permanent gangplank which ran onto her stern. A little empty space showed between the outthrusting lip of the stern and the hanging gangplank.

Now, if Johnnie Tanner had had a chance to pause and think, he would never have dreamed of doing what he then attempted. But, sprinting forward at full speed, he did not think at all. He thought no more than a young wildcat, half starved in the early spring, when it sees a possible meal of red meat before it.

As for the massive chain which barred the way of the gangplank, he hurdled it and went on the downward slope with undiminished speed. A guard shouted at him. A woman on the ferryboat screamed. On the verge of the stern of the boat itself, stood a fat, uniformed fellow holding up both hands, as though sternly forbidding the mad attempt of Johnnie Tanner.

But John was not deterred. He saw a twelve-foot gap between the end of the gangplank and the rear of the boat. It seemed a vast distance, but he merely gritted his teeth and squinted his eyes with resolution. Coming at the end of the gangway, he hurled himself high into the air and tucked up his legs, beneath him. Below, he felt rather than saw the dark, dank face of the water, the shimmer of reflected lights among the forest of piles that supported the wharf on either side. And then he struck the very outermost edge of the deck and pitched forward.

He rolled like a compacted ball rather than a human creature. He rolled straight past the shouting, angry guard and into the tangle of legs of the watchers.

They stood away from him, shouting with excitement, some of them laughing, as Johnnie Tanner staggered to his feet. The guard collared him at once.

John Tanner looked up at him and saw a face round and red and raw-looking. Only the forehead was browned by the weather. The rest of it seemed without a skin. He had a little, short, turned-up nose and tiny eyes put close together under a fat frown. Altogether, it was the face of a pig—an angry pig, at that moment.

"I'm after a man," cried John Tanner. "I'm after a man who—"

"Maybe you'll find him in the jail that you're going to," said the guard. "And if I don't give you a dressing down, young feller, before you're out of my hands, my name ain't Will Chalmers!"

Johnnie closed his eyes with a groan. Then he pointed forward. "He's gone up there," he said. "Somewhere he's hiding. He's a thief! He's a thief! Why, he's stolen—"

The guard, with a grin, half fierce and half complacent, looked around him at the massed faces of the crowd.

"Look at him," said he, breaking in upon Johnnie's speech. "Look at him and listen at him! He ain't old, but he's got some old ways. He's hunting for a thief, he says. Look in the mirror, say I, and you're likely to find that thief, you young sprig!"

Some one in the crowd laughed loudly.

"It's a pretty old dodge," said another.

"Look at the face of him," said a third. "You can see! There's the criminal look. See those eyes!"

Indeed, the gray-green eyes of the boy were fairly blazing as he glanced around him, swiftly, and then he looked back to his captor. He thought of driving one of his hard fists into that great, soft pillow of a stomach, but then he realized that the thing would be useless. He might get out of the hands of this brutal fellow quickly enough, but a hundred hands were ready to collar him again, afterwards.

There was no use arguing with this pig-faced fool.

Said Johnnie Tanner: "Let me see the skipper. Let me see somebody who runs things. I'll talk to him!"

"Look at him! Listen at him!" said the guard with a mock admiration. "He ain't old, either, but look at the way that he acts it out!"

He shook John.

"You young tramp, you vagabond, what you been up to?" he demanded.

Johnnie Tanner felt blood rush to his brain; he grew dizzy with rage and with helplessness.

"I want a chance to talk to somebody who's in command," said he. "Right this minute, he's on board the boat. Right this minute he's got the thing with him!"

They were well out into the stream, now, and making rapid progress, and as the naked, glibbery face of the water behind them grew broader, a sort of despair came over the boy, for he felt his utter powerlessness.

An official in a blue uniform with some golden markings about the collar now came brushing his way through the crowd. He paused before John Tanner, a little, grim-faced, bitter-looking fellow. The heart of the boy sank farther than ever.

"Where's the stowaway?" said the officer. "This is he, eh? Reform school and a diet of bread and water is what he ought to have, breaking through like that."

The guard laughed. "He says that he's after a thief," he explained. "I told him to take a look at himself in the mirror. After a thief! Look at the way of him, though. He's a young old one, this kid!"

The little officer pointed his finger in Tanner's face.

"What's your name, you?" he demanded.

"John Tanner."

"Where d'you come from?"

"No. 78 Linden Street, east."

"What?" said the officer.

"Yes. That's where I live."

"Why, I know that neighborhood."

"My aunt keeps a boarding house there. She's Margaret Tanner."

"Ha?" said the officer.

He looked at the guard with a scowl.

"Wouldn't believe a word that he says," protested the guard.

The boy turned a savage look on him.

"I don't care what you do to me," he told the little officer. "You can beat me, send me to jail, do anything, but search the boat for the thief!"

"What sort of a looking man?" asked the official, who was plainly more and more impressed with the directness and the conviction in Johnnie's voice.

"He looks like a scarecrow," said the boy. "He's dressed in rags, almost. He's got little eyes, and they're bright. They're like the eyes of a bird. He's tall and he's narrow—"

"Why," said a voice in the crowd, "I saw a fellow like that come onto the boat. And he looked like a thief. He looked like he might be almost anything."

The speed of the ferryboat was slackening. John Tanner, feeling the change of pace, looked feverishly forward and he saw that they were gliding into the slip on the farther side of the river. The big piles stood up high, their sides gouged and rubbed to splinters where the fenders of the ferryboats had ground against them.

"If you do anything, do it quick—quick!" said Johnnie. "Because we're almost ashore!"

"I believe that the boy's right," said the officer. "What did the crook steal?"

"Something of my father's."

He hesitated to use the word "revolver." There might not be any man who had so much as heard of such a weapon.

"We'll get forward. We'll block the landing, and then we'll have him bagged," said the officer.

Straightaway, he started forward. Johnnie, now set free by the disgruntled and doubtful guard, went with him to do the identifying. They reached the forward end of the ship, luckily, before it quite made the dock.

"He's in our hands," said the officer, contentedly, "and if—"

"Look!" shouted Johnnie Tanner.

He pointed up toward the tops of the piles. At this point, a high platform extended beyond the line of the piles, used for loading and unloading freight. At about the same level was the awning deck of the ferryboat, and at this moment John Tanner saw the familiar figure of Harry run along the awning deck and leap for the freight platform.

Undoubtedly he had been so placed that he overheard the trial and the acquittal of the boy; he himself did not choose to undergo a similar ordeal; so he had gained the upper awning deck and, as the boat slid into its pier, he did not wait for the landing to be accomplished.

Against the sky his gaunt, awkward figure was seen. It appeared to hang in space for an instant. Then it dropped down upon the freight platform and instantly dodged out of view among the piled barrels and casks which were heaped upon the platform.

"We'll get him still. The wharf police will bag him!" said the mate of the ferryboat.

He pulled out a whistle and blew several sharp blasts upon it, as the boat put its nose under the landing apron. Up the apron he ran and Johnnie beside him.

Two or three uniformed private police came sprinting to answer the alarm and, as he ran forward, the mate shouted back to them the description of the thief.

"He's got through by this time," said Johnnie Tanner. "He's sure to go like the wind. He's got through by this time."

"We'll start the police to work," said the mate. "We'll give them the word on the outside, too."

They passed out from the shadow of the ferryhouse into the brilliance of the sun beyond, but here their way was blocked for a moment by the passage of an engine pulling a string of empty freight cars. The locomotive was coughing up a shower of sparks and thick puffs of steam and smoke commingled. It was only getting up speed on the slight grade which it was climbing, and Johnnie Tanner danced with impatience, for the thing to get out of the way. He wanted wings to fly across and over the obstacle. And then, in the midst of his impatience, through the open side door of an empty car, he saw among the shadows what looked to him like the form of a lanky man, curled up in a far corner.

It was only a glimpse, no more; but the very leap of his heart told him that this was Harry, the thief.

7 · NIGHTS OF TORTURE

HE saw the train shooting past, with a gathering speed, and he shouted to the mate of the ferryboat: "There! There! He's on that! He's in there! I saw him in one of the cars."

"Well, son," said the mate, "it looks as though we can't run fast enough to catch up with that."

"Are we going to do nothing?" cried Johnnie Tanner. "Are we just going to stand here and let 'im get away?"

"What can we do?" said the mate, scratching his head.

Johnnie looked wildly around him for assistance. Then, gritting his teeth, he rushed for the train.

It was rattling along at a good clip, now, but, he saw, about to pass the spot at which he aimed himself, a car exactly like that in which Harry had been riding with a wide-open door. The bed of the car was low. He high-jumped into the air—high-jumped and dived as if he expected to enter smooth, soft water. And he just managed to hurl himself through the open doorway. He was still in mid-air when the after jamb of the door struck him a heavy blow, spinning him around. Then, in falling, his head cracked heavily against the floor of the car, and darkness leaped across his brain.

That darkness endured for a long time.

When he awoke, the car was bumping over a rough grade, and he, lying in an obscure dark corner, was jouncing up and down, bumping against the floor and the side walls. There was a great noise and uproar in his ears; he thought he was going mad.

He leaped to his feet, but a sudden swaying of the car knocked him sprawling again.

Sitting up, he put his back to the wall and raised his hand to his head; there was a big lump over his right temple and a sticky feeling to the skin, which he knew was blood. His head rang. There was an ache on his right hip. And then he remembered how he had flung himself into the air, and how the edge of the jamb had struck and whirled him, and how he had smashed heavily against the floor of the car.

The door had been open, then. Now it was closed.

As he recalled these things, his mind cleared. Looking about him, he found that plenty of the daylight was streaming in through the cracks in the walls and even in the roof of the car.

By this light he found the door and tried it. But it was locked fast and he could not make it slide.

He went back to a corner and sat there, thinking, or trying to think. Baled hay had been transported in that car, it seemed, or else perhaps it was goods which had been packed in straw, for little piles of the chaff covered the floor. This chaff and dust, dancing up and down as the car jolted along, filled the air with particles that made the boy sneeze; the light, striking this mist through the cracks, seemed to pour like bright water into the interior.

He was shut up like a prisoner. No malice, perhaps, had caused that door to be closed; it was simply that at some way station the door had been made fast; and the agent had overlooked the inert form in a corner. That was doubtless the explanation. But, in the meantime, his efforts were balked, and Harry the thief was safe from him.

Weakness came over him. He forgot Harry. He merely wondered how long he would be confined in that place, that dusty dungeon. Then his courage revived. And he told himself, with a fierce iteration, that he never would leave off until he had brought Harry, the thief, to punishment and had recovered the stolen revolver.

He resigned himself. He knew the long pain of labor; therefore, he was equipped with patience, and he used it to endure the vigil.

It lasted unbelievably long.

He told himself that, when the train stopped and the noise of its going was no longer so great, he would shout and beat upon the door and so attract someone's notice.

So he waited, but it was hours before the train halted.

Then he went close to the door. He shouted. He beat. Outside, he heard people passing, laughing, talking. Some of that laughter drew near to him and grew louder.

He became silent. He realized that those on the outside were laughing at his efforts to escape. That was the source of their amusement and, therefore, he was a fool to persist.

He stopped and, sitting back in his corner, he pondered the thing. It was evening, and the air was cool. He was hungry, he was very thirsty, above all. But then the train got under way once more, and the motion was almost a relief to him. It kept certain horrible possibilities out of his mind.

As the darkness came on, he knew the train was climbing. The air grew colder. It began to have the bite of a knife edge, driving into him, and he had to run up and down the car to weariness, slapping his body with his hands.

For hours he kept it up. He was exhausted, but the instant he sank down to rest, the cold stabbed him to the bone, and he had to resume his exercises. The dread of death cudgeled him on.

Then the train stopped once more, and this time, by the hooting of many whistles about him and the murmur of many people, he conjectured that he had come to a large town. So he went to the door and yelled and whooped loudly.

But the noise was very great around him. There was the shrieking of a whistle, here and there, and the roar of steam escaping. And there was the steady, loud rattling of loaded trucks over cobblestones. He was sure that he was unmarked, when there came a smart rapping at the door of the car, and he shouted:

"In here—I'm locked in here!"

"You'll stay locked in till you rot, or dry up!" answered a snarling voice from the outside. "You'll stay in there till you're done. I'll teach the dirty tramps to ride on this line! I only wish that I'd caught a dozen of you in that same car. I'd run it into the river and let you sink!"

The voice departed, trailing curses. And for the first time young Johnnie Tanner saw that deliberate malice might prescribe death for him.

For a time, he could neither think nor hope. He was turned to ice with fear and despair. But then his courage rallied, and he became stronger once more. As the train started, with many jolts and jouncings, he took thought that no matter how his throat burned with thirst and how his body was weak for lack of food, yet men could persist through all manner of tortures. They needed only to have patience. And that was a lesson, as before said, which he had learned before this time.

The cold grew greater. It was a frightful night. So intense grew the cold that several times he dropped down in uttermost exhaustion and decided that it would be better to give up the struggle at once.

But he had a man's strength of will, and he used it now to force himself ahead. Deliberately, setting his teeth against the pain, he struggled on. Then he saw the red gleam of the dawn through the cracks in the sides of the car.

It was still very cold, but weariness here overcame him and he dropped down. He was so frightfully exhausted that sleep overcame him instantly. He hardly seemed to

39

stop falling, before he was unconscious. There he slept, and when he awoke the air was almost hot.

How close he had come to freezing in the early hours of the morning of that day he would never know, except that in his dreams he had died, and in his dreams he had been borne back to the earth by superhuman powers.

Twice, three times during that day the train halted. Thrice he made as much noise as he could, but never once did he attract notice.

In the meantime, he had made up his mind. There was a good knife in his pocket. It had two blades, one very powerful, the other fitted for delicate work. It was one of his father's gifts to him, and with those knife blades he set to work, cutting at the boards nearest the right side of the door.

They were broad, those planks, and one of them should be enough to permit him to break through. Just above the floor and five feet higher, he started two trenches in the wood.

It was not easy work. The jouncing of the car kept the knife blade jumping from the wood; the wood itself was hard, with a tough fiber and streaks of grain as durable as rock. The point of the good steel wore down. He used the long edges, but even these grew dull.

Then he saw that the trenches which he had opened were too narrow. He had underestimated the depth of the plank, and he had to start again, widening each from the beginning.

It was very hard work. His hands were tough from his work with hatchet and ax at home, but blisters appeared on them, now, as he strove to make muscle take the place of a keen knife edge.

Moreover, the lack of water was fiery torment, by this time. If he stopped work, from exhaustion, he at once fell into a sweat of despair.

But, little by little, the trenches deepened.

Actually, at one point in the upper one, he was able to drive the point of the knife through, as the evening of the day came on. He worked desperately, then, to finish the job by the time of utter darkness. But he failed.

And then, unable to see, he had to resign himself to a second night of the most frightful torment.

This was the worst of all. He grew giddy with the

pressure of thirst, the weakness of hunger. Even if his mind had been at rest, the vigil would have been a ghastly one for a grown man—and Johnnie Tanner was only a lad, still under his fifteenth year.

But those who have suffered in small things are somewhat prepared for the great ones. Somewhere there was fixed in his mind the belief that a man can endure thirst for three days. Then he must die. But in any case, he could live through another twenty-four hours. That is to say, if the cold did not kill him that night, for he had not the strength to battle against it, now.

Luckily, that night was much warmer. He could lie down and sleep for an hour at a stretch, with hideous nightmares which wakened him at last. It was hard to swallow, now. When he fell asleep, his mouth dropped open, and when he awoke he felt as though boiling tar had been poured down his throat.

Dawn came at last. He picked up his knife in his sore hand. The pain was so severe that he had to grit his teeth as he closed the fingers around the haft. While he was doing that, the train stopped; voices sounded outside; the next moment the door of his car was unlocked and flung open.

8 · KIND FOLKS

LIFE came back to him, like death, at a single stroke. And now he found himself agape, staring out through the cool pink of the dawn across a great river, muddy brown, its current slow and powerful. He saw the green of the trees along the farther shore, the morning light twinkling upon their leaves.

Yes, it was life!

The man who had opened the door of the car had walked on down the line of the train of empties, whistling as he went, and young Johnnie Tanner slid down from the open door to the bed of the track. He looked around him dizzily and saw that he stood in a maze of switching tracks. Beyond these stood long warehouses, and beyond the low roofs of the warehouses were the more pointed

41

tops of the houses of a considerable town. To the right was the sweep of the river and the green beyond it. Behind the town, he saw hills going up, and beyond the hills there were ragged mountains.

Early as it was, a number of men were working in the railroad yard. They paid not the slightest attention to him as he walked over to the freight platform. A bucket of water stood there with a dipper beside it. It seemed to the boy the most beautiful sight in the world. If the tin pail had been filled with one entire diamond it could not have been more precious to him. He filled that dipper. He sipped of it slowly, slowly, while the juices of life and hope began to soak all through his body.

He could have drunk the entire bucket, he felt, but instead he contented himself with the one dipperful. He had heard, somewhere, that after a long fast must come a long temperance in all matters of food and liquid.

After that drink, with a new hope in him, he set his teeth and looked about him.

He had not a penny. He had only that absurd masquerading costume, his Indian clothes, and that dull-edged knife. But he was not ashamed of his appearance. There were other and greater problems before him. How, for instance, was he to return to his home, for the very look of this place told him that he had traveled to the end of the world.

He went down to the river, slipped and climbed down the slippery bank, and there washed himself. When his face was clean of sweat, dust and the dried blood, he felt better, though the cold touch of the water made the bump on his forehead ache. So he climbed back up the bank and went into the town as the sun put its red-gold rim above the top of an eastern hill.

Early as it was, the town had commenced to stir. There were many people about and, striding down a side lane, he saw a sight which startled him more than had the sight of those painted Indians in the streets of New York. It was a tall man dressed from head to foot in deerskins. But what deerskins they were!

The trousers and the closely fitted jacket were worked over with bright beads and stained quills. The moccasins in which he walked flashed like fire with the same adornments. On his head there was a fur cap; over his shoulder balanced a long rifle. And, most strange of all, when this odd figure passed among the others in the street, no one so much as lifted a head to stare at him as he went.

"I've got West!" said the boy, suddenly seeing the light. "I've landed West!"

He turned suddenly about toward the east, and there he saw the mountains rising. No wonder the nights had been cold. Those mountains lay between him and his father, between him and his home!

His heart sank a little. But the next moment the smell of food reached his nostrils and banished all other thoughts. The doors of a small eating place on the corner had just been opened, but food was already prepared, for the steam of it rolled out into the street. So he walked in.

At the back there was a small counter heaped with homemade cakes, great loaves of bread, brown as could be, whole stacks of doughnuts and trays literally piled with pies of all kinds.

To Johnnie Tanner, it was like a sight of the central treasures of heaven. There was only one discouraging feature. Behind that loaded counter there was a man as tall and as lean as Harry, the thief, with a nose like a hawk's nose and a jaw that seemed capable of taking hold on chilled steel and never letting go. With a bright, savage eye, he stared at Johnnie Tanner. And Johnnie approached him.

He took from his pocket the knife and laid it on the counter. "Good morning," said Johnnie. "Will you give me something to eat for that?" The restaurant keeper said not a word. He looked at the knife, raised it, opened it. He thumbed the blunted points of the blades and the rounded edges. He weighed the knife as though it might have a value by weight.

Then his other hand darted out and caught Johnnie's right hand at the wrist. It was a vise, that grasp. But John Tanner was too tired to offer resistance. Weakly he allowed his arm to be turned until the hand was palm up.

And the other looked intently into the swollen inside of the hand and at the blisters along the fingers.

He dropped John Tanner's arm after a moment. It fell limply to the boy's side, while the restaurant keeper rubbed thoughtful knuckles across his chin. He smiled and a sneer seemed to be mingled in with the smile.

43

The knife he put on the counter and pushed toward his intended patron; then he turned his back and stooped above the warming stove which stood behind the counter, loaded with more articles for the hungry.

John Tanner took up the knife and dropped it back into his pocket. He had met rudeness, here and there, many a time in his poverty-stricken life. But never had he met with such a contemptuous dismissal. Fierce words of resentment came bubbling up hotly into his quivering throat.

He was on the very verge of an outburst when the long, crooked back of the other straightened. He turned with a great bowl of porridge in one hand and a pitcher of milk in the other. Both of them he pushed across the counter to the boy.

"Hold on," said Johnnie Tanner, when he could get his breath. "Those are not for me, sir, are they?"

The other shrugged his shoulders. He merely dipped a spoon into a bowl of granulated sugar and scattered the contents over the top of the bowl of porridge.

And Johnnie Tanner could wait no longer. A fierce pang gripped his very vitals. His mouth ran; he was half blinded with eagerness. So he took up that bowl and the spoon beside it, and the pitcher of milk. He sat down at the nearest table, and presently he was eating as he never had eaten before.

The bowl was large. The porridge was cracked wheat, cooked to a turn. And the milk was crusted over with an inch of cream. To the boy, it was Olympian nectar and ambrosia, but, after the first heaping mouthful out of the big, iron spoon, he began to control himself. People who have starved so long, how much and how fast dare they eat?

He looked up to the man behind the counter with the question in his eye, but he was met by a scowl so fierce that he dared not say a word. So, quietly, methodically, he got to the bottom of that bowl of porridge, and the last drop of milk he drained from the pitcher. Then he sat for a minute with his eyes half closed, stupefied for the instant, like a snake which had gormandized a week's provisions in one long act of swallowing.

He stood up; he replaced the bowl on the counter. "I'd like to pay you. I've got nothing but the knife," he said.

44

He waited, but the other, without a glance or a word at him, swept the soiled articles off the counter. And, since other people were streaming into the place and calling for food, Johnnie went out into the open air again.

Where had he read, in books, that hospitality is not even a virtue in the great West? It is only a common matter of fact!

But the heart of young Johnnie had been touched. This sea of forested mountains no longer seemed so wild and strange, so overwhelming to him. One bit of kindness had warmed him to the whole face of nature.

He could not pay with money, but he was determined, with a bulldog steadiness of temper, that the restaurant keeper should not look upon him as a mere beggar.

He went around behind the store, and there he found, like a formidable answer to his question, a great stack of logs with a sawbuck, under one end of which appeared a heap of sawdust, the upper part white and fresh, the lower edges rain- and weather-stained to brown.

Well, there was the answer placed providentially under his eyes, so he lifted off a top log, dragged it to the sawbuck, and placed it on the crosstrees. Then he picked up the saw. It had huge, ragged teeth and seemed more fitted to the power of two men than a single boy. Beside it was a broken half of an earthenware pitcher, containing some fat scraps of bacon rind, for the greasing of the sides of the saw.

He looked down to his hands. They were very sore, but after he had wrapped his handkerchief around the saw-handle, he grasped it and began his work.

The blistered hands, after all, did not bother him so much. After the first drag at the saw, he saw that sheer physical torment was likely to be his chief trouble, the weight of the blade was so great and the teeth bit so deep.

However, even to this he strove to adjust himself, with more or less success.

It was chiefly a trick of balance. If the saw blade could be worked with such a delicate stroke that it did not begin to shudder, and tremble from side to side outside the cleft which it chewed into the log, he could draw it back and forth without too great an effort; the instant that it began to make friction, however, and came out of the true, it lodged in the cleft of its own making.

45

Thought, a steady touch, a careful eye had to help him. And he used them, all three. Besides, it was not the first time that he had used a saw—never a saw like this, to be sure, but then this seemed a country of giants! He shrank. He grew smaller and smaller in his estimation of himself until, at last, he saw that he actually could master that huge tool with some degree of expertness.

He braced himself, he established the easiest position, he inured himself to a steady and rhythmic swing, his eye always sighted along the back ridge of the saw, as down a gun barrel. Then the sawed pieces began to come off the logs with a reasonable degree of regularity and of speed.

The sun grew hotter. It was midmorning when his knees began to fail him, shuddering beneath his weight. He threw himself down flat on his back, his arms thrown out wide, and rested for half an hour in the shade of a tree. Then he got up and fell to work again until a door slammed at the rear of the house, and he turned to find a woman watching him with a curious expression on her face.

9 · FOOD AND SLEEP

SHE was a big woman, garbed in calico which had once been blue and now was faded almost white; the original pattern was merely a shadow, here and there. She stood with her arms akimbo, in the attitude of one who judges and judges with severity. Her face was darkened by a frown. This gloomy expression made him connect her at once with the man who had stood behind the counter in the front of the restaurant.

"Who told you to be cutting at that wood?" she demanded.

"I thought it looked like it was waiting to be cut," said the boy, and he glanced at the considerable dimensions of his heap of sawed wood with quiet pride and something of a smile.

"Nobody'll ever use them logs for building now," she said sourly.

46

"My gracious!" exclaimed the boy. "D'you mean to say that they were for building, and not for sawing?"

"Didn't you see how straight they was?" she asked him.

"Yes—y-e-s," stammered poor Johnnie Tanner. "Now you speak of it, they were all pretty straight."

"And all about of one size?"

"Yes," he said.

His heart fluttered; he could have sunk into the ground.

"I guess I've done a terrible lot of harm. I've been a fool," said he.

"Yes, you been a fool," said the woman. "You would've been a fool if that wood had been meant to build with. But it wasn't. It was meant for a fire. But you might've asked."

"You mean that it is firewood, after all?" he asked her.

"Yeah. You've saved pa a half day's work, pretty nearly. That's all that you've done. Come here to me."

He went to her.

"Hold out your hands," she commanded.

He did as he was told.

"What you been doing?" she asked. "Did the sawing work up all those blisters?"

"No, only a part," said he.

"Go and wash them hands and bring them here to me," said she.

He washed his hands, pumping the icy water from the well over them, and the fever departed from them and the flow of the water over his feverish wrists made him almost groan with relief. Then he went back to the house and the big woman who stood waiting at the back door. He was still in some doubt; but he felt that she would not be as harsh as she seemed.

She waved him in before her, and he entered the kitchen. There was a big stove in it, and on top of the stove was a crowd of pans and dishes and kettles, giving out clouds of fragrant steam.

"How many breakfasts have you traded that old knife of yours for?" she asked him.

"Ma'am?" said the boy.

He looked at her curiously, frankly. He was so very tired that his natural sensitiveness was rather blunted—so tired that the sinews throbbed and ached and trembled down the back of his legs, and a weight rested against the

47

base of his brain. That morning's work, after a two days' fast, had been far too much for him.

She replied to this gaze of his with her usual scowling look.

"Nothing," said she. "Maybe you ain't— Well, gimme your hands."

She poured over each hand a briny solution. It stung like fire. The pain of it mounted like a smoke into the brain of the boy, but he set his teeth firmly and endured the thing. He had to smile a little, so intense was the torment as the brine worked through the outer skin to the bottom of the blisters, which had broken.

She, in the meantime, surveyed him with a sneering, almost exultant look which changed, gradually, to a nodding satisfaction and wonder.

"Set yourself down there. D'you know that it's noon? D'you work all day and never stop to eat, in your part of the world?"

He sat down in a corner. The smell of the food drenched the air. Now, that breakfast he had eaten seemed an infinite time past. He would have sworn that days had passed since he had tasted any substance whatever, and the woman, pulling up a small table before him, covered it with all that was delectable. There were minor details enough to have made a meal for two ordinary men, perhaps. But the central fact was a great steak, not overdone.

"You ever taste anything like that?" she demanded while he was in the midst of his gormandizing.

"No, I never did," said he.

"That's venison," said she. "I reckoned that you'd come from one of them mean, contemptible parts of the world where they don't know the taste of venison. Here's another slab of it. Don't you hold back. You can eat the whole deer, if you got room to swaller it."

But at last he could eat no more. He lingered for a moment over his third cup of coffee. Then he stood up, helping himself by pushing with his hands.

"I'll get back to the woodpile," said Johnnie.

"You won't," said she. "You'll not go back to the woodpile. Stand right there still, in front of me. There! I knew it! Look at how you wabble. You come here with me."

She took him by the shoulder; there was no will or

48

strength in him to make him capable of resistance. She literally dragged him into the adjoining room. There was very little furniture, but a small white bed looked to the boy as beautiful as a single snowy cloud when all the rest of the sky is burning with an August sun.

"You go to sleep," said she, and gave him such a push that he toppled over upon the bed.

He tumbled upon his back, with his arms thrown out wide. He did not move from the first posture of his fall, but sleep, with a single bludgeon stroke, dropped him senseless.

He awoke with rosy light falling slantwise upon his face and sat up with a guilty start. For a moment his head spun; vaguely he realized that it was late in the day; that Aunt Maggie would be furious with him because he had indulged in an afternoon nap. Then, with a further shock, he remembered everything that lay between him and New York.

The lost revolver, Harry, the thief, the imprisonment in the empty freight car, the long torture of thirst and hunger and now at last he was both fed and rested. The strong and supple young nature had thrown off the effects of fatigue. He stepped out of the door of that bedroom as fit as a fiddle.

The woman was at her work, washing a great pile of pans at the sink.

"Suppose that I help you, ma'am?" suggested Johnnie.

"Those hands of yours getting into soapy water? I reckon you better keep 'em to yourself, for a time. You go and take a walk around town. I'm glad that you've finished snoring the house down. You go and take a walk, and come back here for supper time, if you got no better place to go."

He went outside. It was not yet sunset, but it was the time when men stop work and relax for an hour or so before the evening meal. It was a time of good feeling, with the sense of completed and finished labor well behind one. So felt the town, and Johnnie Tanner suddenly remembered, as he walked down the street, that he did not even know what the name of the town was; he did not even know the State!

This thought made his brain spin for a little, but he went along with a brisk stride, for he felt that, after all, perhaps he had not everything to do with the control of his destiny. He had started to chase a thief; he had crossed a river in the pursuit. He had entered a train; and Fate had taken charge of him and whipped him how many hundreds and hundreds of miles away?

He came down to the wharves along the river. Two river boats were there. One was still loading; the other had its complement of goods and of passengers. The latter crowded the decks. They had friends along the docks who waved and shouted to them, and there was quite a carnival air of gaiety about the scene. The boat was bound westward, he learned from the chatter of the crowd.

"How far west, if you please?" asked he of a man near him.

"Right down the old Ohio to St. Louis," said the stranger.

He gaped as he heard it. This was the Ohio, then?

The two names were like thunderclaps. The distance that separated him from his home and his father seemed to be something more than a mere physical fact. It was like a spiritual separation, as well, an unsurmountable thing.

They began to cast off the lines which fastened the boat to the dock. There was a fresh outbreak of shouting, louder than ever. And as the boy watched, still amazed, his eye was taken by a slender figure on the deck of the steamer, at work coiling down a heavy, dripping rope.

There was something about the length and the narrowness of that back which attracted the interest of young Johnnie Tanner. Then the fellow straightened and turned from his task, and he saw the face of Harry, the thief!

10 · MORE WILD TALES

HE digested that miracle for a long instant, while the explanation shot through his mind. Harry had stuck to the same line of empties which carried the boy. He must have stuck to them because they took him where he wanted to go—West! That was the country which he seemed to know.

What more likely than that he should return to it? Now he had found work on the river boat to take him down the flood.

But the strangeness of the meeting stunned the boy for another moment. Fate, about which he had speculated before, he now was sure of. Fate had charge of him.

Then he saw that the boat was cast off. From the twin funnels there burst out more energetic clouds of black smoke, boiling and swelling in the sun-stained air. The big side wheels began to dash the water white and the flat-bottomed hull slid out into the river.

Then Johnnie Tanner awakened from his trance.

He pushed frantically forward.

"Stop that boat!" he screeched. "Stop that boat!"

His voice was almost drowned in the uproar of the crowd, as it shouted farewell to the departing friends. He stepped on something soft, as he struggled forward, and heard an oath in his ear.

Then he was seized by mighty hands.

"Look where you step, son!" exclaimed a voice.

He looked up at the vision he had seen that morning walking through the streets of the town, the fur-capped, skin-clad form of the rifleman, the sweep of beard, cut off short and square, the long, flowing hair.

"Look where you step while you're a-stopping of that boat," cautioned the hunter, upon whose moccasined foot the boy had trodden.

"There's a thief on board of her! There's a thief on board that stole my father's—"

"There ain't any way of stopping that boat," said the hunter. "You can't rope it and hold it; you can't still-hunt it; you can't ride it down. It's the fastest-footed boat on this here river. Mind what I say, that you can't catch that thief this side of St. Louis. Are you gunna hunt him that far?"

"I'll hunt him to the edge of the world!" cried the boy, in a sudden frenzy.

The iron grip which held him by the shoulder relaxed a little. Even in his agony of impatience and regret, the boy could see that the hunter was smiling.

"How far you trailed him already?" he asked.

"From New York," said Johnnie Tanner, almost absently, staring sadly at the widening gap between him and the boat.

"New York, eh?" said the deep, quiet voice of the hunter.

The crowd around them was scattering. Presently they stood alone, Johnnie Tanner staring with sad eyes after the dwindling boat. He saw a swirl of the current twist it somewhat to the side; then with the full force of the current and the drive of the powerful wheels, it slid out of sight around a tree-clad curve of the shore.

"You've trailed him from New York, have you?" said the stranger.

The boy did not answer. He merely sighed.

"You wear this kind of clothes in New York?" went on the hunter.

Johnnie looked at him with a troubled, desperate glance.

"I was playing Indian," he said, "and a tramp came and stole—"

He stopped. He flushed a hot red. It was partly from shame that a boy of his manly frame and size should confess that he had been doing so childish a thing as to play Indian! Again, he saw suddenly that his story was too wildly improbable. People would not believe him.

"All right," said the other coldly. "If that's your story, you stick right close to it. My pa, he used always to say to me, that a long lie was better than a strong one. Not that you're lyin' to me, of course."

Johnnie turned about, took a breath, faced the stranger by sheer force of will.

"Look-a here," said he, "you have no right to call me a liar!"

He was afraid. But it was stern, patient Aunt Maggie who had taught him that every difficulty and every shame must be faced resolutely.

"I took it right back," said the huntsman.

And suddenly he was smiling broadly. This smile made his beard and mustache spread in a rather ominous way, but the blue twinkling of the eyes made up for that. Johnnie sighed with relief when he saw that the tension was over.

"Well," said he. "It's all right. And I'm mighty sorry that I stepped on you."

"You was in a hurry," said the other, "and I reckon that you're too young to know how to hurry slowly. I'll forget it quicker than my foot will. That foot of mine has always had kind of special ideas of its own, since I got an arrow through it one day."

"You?" cried the boy. "An arrow?"

He looked at the stranger with bewildered delight. A man who had been wounded in actual combat with Indians!

"A real Indian arrow?" cried Johnnie.

"A dog-gone Osage war arrow, with barbs onto it," said the other. "It sure was an Indian arrow, if the Osages are Indians; and I reckon they's more Injun to the man among the Osages than any other tribe!"

Johnnie caught his breath.

"I would like a lot to know how it happened," said he. "I guess there was a terrible fight."

He looked at the keen eyes, the powerful shoulders, the supple, strong, well-wired body of the stranger. "I'll bet there was a whale of a fight!" repeated Johnnie.

"There wasn't any fight at all," said the stranger. "There was only a run. I done the running in front, and the Osages done the running behind."

"Oh!" said Johnnie, and strove not to allow too much disappointment to appear in his voice.

The other, however, was not deceived; but he went on: "I always run from an Injun."

"I suppose you have to, when there's a crowd," said Johnnie.

"They don't have to be a crowd," said the huntsman. "I run from any stray old Injun that I find lyin' around loose on the prairie. It's a way that I got. And you can bet that I was runnin' from them Osages!"

Pity, contempt, disgust swelled the heart of the boy. He could hardly meet the eye of this man, for fear that his scorn would show darkly through.

"Aw," said Johnnie, "I guess you wouldn't. But why did the Osages chase you, that time? Just plain meanness?"

"Mostly because I was down there to steal hosses from 'em," said the stranger complacently.

"Stealing horses? Stealing?" cried the boy, the disgust ringing in his voice.

"Yes," went on the other, as though he had noticed

53

nothing. "It's one of the best kind of jobs that you can do. That way, you get lots of hosses, if you're lucky, and you only lose a little hide now and then—if you're lucky. And the Osages had a horse that I wanted pretty bad. He was a coal-black son of Satan, and I reckoned that I would feel pretty good with the wind he raised on my face. So I went and got him."

It sounded like a very dishonorable practice to the boy. But he was fascinated, nevertheless.

"It was night?" said he.

"Not a bit it wasn't night," said the other. "I was right in the open middle of the day, and the brightest kind of a day, and right out on the plain near to the camp. I got up and laid my rope onto that black streak of lightning. And the boy that was herding him, he raised a yell and started for me with his bow and arrows, but I scared the lad off with a bullet out of my rifle, and then I shifted my saddle onto the black.

"By the time I got that saddle cinched up, they was coming; about every man in that tribe was heading right for me and raising a dust and a yelling that slapped the sky right square in the face and took the wind all out of me. So I hopped into the saddle; and that black, he began to pitch.

"He didn't like the smell of me. It wasn't homelike to him. And he didn't like my long knee-grip, maybe. Anyways, he began to buck, and nearly he had me out of that saddle—and the Osages coming up every second!"

"My gracious!" gasped the boy.

The other almost gaped at him, bewildered.

"What did you say?" he demanded.

"I said: 'My gracious!' It must have been terribly exciting."

"You said 'My gracious,' did you?" echoed the other. Then, as though gradually recalling his scattered faculties, he went on: "It wasn't exciting at all. It was just plain sickening. I seen that bow-legged bean pole of a chief, Red Feather, scooting out in front of the tribe. Red Feather was the one that owned that black stallion, d'you see? Well, I felt that I was about done, but just then the black seemed to have bucked the kinks all out of his system, and he started in to run. It just happened lucky for me that he started running away from the Injun

54

town, instead of through it. Because I couldn't guide him a mite. He had a mouth like a bit of steel gun barrel. You couldn't bend it. It would've taken a giant to bend a corner of his mouth. I can tell you."

"It was terribly lucky!" said the boy.

"You bet it was! He started running, and in a half a minute we had that tribe trailed out behind us like the tail behind a comet. And still we were gaining and looping it away at a rate that I never saw a horse go before. There was a regular gale whipping into my face. I ducked my head into it and thanked my stars, and already I began to count up the money that I would win when I matched that greased bit of downhill lightning against any other horse on the prairies. But just then the black doubled around and ran straight back."

"Right straight back toward the Osages?" cried Johnnie, on tiptoe and straining with excitement.

"No, but straight back towards the Osage village. He come straight at it, with me leaning to the left and pulling, and then leaning to the right and pulling. But I couldn't even saw a dent in his nose, he was so dog-gone hard and mean.

"Well, son, I had a picture of myself frying over an Osage fire, after the squaws had finished shooting play arrows into me, and after the boys and the girls had finished sticking splinters under my finger nails and setting fire to the splinters. I had that picture mighty bright in my mind, and I could smell myself burn, like bad bacon. And then we hit that town."

He paused. Johnnie was breathless and starry-eyed. Yet the other deliberately, through a long moment, worked at a corner of a plug of chewing tobacco, until he had chewed off a good mouthful.

All talking was impossible until that lump had been moved across the tongue and tucked into one cheek, and the stray bits, the end and the shreds of the tobacco had been spit out. Then, slowly masticating the chew, the other went on, speaking with gaps between his words:

"We hit that town so fast that we kind of blew it all into a lump, like the way that a sand storm turns everything red-brown. It was a funny thing, sort of, the way that the speed of that hoss made that town a solid wall of tepees on each side of me.

55

"I tell you what. I could see them open their mouths to yell at me as I went by, but the sound never caught up to me. I never heard a thing except the whiz of the wind as it went screeching past my ears. You look and you'll see where they look kind of peeled at the edges. That's what the wind done that day to me. And I went clean through that Osage village in three jumps and a scatter. And, just as I was hopping the black into the middle of the blue of the hills beyond, there was a mean-faced old man that put an arrow on the string and give me that arrow right through my foot, barbs and all."

He paused in his narration.

"You got away?" cried the boy.

"Do I look like a ghost?" said the hunter. "Well, sir, there wouldn't have been a ghost left after them Osages had got through with me, supposin' that they'd caught me. But they didn't, and here I'm standin' on the banks of the Ohio, swappin' lies with you, that's come all the way from New York to hear what we can tell in this part of the world!"

"The horse!" said Johnnie Tanner. "What became of the wonderful horse?"

"The horse is what I'm starting back to see," said the hunter. "The horse is what's takin' me back there, and inside of half an hour, I start."

11 · A FAREWELL

JOHNNIE sighed. The thrill of the narration still was tingling in his very finger tips. "Oh, well," said he, "I guess that was as close a call as you could come to."

"I guess that it was close enough for me," said the hunter. "I was only a comparative boy, as you might say, when that happened. I was hardly more'n as old as you are, son, when that happened a couple of years back. And look what it done to me? I wouldn't mind nothing else, but it sort of sickens me the way that it growed me a beard for a windbreak and turned that beard gray around the corners, so's I mostly look as though I'd been kind of careless with my tobacco juice."

56

The boy stared. Then, suddenly, he laughed; and his hearty peals of laughter rang across the river water. He laughed and still he laughed, and his eyes shone at the hunter.

"I'll bet you don't run away, every time you see an Indian," declared Johnnie.

"Don't you be putting up your money rash and free like that on a man that you never seen before," said the stranger.

"My name's Johnnie Tanner, sir," said the boy.

He held out his hand, tentatively. It was instantly taken in the strong, brown grip of the other.

"My name's Hank Raney," said he. "I'm glad to know you, Johnnie Tanner Sir. Do you always use all those three names?"

"Why, there's only two names and—" began Johnnie.

Then he saw the point and he laughed again, still more merrily. The other did not laugh in sympathy; but his eyes twinkled like blue stars in a brown sky.

"The 'Sir' family ain't very big, out here," said Hank Raney. "It come over from old England, and it went and got a pretty good start for itself along the coast, and in Virginia kind of specially it come along famous. But when folks begun to come West, the Sirs didn't do so good. They didn't seem to like the mountain air, crossing over. And the mountain air didn't seem to like them. There was many of the Sirs that never got out of Virginia at all, but went back home and growed a longer set of whiskers and laid in a new stock of Bourbon.

"And the Sirs that got over the mountains and onto the plains, they got sickly right away. I dunno what it was that done the thing. I guess maybe that the Sir family has gotta be pretty close to the sea. They need the salt air, maybe, the same as bacon needs a smokehouse. But lookin' far and wide, I dunno that I recall more than half a dozen of that whole big family that I've met up with this far West! And even that half dozen was feelin' a little sickly, and yaller around the gills."

This long explanation kept Johnnie Tanner chuckling and bubbling with laughter. "Well, Mr. Raney," said he, "I won't call you sir. But my aunt told me that I should speak to older men that way."

"Why, I ain't so much older," said the other, "except

57

for that ride I was telling you about that put the years onto me and raised me this here crop of windbreak on my face. But you ain't told me how come that you're gunna catch up with the thief that you've trailed from New York. Gunna charter a private boat and go down the river fast and unloaded, to skip over the mud banks?"

"No," said the boy. "Unless you can charter a boat for this much."

He held out the pocketknife.

"That's all you got?" said the hunter.

"That's all I've got," said Johnnie cheerfully.

And he made a gesture as though to indicate that he also had his hands and that they were enough.

He found that the glance of Hank Raney was clinging to the hand which had gestured, observing it keenly.

"Looks like you've walked from New York on your hands," said the other.

Johnnie looked him straight in the face.

He spoke slowly, as though to allow Raney to break in with an interruption whenever he chose.

"I got into a box freight car. The car was locked while I was asleep. I was in there every lick of the way."

"No food; no liquor?"

Johnnie flushed.

"No," he said stoutly.

At this, the eyes of Raney narrowed until they became single beams of blue light, which almost disappeared. Then they gradually widened again, and he said suddenly: "I believe every word that you say, son."

"Thanks," said Johnnie. "I'm mighty glad that you do. Thanks a lot. I know that it doesn't sound like a true story."

Mr. Hank Raney began to frown at the planks of the wharf.

"Look-a here," said he suddenly.

"Yes?" said the boy.

"There's the *Cyrus B. Oliver* that's going to start down the river in about fifteen minutes. If you want to, I'll take you down to St. Louis with me. I'll pay your way. Don't worry about that."

Johnnie shook his head.

"I couldn't pay you back right away," said he. "I
58

couldn't let you pay my way. It's a mighty kind thing of you to offer, though."

Hank Raney cleared his throat. He glanced up as though in sudden curiosity toward the sky.

"Matter of fact," said he, looking back to the boy and speaking in a most confidential tone, "matter of fact, that talk of paying your way was only a kind of a manner of speaking. You see, the captain on that boat is a friend of mine. I'll just speak to him, and he'll let you ride free."

Tanner's color rose. His heart beat fast and high at the thought of following again on the trail of Harry, the thief. With a fierce joy, he imagined the picture of a street in St. Louis, the long, lank saunterer idling up the street, and he, with big Raney and a policeman, softly coming up behind. He could see the hand of the law fall upon the shoulder of the wretch. He could see the long face of Harry turn yellow-green in terror as he recognized the lad whom he had robbed on the farther side of the continent. Ah, that would be a sweet moment for Johnnie Tanner! A sweet, a glorious revenge! It would compensate, at a single stroke, for all his sufferings since he left the great city.

This was the golden vision of his mind and yet he still hesitated. There was a good strain in Johnnie which forbade the easy acceptance of favors.

"You'd be begging for me," said Johnnie.

"Begging?" said Raney, opening his eyes in apparent frankness of soul. "Why, the way of it is that the captain is mighty glad to have the decks of the ship as full as he can get them. He says to me: 'Raney,' he says, 'it's a thing that I don't like to let out. Only to a few old friends like you. But a good many times I've wished to see the old *Cyrus B. Oliver* heavier loaded with passengers. It gives her the look of a popular boat. It makes folks think that she's a great money-maker. The more crowdeder she is, the more folks will fight and pay to get onto her. You know how the way of it is, don't you?'

" 'Sure I know, Captain,' says I.

" 'Well, then,' says he, 'seeing that you're such an old friend of mine, any time that you want to, you can slip a man or two on board, and give the wink to me, and I'll be glad to have 'em along. Only, just keep the thing under your hat, and don't go to talking any too free about it.'

"So that's the way of it, son."

"It sounds like a sort of a strange thing to me," said Johnnie.

"Business is always strange," said Hank Raney, with a feeling nod. "It starts funny and it ends funny. The funnier the ways of a business, the more money it's sure to make. I've always noticed that."

"Well," said the boy, "I'd be mighty grateful to you, Mr. Raney. There's nothing that I wouldn't do for you, if I could get down to St. Louis."

"And what would you do to him, if you caught the thief there?" asked Raney, with a flash of curiosity. "Suppose that you didn't have a policeman around handy, I mean."

The boy thought, and his teeth set hard, his lips twitching back.

At last he said, not loudly: "I'd kill him, if I could. I think that I could!"

The hand of Raney dropped on his shoulder and patted him. "Now, son, would you do that?" said he. "Would you really do that?"

Young Johnnie waited for a moment, considering the half-amused and half-serious expression of his friend.

"Well," he said, "I guess that. I've talked a good deal."

"You've talked a good deal," admitted the hunter. "It's all right to talk a little, only, it's better not to talk at all. But you're new in the West and the West has its own ways. Now you get your things together and we'll go aboard."

"I've got nothing with me," said the boy. "Only—I have to see two people in the town here."

"See them quick, and come back here on the run. It's only fifteen or twenty minutes before the start."

Johnnie Tanner turned and sprinted back through the town. He was puffing and panting with all his might when he came to the restaurant. There the supper was under way; the place was well filled; but when the sour-faced proprietor saw the boy he hooked a thumb over his shoulder.

John Tanner scuttled around to the rear of the building, and there he found both the man and the woman waiting for him, looking more dour than ever.

"What you found in town?" said the wife gloomily.

"What you found that's brought you back here looking so scared?"

"I'm not scared," said the boy, "but I've found a way of getting further west, and I've got to take the chance. I just came back to thank you, a lot."

"You're going further west? You're going to be a fool!" said the proprietor. "This is far enough west for any man to be. Farther than this is too far west for a boy. You stay here. You stay here and find yourself in a home, my lad."

The woman suddenly laid her big, red hand upon John's shoulder in a kindly way.

"We like you pretty well, son," said she. "You might be better off with us than you think!"

Johnnie Tanner looked up at them in bewilderment; his heart was softened.

"You're mighty kind! You're mighty kind!" said he. "Only, I've got to go as far as the trail leads."

"Young man," began the woman.

"Be quiet," said her husband. "Be quiet and leave him go. You can't keep a colt in a sheep pasture. He either starves or jumps the fence. Good-by, son."

And away went John Tanner, looking back toward them once and smiling over his shoulders.

12 · DOWN THE OHIO

AN engine was getting up steam in the railway yard when Johnnie Tanner returned to the wharf. He had a choking feeling of dread, when he heard the locomotive puffing and panting from a distance, for he told himself that the steamer was surely gone and was sliding swiftly downstream.

But he was wrong. It lay placidly at the dock, with the big form of Hank Raney standing by the gangway. He waved to Johnnie and called something to the guard who stood ready to accept tickets.

"That's the boy that's fixed," said Hank Raney. And John Tanner was permitted to walk up the gangway to the deck of the boat.

He stood close beside Raney as the final preparations were completed and the ship cast off.

An odd feeling came to the lad. It was as though this were the last shore of his native land, and as if this river were a great ocean across which he would be at an irrecoverable distance from home. Raney dropped a hand on his shoulder. He said, briskly and coldly, "Now's your last chance to change your mind. If you stay here till that gangway is pulled in, you'll be an older boy than you think before you get back this far east. Take one think, and make it strong. There's plenty that travel this road out, but there ain't so many that come back by it!"

John Tanner actually made a step toward the gangway. But he hesitated, and the next instant, with a whoop, two dock hands shot the long gangway on board. Immediately, the current and the first powerful turn of the sidewheels carried the ship into the stream. A narrow strip of gleaming water separated them from the bank; the strip widened; presently the whole vessel heeled a little and the boy knew that the more powerful central current had seized upon her.

There was a relief, in a way, to being thoroughly committed to the adventure, placed so that he had to keep his face turned forward. And yet, at that moment, he could only think of the rough and kindly ways of the restaurant keepers with a bitter regret. It was a place for hard work, but it was also a place of plenty.

When he turned from his own sad thoughts, he found that Raney had disappeared, and his heart leaped, suddenly, with cold fear. He reassured himself quickly. Hank Raney had not established himself as a post upon which a strange youth could lean. He was neither an adviser nor a comforter. He was simply a good-natured stranger who had been willing to help the boy make a start down the river. But the entire weight of the battle was on himself, Johnnie Tanner.

He accepted the truth of this position with a settled gravity; then he went to the bows of the ship.

How long would it take them to shoot down the rapid Ohio to the Father of Waters?

He had not the slightest idea. He only knew that the way was long. In the meantime, though he had been presented with a chance to ride free upon the steamer, how was he to find food?

The thought troubled him but little. After that experience in the closed car, he felt that he could endure a whole month of starvation—if only he could enjoy water and fresh air!

There was a mass of unstowed freight in the bows of the steamer. A cursing foreman directed a gang of workmen who piled the freight and made it ready for covering with a tarpaulin.

"D'you want an extra hand?" asked John of the foreman.

"I want room and no lip from a kid," said the foreman. "Get out of my way."

The boy went out to the tip of the prow. Leaning over it, he saw the cutwater turning up a transparent furrow on either side and this ever-rising arc was tinted a rosy gold by the evening sky. The colors, however, were fading rapidly. Here and there a dull glint of crimson or of gold gleamed on the face of the river and died out, and the shores drew away to a cloudy obscurity.

He turned and looked back at the staterooms, and the pilot's cabin high above all. He could see a dim shadow above in that cabin behind the big forward window. Yet loftier, above the entire structure, stood the twin funnels, held firmly in place and attached by two big braces. It seemed a miracle to him that so great a ship could float on river water; it seemed still more strange that engines could be built big enough to make the entire hull tremble with the power of their thrusting. But he could hear the dull roar of the monster in the hold and the cool, dashing sound of the torrents that tumbled back from the churning paddle wheel. Two vast plumes of black crowned the boat, towered in the air, and gradually fell away behind, to be lost in the darkening sky.

"She's been a good one in her day," said a voice out of the night beside him. "She's been good, but she's old, now."

He turned a little and saw for the first time an impassive figure seated on a small keg. He could not make out the face of the man until the latter pulled at his pipe. Then the dull glow enabled Tanner to see the face of a man of middle age, furnished with short-cropped whiskers.

"She's strong," said the boy. "She seems pretty strong."

"She's too strong," said the stranger.

The boy was silent, waiting to have this odd expression explained.

Said the other: "A hundred and thirty feet of her, and nineteen foot beam, and a model hull with a six-foot draft. That makes too much. She's too strong. She rides too deep. She's bound to be dragging her keel over the bars. She's bound to be hunting for trouble that a pilot ain't able to see. Like some wives, I've heard of, that are always finding snags out of their husband's sight. This boat, she ought to be on a lake, and a big lake. She ain't meant for river work. And only one engine; that's another bad idea. And the flywheel's too big a weight."

Then he added: "Where are you bound for, young lad?"

"St. Louis," said the boy.

"There's a town for you," said the other. "There's a town, and it's going to be more of a town, too. It's going to be a whale of a place, I can tell you. It's going to be a city the world'll hear of."

"Why?" asked the boy.

"Because it's lying right in the middle of things."

"The middle?" cried John Tanner. "I thought it was pretty far west."

"Far west?" said the other, almost scornfully. "Why, it's only at the beginning."

"Here you are!" said the voice of Raney.

He loomed huge in the dark.

"Yes?" said the boy, standing up.

He was very glad to see Raney again. He was delighted that the big fellow had cared to hunt him up as quickly as this.

"Where you been?" asked Raney again.

He spoke roughly, impatiently.

"I've just been here," explained Tanner.

"Yeah? I thought that you must've dropped overboard and cut out for the shore. I thought that maybe the fish would be dining on you before the morning comes. I've been over every inch of the boat and here you are out here in the dark!"

He turned.

"Come along!" said he.

But John Tanner hesitated. He was pleased by this attention from the big hunter. But he did not wish to follow any man at heel, like a puppy that must come when it is whistled to.

"Where?" he asked.

"Why, you'll be wanting to eat, won't you?" demanded Raney. "Come along, will you?"

Tanner came, but very slowly. He was thinking hard, when his companion tapped him briskly on the shoulder.

"Now, lemme tell you something," said he. "Pride's a good thing, a fine thing, a grand thing for them that need it. But right now you don't need it. You put your pride into a pocket, and you button up the flap of the pocket, too, so's your fool pride won't be getting out and getting in the way. You hear me?"

He spoke sharply, but John Tanner suddenly made up his mind.

"I'll do just what you say, if I can," said he. "I guess you know things better than I do."

Suddenly Raney laughed.

"What were you gunna do?" he demanded. "Set there and wait for luck and a good dinner to drop into your mouth?"

"I tried to get a job with the deck hands," said the boy, on the defensive. "I couldn't land it, but I thought that something else might turn up."

"Deck job, eh?" said the other. "Well, that's the right kind of pride, only you don't need to work with the rats on the deck while I'm with you on this trip. I got eight hundred dollars in my wallet, son, and I don't aim to keep all of it there all the way to St. Louis."

They had reached the deck above, passing into a better-lighted section of the boat, and at this moment a man wearing a long-tailed coat and a broad gray-white hat went by them. He paused a little as he heard the last remark of Raney and, as he turned, the boy saw the glint of a big jewel in his cravat.

He stepped on hastily at the side of Raney. He felt that the keen eyes of the stranger were watching them both—not that there was any danger in this, but that it vaguely disturbed him. In such a manner might a cat have looked after a mouse!

13 · THE CARD GAME

THEY had supper together in the dining room, a small affair, since most of the passengers were likely to take their own food with them. There John Tanner sat quietly and ate like a man—or like two men. His prodigious fast which had ended that morning still had its teeth in him. As soon as he had finished supper, immense waves of drowsiness came over him; his head began to droop.

"You come along with me," said Raney. "We got a cabin, aft. You can turn in there for a good sleep."

"I'd better stay up and see things," said Tanner.

"No matter where you stay, you'll be seeing nothing but your own dreams, in another five minutes," said the other.

So Tanner went, submissively, and found a snug cabin with two berths in it, one above the other. He undressed. At the washstand, he sponged himself off, and Raney, undoing a pack which stood rolled in a corner of the room, threw him a flannel shirt.

"That'll do you for a nightshirt," he said.

Tanner was too far gone with sleep to protest. He put on the shirt which reached to his knees and, smiling sleepily at Raney in comment on that loose fit, he clambered to the upper bunk, and was asleep.

A crashing noise came into that sleep.

It merely made him turn on his side and sleep the harder.

Then he heard voices, laughter close beside him, but still consciousness did not entirely return until, suddenly, he found himself wide awake and a murmur of conversation in the cabin.

The air was thick with stifling tobacco smoke. Perhaps it was this which had choked him and wakened him.

In the room were four men; one was Raney, one the tall fellow of the cravat and the diamond.

At this sight, he forgot the tobacco fumes that had made him dizzy; a keen sense of danger cleared his brain.

Then he took stock of the other pair. One had the

starved, sallow look of a consumptive. One had the face of a bulldog, with a square jaw and square, massive shoulders. They were gathered around a small table. Gold and silver in little stacks stood before them. He of the diamond was dealing cards, and young Tanner was fascinated by his long-fingered, white hands and their deft manipulation of the pack. Now the shuffling was completed, and the cut made, and the cards flowed out rapidly, dropping with a soft whispering sound upon the face of the table.

"I want a change of luck, Marshall," said Raney to the dealer. "I've been playing kind of deep, for me, and I need a change of luck."

"You'll get it," said Marshall suavely. "You ask Harry Bray about the time he told me of."

He nodded his head toward the bulldog. "I was telling Marshall," said Bray, "this evening. I don't play cards very often. Just a kind of a relaxation to kill time on a trip like this. But I was going down toward New Orleans on a boat and I got into a little game with a few gentlemen. I had twenty-one hundred dollars, and in an hour and a half I was down to my last ten. I looked that eagle in the face and gave it a toss and a spin. Heads, I quit. Tails, I'd let it go after the rest. Well, sir, what you think happened?"

"Well?" said Raney, an almost feverish interest in his eye.

"I'll tell you what happened. I bet that ten on a pair of queens, and it won forty dollars for me on the next deal."

"You did?" said Raney, smiling.

"I did, Mr. Raney. And in another half hour, I have twenty-five hundred dollars in front of me. And ten minutes after that, I got four kings, and a planter from Louisiana sat across from me with four queens. You can imagine what happened. I took three thousand from him on that hand."

He laughed a little.

"That's the way the game goes," said Marshall. "Maybe you've had the same experience, Mr. Quincy?"

He of the consumptive look blinked and nodded slowly.

"That's always the way," said he. "The losers are the ones that don't hang on."

"Of course they are," said Marshall. "It's your bet, Quincy."

"Five dollars to draw, gentlemen," said Quincy.

Either he had gone in with big stakes or else he had won a good deal. There were thick stacks of yellow metal before him. But Raney, whose turn it was now, had been diminished to a single pile. Two hundred dollars, the boy estimated, stood before Raney. He hoped that the rest of his eight hundred had not gone across the table. Part of it, surely, must be in his purse.

"I'll up that five a little," said Raney. "We'll make it twenty to draw."

"It's high for me," objected Bray. "But—well, here's for luck."

He pushed in the money. Marshall contributed the same sum and began to deal.

At this moment, the boy took note of a curious fact. Beside the hand of Marshall lay a large gold watch.

At first, it looked to the boy like a flake of living flame, there on the table. But now he saw that this illusion was caused by the highly burnished state of the metal. It was so polished it gave back a flaring reflection. It was smooth as a mirror, and like a mirror it reflected the ceiling of the stateroom. The oddity lay, chiefly, in that the watch was turned face down. A man who wished to keep track of the passage of the time would, surely, have preferred to leave his watch face up.

"Cards, gentlemen," said Marshall, and held the pack ready in his hand, flipping the farther end with the tips of his agile fingers.

The boy, hanging over the edge of the berth, could clearly see the head of a "jack" on the uppermost corner of the lowest card in the pack.

"Three to me. I'm an honest man," said Quincy, smiling.

Without haste, with an almost undue precision and gravity, as it appeared to the boy, Marshall made the three cards fall one after another in front of Quincy. One was a queen. The boy was sure of that.

"Two for me," said Raney.

Clearly Tanner saw them, this time, as his sharp eye grew more practiced in staring into the yellow, mirrorlike face of the watch.

Hank Raney got a nine of spades and a jack.

Was it not the very jack which, a moment before, had appeared on the bottom of the pack, as it was held over the watch?

He stared hard.

Yes! That lowest card—its reflection was perfectly clear and bright in the burnished surface of the gold—was now an ace of diamonds.

He took a quick breath.

He did not know much about cards, but like most curious youngsters he had picked up a little of the ways of a poker game.

At least, he knew that cards are not supposed to be dealt from the bottom of the pack.

He changed his glance to the face of Raney, and saw there a sudden tightening of the lips, as though to suppress a smile. And again, though Johnnie was no expert at the game, he knew enough of all games to guess that Raney had not the facial control necessary for a gambler.

Bray had taken three cards, in the meantime, and the dealer then discarded all of his.

"I'll take a longer chance," he said.

And he slowly dealt himself an entirely new hand of five cards. Young John Tanner saw those cards one by one; but there was only one card which was of special importance to him; that was the ace of diamonds. Three other aces, he saw, went into that hand, but the ace of diamonds could only have come off the bottom of the pack.

It did not need a mind reader to tell exactly what was happening at that table. The gull, Raney, had been given three jacks in the deal, and another jack in the draw. He would bet his last penny on such a hand as four of a kind. And, in the meantime, there sat Marshall, cool and calm and smiling, with four aces out of the draw!

The very brain of the boy turned giddy. A great heat fumed upward in him and clouded his brain. Then he began to speculate.

What should he do?

That the three visitors were all rascals and that they all had joined hands in the plucking of Raney, he had not the slightest doubt, any more than he had that Marshall was the leader and organizer of the pack. He ground his teeth. If he warned Raney, there would probably be a fight and, in case of a fight, there would be the frontiersman against three fellows, every one of whom looked as dangerous as a snake.

Besides, it appeared from Raney's own account, that he was by no means a hero. He fled, he had said, from a single Indian. He never took the chances of personal combat. And, even if he were able to take care of himself on the open prairies, the dangers of a fight in a small, closed room were infinitely greater.

So young John Tanner lay there in the berth, his jaw set, silent, and saw the betting begin, saw larger and larger sums put in, saw his friend Raney put in the last of his money and find it insufficient to call the last bet which had been made against him.

Would his rifle be accepted?

Of course, it would at a reasonable price. He laid a pair of fine pistols, also, both double-barreled, and apparently beautifully made. Marshall looked them over with a professional eye.

Yes, they would be accepted, also, and they would just make up the right amount.

So the bet was made which would probably turn Hank Raney into a beggar.

"Hold on!" said the boy.

Raney looked up with a frown; but the other three jerked about in their chairs with sudden suspicion and malice.

"What's this? A plant?" demanded Quincy savagely.

"A plant is what it is!" declared Bray, putting a hand inside his coat and looking about him with dangerous eyes.

"Well," said Marshall, "don't tell me that you've had a helper up there all the time, Mr. Raney? Not a helper up there, ready to read my hand over my shoulder—because he could see my cards, of course!"

The boy pointed furiously straight at Marshall.

"I can tell Mr. Raney's hand, too," said he.

"You can do what?" said Marshall, flushing and suddenly scowling.

"I can tell what's in Mr. Raney's hand," insisted the boy.

"You can't do that, Johnnie," said his friend. "You've been seeing things in a dream."

"No," said the boy, "but I've been seeing them just where Mr. Marshall sees them. I've been watching the reflections in the back of that gold watch. If it was only the time that he wanted to see, why didn't he have it face up on the table? It's as good as a mirror, and he deals the cards over it!"

Raney, slowly, as though an invisible hand were lifting him, arose from the table.

"It's kind of a funny idea," he said, through his teeth. "Suppose that you try to tell me what I had?"

"You held up three jacks," said John Tanner, "and he passed you a nine of spades off the top of the deck—and a jack of clubs off the bottom of the pack."

Raney gaped. It seemed as though he could not comprehend, at once, such infernal meanness and chicanery.

But Marshall flew into a fine passion. He thumped a hand upon the top of the table. "You're right, my friends!" said he to his companions. "We've been trapped in here, all together. Raney's a villain and the boy's his confederate. Get the table stakes and get out of here onto the deck! Scoundrels, for gentlemen to fall into their hands—professional gamblers, I take my word!"

At the command to take the table stakes, there was no hesitation. The thin-faced Mr. Quincy, as though he had been waiting for that very instant, presented his hat to one corner of the table and, tilting the table top, he caused all the piles of money to fall into a musical confusion, sliding in heaps and strings and masses into the crown of the hat.

That would not have gone unresisted by Raney, perhaps, but the alert Bray, at the very same moment, drew a short, double-barreled revolver and pointed it at Raney's head.

14 · THE FIGHT

THE boy did not hesitate. He saw only two things, the smiling, sneering face of Marshall and the savage look of Bray as he held the gun leveled at Raney.

There was one more thing that might be of importance. Since the boy had last spoken and precipitated the crisis, none of the three had given so much as a glance to him. And yonder stood their gull, Raney, his face convulsed, the purple veins standing out on his forehead.

Once the three were out of the cabin with the spoils, there was nothing that Raney could do. Even if the captain of the boat were his friend, the words of three individuals, all well dressed and apparently of some education, would be enough to beat down the testimony of the frontiersman and a ragged boy.

Tanner could see these things at a glance. He could see another thing, also; the leveled gun was the only drawn weapon, and he hurled himself from the height of the bunk straight at the shoulders of Bray.

He doubled himself up in the air. He aimed his doubled knees at the small of the other's back. He aimed his sharp elbows at the back of Bray's neck. And with both knees and elbows he struck home.

Marshall managed a hasty exclamation of warning. But it was too late, and Bray dropped forward with a crash upon the floor. So great was his surprise that he did not even fire the pistol, however blindly. The blow shocked him. He lay still where he had fallen.

While the boy pulled himself together and got on his hands and knees, he saw the long legs of Raney stride past him, and the iron-hard fist of the frontiersman smashed into the face of big Marshall. The latter reeled back a step. But he was not quite stunned. He got out a bowie knife longer and more curved than the tusk of a walrus.

John Tanner saw the flash of it. He also saw a more immediate danger behind his friend, for there was Quincy, his lip curling back from his yellow teeth, swinging Raney's own rifle like a club to brain its owner.

John Tanner leaped as a cat leaps, from hands and feet, and hurled his weight against the knees of Quincy.

The little man toppled over him, and Johnnie kicked himself out from the wall with both feet, like a swimmer, and grappled with the enemy.

He was big, strong, capable of endurance, and now that the first blow had been struck, his courage was at the fever point. But Quincy was like a wildcat. In a scant second, he had caught John Tanner with a strangle

72

hold which was a full nelson, and the head of the boy jerked back, breathing became impossible, a black mist covered his eyes.

Through that mist he saw Marshall fall like a tower, catch at the edge of the table, miss it and topple loosely to the floor. Through that same mist he saw Raney come with a bound, and suddenly the pressure was released from about his throat.

He was able to sit up, gasping; not even water after his long famine tasted so sweet as the smoke-tainted air of that little cabin.

"Get up!" commanded Raney.

He staggered to his feet.

Then he could see all that had happened. In the first place, in the far corner of the cabin stood his friend, Raney, erect, at ease, even smiling. And the cause of his smiling was, no doubt, the pair of long-barreled pistols with which he covered the others in the room.

Of these, Quincy was struggling back to his feet from the lower bunk, where he had been hurled or knocked flat with a blow. Marshall began to sit up, with blood running in a steady stream down one side of his face, a very wild-eyed and different man from the smooth gambler of the moment before. And even the stocky Bray now pulled himself to his hands and knees where he stuck, swaying. He had fallen so that his whole weight came down fairly on his nose. It was broken, and the flow of blood from it was amazing.

In spite of his suffering, he reached for the pistol which had dropped from his grasp. But John Tanner saw the move. It was a cruel thing to do, but he brought his heel down on the back of Bray's hand—brought it down with all his might—and, as Bray jerked his hand away with a sharp screech of pain, Johnnie hurriedly scooped up the weapon.

He stood back beside Raney and, like him, he leveled the pistol.

"Now, Johnnie," said the tall man, "if you see one of them make a shady move or so much as reach into a coat pocket, let him have both of the balls that are in your gun. D'you hear?"

"I hear you, sir," said Johnnie. "And I'll do it," he added through his teeth.

"Aye, and they'll take your word that you'll do it," said Raney, grinning.

"Marshall, it don't seem to've turned out the way you expected."

Marshall, a handkerchief pressed against his bleeding and swollen cheek, where the hard knuckles of Raney had bitten through almost to the bone, was mastering himself as fast as he could.

"Raney," he said, "this is an outrage that you'll hear of later on!"

"I kind of think I will," said Raney. "Other folks are going to hear about it, too!"

"There's law on the boat," said Quincy, rubbing his arm gingerly, which had been bruised and almost broken by his fall into the bunk. "There's law on the boat. The captain has the right to act. We'll see how long it takes to get this fine pair into a set of irons. The next sheriff can handle them better than we can!"

Johnnie Tanner began to grow alarmed.

It was true that the three rascals could testify against two, one of these a mere stripling.

What, then, would happen in case they appealed to the authorities of the law? They would do that. They would do anything, so long as they had a chance to damage the two who had foiled them so completely. It was odd to see how the passion of hatred gripped them.

Bray, with the face of inconceivable ugliness, with the blood running in streams from his nose, thrust out his lower jaw through the blood, and with the glare of a prize fighter seemed about to rush in for the attack at the next instant. His friend Quincy, on the other hand, had turned from sallow to a sort of yellow green, and he trembled from head to foot. One might have thought that it was terror which controlled and unnerved him, but his eyes glared like the eyes of a madman.

Finally, big Marshall had grown white, calm, dignified. His eyes seemed to have sunk into his head, and it was plain at a glance that his malice, unlike that of the others, would last through a lifetime. He controlled himself perfectly, after his first brief outburst.

"Gentlemen," he said to the other two, "since it appears that we've fallen into bad hands, the thing for us to remember is that such insults as these have to be revenged personally. For my part, I should be reluctant to call in the powers of the law. I prefer to take the responsibility to myself."

"And me!" growled Bray, his voice hoarse and bubbling in his throat.

"You need only return to us the money—"

"Why should I return your money? What money's yours?" asked Raney sharply.

"You hear?" snarled Quincy.

He appealed to his two friends. He was half hysterical with his fury.

"What money's ours?" asked Marshall, raising his brows. "Do you actually ask what money's ours, my friend?"

"That's what I ask," said Raney.

"You mistake," said Marshall. "You think that we wish to take away our just and fair winnings from you. No. For my own part and personally speaking, I have nothing to do with men of your kind. I play at cards for small stakes with my friends and with gentlemen whom I consider worthy of being my friends. Mr. Raney, I am frightfully deceived in you. I shall never again consider that I am a judge of character. I could have sworn that you are a gentleman. I am still ready to be convinced. The little fool, yonder, precipitated matters in such a sudden manner that, of course, you did not have a chance to think calmly."

"That's enough of the guff," said Raney, breaking into this calm-voiced speech. "You don't win yourself anything here with that sort of talk, friend. You've made your play, and you've lost. Are you gunna start howling now, like a cur?"

"Like what?" said Marshall. "Mr. Raney, you know in what manner you can be held accountable for such language used to a gentleman with a gentleman's standing?"

"Come along!" said Raney impatiently. "I know what you are. You're a gang of thugs. Don't try to pull wool over my eyes any more. You trimmed me. I was a fool, and the boy saved my money and my face for me. Now, get out of here!"

"It's not possible!" said Marshall, in apparent astonishment. "Are you driving us to the captain to tell him that we've just been robbed in your cabin, and that we must invite him to throw you both into irons?"

Raney looked at the cheat with a broad grin. "Marshall," said he, "you're pretty smart. You ought to be a politician. But you've lost this hand, and you ought to know it. You wanted my money. You were crooked to get it. Well, by rights, I should take every penny off of both of you, and your watches, too. You wouldn't howl to the captain. He's not fool enough to believe you. One man and a boy don't tackle three roughs like the set of you unless they're cornered first.

"I'm leaving you the coin that you've still got in your pockets. I'm only keeping the stakes that were on the table and the gun that the boy took from Bray, yonder. He's got a right to some sort of a commission; call it a kind of a keepsake, if you want to. Now I've told you what you can do. Get out of this cabin, or I'll kick you out!"

There was a slight pause after this, and during the pause a low whine was heard forming in the throat of Bray, like the shrill noise which a bull terrier makes when it is begging for trouble.

Quincy, too, looked quite ready for anything, and at a word or a mere sign from Marshall a desperate attack might have been made, even in face of the leveled guns. But Marshall was not a fool. He spent only an instant surveying the two who stood ready there on the farther side of the little cabin.

"Quincy, Bray," he said at last. "We'll leave here. This is only the beginning of the story. Mr. Raney will realize that, later on. Now, go ahead of me through that door."

They hesitated a little. But it was apparent that they were accustomed to the domination of the taller man, and now they filed sullenly, silently through the door and out upon the open deck. Young Johnnie Tanner closed the door on the three of them and securely bolted it.

15 · THE GENEROUS HUNTER

WHEN he turned toward his friend, he expected some outburst of emotion, some suggestion of gratitude, at the least. He had saved Raney eight hundred dollars and he had done it at the risk of his life.

But Raney merely said: "Sit down there and count out that money."

Johnnie Tanner was hurt, but he did as he was told. He quietly spilled the heavy contents from the hat of Quincy onto the table. Then he checked off the contents into piles of ten. Most of the money consisted of ten-dollar gold pieces, with a few double eagles thrown in. There was a quantity of fives, also, but the ten-dollar pieces were predominant.

Every little pile made a hundred dollars. A hundred dollars!

He had heard his father speak of large sums. He had seen the bright face of the Daughter of the Moon. But this was actual gold, the current coin of the land, not a story, not a jewel. In one hand he could hold more solid cash than ever had passed through his fingers in all the days of his life.

A strange, cold fever began to run through the veins of the boy. With narrowed eyes, he checked off the bright little piles. They made a sensible weight upon the table. Money, to John Tanner, had been a dream, a name, rather than a reality. Now it loaded the table before him.

Raney alone had put a little more than eight hundred dollars into the game. The other three had averaged even more, as though to encourage him by the sight of what he might win if "luck" should turn his way.

Altogether, there were twenty-nine piles of ten-dollar gold pieces. There was six hundred and fifty dollars made up of the larger and the smaller denominations.

"Thirty-five hundred and fifty dollars!" said the boy.

And he pushed back his chair with a gasp.

"Why, Mr. Raney, you're rich, I'd say. Thirty-five hundred dollars, that's enough—"

"Enough to fit out a whole trading outfit, mules, horses,

trade goods, and wagons!" exclaimed Raney enthusiastically.

He continued to pace up and down the floor for a moment.

"Now count eight hundred out of the lot!" said he.

The boy obeyed and stacked rapidly eight of the hundred-dollar piles upon a corner of the table.

Raney swept it off and poured it into the mouth of a capacious purse of soft leather.

"You see the rest?" said he.

"Yes," said the boy.

"How much is it?"

"It's twenty-seven hundred and fifty dollars, I suppose."

"It's twenty-seven hundred and fifty dollars," nodded Raney.

"And who does it belong to?"

"Why, to you, Mr. Raney."

The same fire that had been in the eyes of the boy was in those of his friend now. And Raney, resting his knuckles upon the edge of the table, leaned loftily above John Tanner.

"Don't you get a part?" demanded Raney again.

"Don't I get a part?" echoed Tanner, amazed. "Why, I'm only a boy, and I don't count when it comes to money."

"Don't you?"

Suddenly the big man laughed, though the laughter came groaningly through his teeth.

"Blast me," said he, "if I don't almost wish that I was a crook. That's what I wish. I'd fit out the neatest little trading party you ever seen, and I'd have some of those buffalo robes off of the Sioux or the Cheyennes. They know how to tan 'em, and they know how to paint 'em, too, for the fools that want to collect curios! But I can't be that big a crook. Have you got a purse around anywhere?"

"No," said the boy.

"Get one, then," said the other. "Or a little sack of leather, that would be better. And load that money away into it, because it's all yours!"

John gripped the edge of the table, and his eyes were as big as moons. "All of that?" he breathed softly.

"Yes, every penny of that!"

Johnnie shook his head.

"It really couldn't be all mine!" he said.

"Why not?"

"Why, a boy couldn't—"

"Couldn't he?" said the other. "No, he couldn't. A boy couldn't make himself into a cannon ball and jump onto three armed crooks and save the life of a partner that he's known less'n one day. A boy couldn't, hardly— jump in his nightshirt and fight like a young demon, like a wildcat—a grown man wouldn't hardly do that, and how could a boy do it?"

He nodded. His grin was almost a sneer.

"No, I guess that you didn't do it, Johnnie. I only dreamed that I saw you come out of that bunk like a chunk of lead and floor Bray. It wasn't a fact when that Quincy was about to brain me from behind, that you tumbled him. It wasn't a fact that you let yourself get about choked for my sake. No, I just dreamed all of them things, son. None of them really happened?

"No, you get that twenty-seven hundred and fifty. If it was twenty-seven thousand and fifty, I've had my share. I've got back the eight hundred that I don't deserve to get back, because I was such a fool, and I get a whole skin and a head that ain't been cracked open, which it sure would've been, except for you. Pocket up that money, son, because I'll never touch it!"

Johnnie reached out suddenly toward the treasure. He jerked his hands away, as though he had touched fire.

"Suppose," said he, slowly, "that when I was being choked—well, in another minute I would have been dead. Then you came."

He grinned.

"I wasn't seeing very clearly," he said, "but you looked pretty good to me, you and your long legs, Mr. Raney, as you came stepping across the floor."

Then he shook his head, firmly, decidedly.

"I like money as well as the next one," he said. "But I can't take more than a share. I'll take eight hundred, the same as you did. Then the rest we split. Like partners. Because we fought like partners to get it."

"I won't have it," said Raney.

"Then I'll throw it away," said the boy firmly. "I'll give back the rest to the three of them."

"Not a penny!" cried Raney. "Those yellow dogs!"

"Then we make it share and share about?" insisted the boy.

Raney sat down on the edge of the lower bunk and stared for a long moment at the youngster.

"I see where I been wrong," said he with a sigh.

"How?" asked the lad.

"I been trying these years to get a partner. I've tried to get them where they was as old as me. But years, they spoil a man. Years, they turn his brain all wrong. And now I can see it. I should've tried to get a kid, like you are—if there are any more like you."

He paused, and a hot flush went over the face of Johnnie Tanner. Aunt Maggie had been rather sparing in praise. It was a thing for which he was not prepared. He felt as though he had been knighted by the accolade of a king.

"How old are you, Johnnie?" asked the frontiersman. "Sixteen? Seventeen?"

"I'm fifteen, pretty nearly," said Johnnie.

Raney leaped to his feet.

Then he sat down again as suddenly.

"Fifteen!" said he. "Fifteen—nearly!

"Aye, aye, aye!" said Raney slowly. "I begin to see. Sometimes you come across 'em, the one in a million. I guess that you're one of those, son. Now, if I could have my way, you and me would team together from this point on, and we'd do something together. Why, we could move the Rockies right out of our way, and run rivers through the desert, and melt the whole of the snows in December. That's what we could do. But, instead of that, you'll get off this boat and take the next one back to your home—or the one that starts you on the quickest way along."

"You mean, because of all of this money?" he asked.

"Well, and wouldn't it almost set you up in business?" said the other.

"It's nothing, compared to what I'm after," admitted the boy.

"Hold on? What was stole from your dad, then?"

"What?"

He hesitated. Then, still blushing, he said: "Look here, Mr. Raney, there's no business in the world that I wouldn't tell you about—I mean, no business that has to do with me. Not since the second when I saw you jump across the room to knock Quincy sky-west and crooked. But this business isn't mine. It's my father's. So I don't dare to talk even to you about it."

Raney frowned, but the frown lasted for only a moment. And then he was smiling again.

"You've got the right," said he. "And that makes you twice the man that you were. Because why? Because a man that can keep his tongue still is the man that's worth twice as much as the talking fool. The Injuns know that! Even the Injuns. But tell me, Johnnie. Are you still going to keep on the trail of what was stolen?"

Johnnie drew his breath in, and then he nodded soberly.

"I have to," said he. "And now I want to, more than ever before. If only I can manage to find the trail again!"

"Tell me. You feel kind of lucky, after to-night?"

"I feel mighty lucky," said the boy. "And sort of safe, being with you, Mr. Raney."

The big man grinned. "You feel safe with me, do you? I dunno why, when I've got you nearly brained and very nearly choked to death inside of one day. But if you want, I'll stay with you, son, until you get to the finish of that trail, if it takes us ten years together to turn the trick."

"Hold on," cried the boy. "You wouldn't want to promise a thing like that."

"Wouldn't I?"

"No, because it's only my business, and not yours really. It's only my business, and you wouldn't want to give up your time."

"Wait right there," said the other. "Partners don't have business outside of each other. Do we shake on that?"

He stood up. The boy rose also. They joined their hands in a long grip.

"I'm mighty proud and happy!" said the boy.

"So am I," said the other, "and more than you!"

16 · THE THREE PAWNEES

THERE was not one word of comment from the three disappointed gamblers after the fracas of that night. They carried their disappointments and their sorrows away with them when the ship arrived at Cincinnati and, going ashore, they merely turned to give that unlucky steamboat a final glare of hatred.

Johnnie Tanner and his friend went ashore at the same point. It amazed the boy to find such a city so far west. It was said that the population of this swiftest-growing of cities was now over fifty thousand and the town looked it! It was said that there were more than forty churches, a college, an asylum for the insane, all the advantages of a big community. The town had grown up like a weed.

"You know why they've got to have an asylum for the crazy ones out here?" said Hank Raney.

"Why have they, Hank?" said the boy.

"Because so many folks go off their heads when they see the way that luck has passed 'em by. They see so many folks get rich while they're still doing day labor, that they can't stand it. I recollect down on the other shore, down there in Lexington, or thereabouts, where they sell mules for a hundred and fifty dollars and a she-ass for six hundred—I recollect that down there was a fellow who sold his right to two thousand acres for a rifle."

"What?" cried Johnnie Tanner. "For a rifle?"

"Why not? Fifty or sixty years back, all that the land amounted to was to give you a chance to break your back and spoil your good nature. Suppose that you cleared off a lot of it and raised a stack of corn. Suppose that you had a lot of acres and that the yield was big. Well, what would you do with it? You might load it partly into your little hand mill and make enough flour to carry you through the winter. And you might save some more for seed for the next year.

"But what about all the rest? Well, you could feed it to hogs, say. Those that the bad luck of sickness didn't carry off, and those that didn't run away and turn wild in the woods, you could slaughter 'em, and turn 'em into ham and bacon, and load the pork onto a flatboat and start on the trip down to the market. But where was the market? Why, it was clean down to New Orleans! You had to float down all that way. Maybe you got nearly there, and the river pirates scooped you in. Maybe you got halfway, and you hit a snag and good-by to your boat and the load on it.

"When you got to New Orleans, maybe the market was full of just such fellows as yourself, and it was pretty hard to even give the stuff away. Well, that's why there was no value onto the land out here. No railroads. No roads of hardly any kind. A good, fat soil to set down onto and make yourself a fine homestead, but more than you raised for yourself was clean wastage. So what was the good of having more than forty acres, say?

"Well, that fellow I was speaking of, he traded in two thousand acres for an old rifle. Right now that land is worth sixty dollars an acre, and there's buildings on it and improvements worth another fifty thousand. And when the old fellow came back and seen what the other man had made out of what he's practically given away, he lost his wits clean and never spoke a right word after. That's what this country is likely to do to you. It goes past you so fast that your eye gets blurred. It grows the way that a tree grows."

They found a clothing store with a very complete line of goods, ready-made, and there they bought clothes for Johnnie. Big Raney advised him, and he got tough, durable homespun of a gray color, stout boots, a hat, and all the necessary incidentals of an outfit.

They went back to the boat, keeping a wary lookout for Marshall and his two companions, but the precious trio did not appear. One trouble haunted the mind of the boy; it was the fear that Harry, the thief, might have landed at some such place as this, without going on to St. Louis, the natural end of the river voyage, but Raney was very optimistic. He argued that Harry had a job on the ship which was carrying him and, therefore, he probably had signed on for the entire trip. He would not be employed for merely a short portion of the run. Besides, Harry's talk about the Far West and the Indians was in itself almost a sufficient proof that he intended to go out to his old stamping grounds.

"He's been to the big cities and had his kicking," said Raney. "Now he's sick of 'em. He wants to get out into the open once more. He looked like a poor tramp to you, there in New York. Well, he may be a good deal of a man out on the prairies. If he's once lived fat and easy and big in an Indian tribe, he's likely to hanker after the same kind of a life again. If he won out before, he's likely to try to win out again. No, no, son, don't you worry. We're on the right trail. I only hope that we can get to St. Louis before he's branched out and left the town for parts farther west still, or north or south."

Such talk as this made Johnnie feel far more at ease. But every night of the trip he was dreaming about the final meeting with the enemy. And every night he imagined that he had collared the flying thief, and that big Hank Raney was speeding up from the rear to come to the rescue and terminate the fight.

The river, the river life, the towns they passed were enough to occupy him during the day. At Cincinnati the stream was nearly half a mile wide, and it grew by degrees. At Louisville it was a mile and a half across!

After the wild procession of the forested bluffs and rolling banks of the river, wild as the end of the world, it was a strange shock to come out on the big towns, like Louisville and Lexington. There were twenty thousand people in Lexington. It was a center of rich, level grazing and farming country. The wealth of the soil, said a planter who came on board here, was inexhaustible. It was composed largely of alluvial deposits and could never be drained of its productive qualities.

Raney used to listen to such talk with a smile of content. "Back there in the East," he was fond of saying, "they's a string of big towns, a lot of shipping, a lot of noise. They think that they're the whole United States. But they ain't. They're only the fringe. You're getting into the heart of the country now. Not right the middle of the heart of it either. There'll be a thousand miles more to travel, before you get to the center of things. I'll tell you a little thing. There'll one day be a hundred million people in this land of ours."

"One hundred million?" gasped Johnnie Tanner. "There couldn't hardly be that many people all of one nation!"

"All right. If you can wait long enough, you'll see. Two hundred million, maybe, some day."

They passed out of the mouth of the great Ohio, the "beautiful river" of the early French, into the stream of the Mississippi, and since it was early morning, Johnnie Tanner was on deck in a state of the greatest excitement. He hardly knew what he expected to see. He rather thought it must be like a limitless ocean of inland waters, flowing. But he was vastly disappointed.

It seemed hardly larger than the Ohio itself, and it was a frightfully dirty tide that he saw rolling south. They turned up into the current, and the speed of their going at once diminished perceptibly. The green shores of the Ohio had slid smoothly, sweetly by. This slower drudging up the stream was, compared to the former part of the trip, like the difference between walking and flying. The shores, too, were at first low, uninteresting. But gradually they grew loftier, more noble, more imposing. And when they finally reached St. Louis, the boy was more astonished than ever.

It was a big and growing city. East St. Louis was hardly existent. But on the rolling ground of the western bank of the stream, as one went north, appeared the serried ranks of the houses, substantially built and arranged in squares.

Johnnie Tanner had to rub his eyes and stare at the thing as at a mirage, which may be described in the most minute detail, but which cannot be given credence. It seemed to him that they had journeyed halfway around the world, and here in the heart of the wilderness was a flourishing metropolis!

They slipped into a wharf on the big docks. They stepped ashore. And the very first thing that met the staring eyes of Tanner was a group of three Indians, blanketed to the tops of their heads and walking together with a slow, dignified stride. They wore hair-fringed leggings and dyed feathers projected above their heads.

"Look at 'em, the hair-lifting, cattle-stealing blackguards," said Raney. "Dog-gone me if I ain't sort of glad to see their ornery hides once more. Those Pawnee scoundrels! This here sight of 'em, it puts me right back into the old days."

"How d'you know that they're Pawnees?" asked the boy.

"There's something so ornery and mean about the whole look of 'em," said the other. "Besides, you can see their top-knots. They shave off most of their hair, that section of the Pawnees. They only leave a scalp lock. And I can tell you something. It's a mighty proud Cheyenne or Sioux that's got a Pawnee scalp lock drying in the smoke of his tepee. I know 'em. And, here and there, is some of 'em that know me, pretty good!"

He chuckled as he said this.

They were walking up the street, their packs on their shoulders, for the hunter disdained taking a carriage to a hotel. And the three Pawnees, after crossing the street, turned straight back toward them.

"Watch lively and have your hand ready to yank out that double-barreled pistol of yours—the one that Bray loaned to you, son. It's just possible that those three rapscallions have recognized my face. It ain't likely. White men all look pretty much the same to them; just the same as red men look all pretty much the same to our eyes. We ain't trained to find the differences, d'you see? However, we'll look sharp. But whatever you do, don't start trouble with Pawnees unless you got to! They might try to pass a knife into me; or they might act like old friends."

Johnnie Tanner went on, walking as on eggshells.

The Pawnees came closer. In their enveloping blankets, they looked like grimly mumming figures; and as they drew nearer, Johnnie could see the gleam of bright eyes and the contour of savage features. They moved with infinite deliberation and dignity, keeping their eyes straight before them.

When they came closer, the hunter raised his right hand.

"How!" said he.

They stopped at the same instant.

They made an answering gesture and, speaking almost in one and the same breath, they replied: "How!"

Then they stepped on, as slowly, as deliberately as before, with their eyes fastened straight before them.

17 · MORE HISTORY

BIG Hank Raney, with a step and a manner almost exactly like those of the Indians, went on up the street a short distance without looking over his shoulder. His face wore a distinctly worried expression. At last he stopped short and turned about. The three Pawnees had disappeared.

"No, sir, they ain't forgot me," said Hank Raney.

He shook his head to emphasize his sureness on that point.

"Would they be likely to?" asked the boy, quite at sea.

He received no answer. The mind of his friend was filled with his own thoughts.

"That was old Red Mane himself," said Raney.

"Red Mane?" said the boy. "I don't think that you've ever mentioned him to me."

Still Raney poured out his own reflections and paid no heed to his companion.

"The second one was Two-tailed Calf, all right, but who was the third of the rascals? I've seen him. Wait a minute. By the great horn spoon! That's Bending Bow! Have Bending Bow and Red Mane buried their troubles and become friends? If they have, then look out, Cheyennes. Look out, Dakotas! The Pawnee wolves will be clawing your throats for you in no time! Yes, sir, it's Bending Bow and Red Mane, and together!"

"And they're great chiefs?" asked Johnnie patiently.

"Great? They're as great as poison in the air!" said his friend. "When the Cheyennes think of Red Mane or Bending Bow, they get chills and fever. So do the Sioux. They've taken enough scalps to paper a house with 'em. They've lifted enough hair to make clothes for fifty men. That's the kind of chiefs that they are."

"They're the head chiefs?" said the boy.

"They're not the head chiefs. Old Arrow Flint is the biggest noise in the tribe. He's the medicine man. And he's the old scratch, too, I can tell you. But he does his deviltry inside of a tepee. It's a good tepee to keep out of!"

"Is he a real wizard?" asked the boy.

"I'll tell you; I seen him with my own eyes putting a curse on Trotting Horse, the Cheyenne chief, and the right arm of Trotting Horse withered up to the bone, a month later. I saw that arm with my own eyes, too, before and after the curse. You can make up your own mind. I only tell you exactly what I seen myself!"

Superstition so utterly gross as this in his friend amazed Johnnie Tanner. But big Hank Raney spoke with such conviction that he could not help taking the matter rather seriously.

He stared up at Raney's face, and the latter still looked dark enough. "It's a confounded outrage!" said Hank Raney. "There's enough men here in St. Louis to clean up every Pawnee on the plains, and that's what had ought to happen to 'em. But instead, they let the red hounds come into the town here. I'll bet you that they've wined and dined 'em. Yes, sir, I'll bet you plenty that they've given those two murderers and hair-lifters fine presents, and everything that their hearts desire!"

"Why should they do that?" asked the boy.

"Because," said the hunter, "some of the rich traders want the Pawnees made friendly. They want the Pawnees made friendly to them. They don't care how many settlers and trappers and small traders the Pawnees kill off. The more, the better, matter of fact. That wipes out the competition and leaves them a clean field. All that they care for is to get the Pawnees on their side for a few years, so they've got the three big chiefs in here, and I suppose that they've given them so much junk that nobody'll be able to get so much as a cup of water out of the chiefs, after this, for less'n a barrel of beads! Kind of turns my stomach, Johnnie!"

"But what have they got against you?" asked the boy, more interested every moment in the odd reaction of Raney to this meeting.

"They got hardly anything at all against me," said Raney absently. "They got hardly anything at all against me. Only, one time, a brace of young Pawnees came up and charged my camp, where I was boiling some water to make tea, and then—"

"Jiminy!" breathed Johnnie Tanner. "They charged right in on you, out of the dark?"

"Well, that's what they intended to do. But I was telling

88

you about that black horse that I borrowed from the Osages?"

"Oh, yes! I remember every word of that!"

"Well, that horse has the nose of a wolf and the ear of a rabbit. He smelled trouble while it was still half a mile upward, and he warned me as sure as could be."

"So you could pack and escape?"

"Well, the way of it was that I was feeling pretty lazy and sleepy, son."

"Yes?" said the boy.

Then he added: "But you always said that you ran from Indians."

"Yes. I always run from 'em. But there's such a thing as being too dog-gone tired to care. So I just left the black hoss there to sort of take their eye and fill it, if they came along, and I crawled outside the rim of the brush—I had camped near a little water hole that night—and there I lay down with my rifle and sure enough hoped that I wouldn't be bothered, but that I would have a good sleep there.

"Pretty soon, as I looked toward the fire, I seen the back of a man sliding out from the brush and making for a place where I had rolled up my blanket, to make it look like there was a man inside of it. He went sneaking along toward it, and another red demon of a Pawnee, he came out, too, and started for the stallion, which the Osages called him something that means midnight, so that's his name.

"And Midnight, he lets out a snort and rears up. And just then I get my bead between the eyes of the second Pawnee, and I let drive and land him deader than a fish. The other Pawnee, he scoots for it, and he gets away, but he leaves a trail of blood for quite a ways."

"Did you load so quickly that you were able to get in a second shot?" asked the boy.

"No. I didn't have time for that. Three jumps, and he would be behind a black wall, it was so dog-gone dark. He was already just sort of wavering like a shadow on the rim of the firelight when I threw my hunting knife after him, and it just managed to nail him in the leg."

The boy squinted his eyes a little and shuddered.

"Did the knife stick in?"

"No. That knife had a weighted head. And after a

couple of his jumps, it worked its way out, but he didn't walk very good with that leg for a long time after, I reckon. So I went out and picked up the knife and came back to the horse and the dead man. And the minute that I seen him, I was sorry."

"Yes," said the boy. "It must be a terrible thing to have to kill a man, and then to stand and look at what you've done."

"Son," said the other, "sometimes you talk a kind of a way that bothers me a lot. After you get to know the Pawnees as good as I know 'em, you'll wish that the whole dog-gone tribe was dead, the way that I wish 'em. I'd even like to have the killing of them myself, if it was all handy and safe, d'you see?"

"Then what troubled you about the dead man there by the campfire? Was it some one who had been a friend?"

"He'd been a friend to himself, and to nobody else," declared the hunter. "That's the only person that he'd been a friend to, my son. But when I seen him, I knew that he was Walking Afternoon."

"That's a strange name," said the boy.

"Yeah. They got some funny names, those Pawnees. Walking shadows of the afternoon, perhaps they might've meant. I don't know. Besides, when you translate the names out of the lingo, they sound pretty much different. Anyway, there was Walking Afternoon with a bullet between his eyes that had let out the most of the little brains that he had. And all at once I remembered that he was the nephew and the favorite nephew of Bending Bow. Wow!"

He uttered a loud groan.

"Bending Bow," he continued, "was the brother of Walking Afternoon's mother, and that's a mighty close relationship among the Injuns. Almost closer than father and son, I guess. And Bending Bow loved that dog-gone hoss-stealing, worthless, ugly redskin of a nephew of his. He loved him so much that he set him up with the price of three wives, but Walking Afternoon was so mean that they wouldn't stay with him, and the whole three of them up and left. Well, Bending Bow staked him again, and always treated him fine. And there was Walking Afternoon dead, and there was that other ornery Pawnee with the knife cut in his leg, galloping off to tell Bending Bow the favor that I had done to all of them!"

He groaned again. Then he added: "Well, son, I didn't mind so much the Osages being on my trail. But it was a different thing when the Pawnees began to want my hair. So I figgered that I'd go back and take a rest in the mountains for a while and do some little shooting for fun; deer shooting is what I mean. And the memory of that horse Midnight, it's pulled me back here to the rim of the troubleland! Now I can see that I've been a fool. All the three of 'em spotted me, and they'll start their monkeyshines right away to knife me!"

"But you won't leave," said the boy. "I don't think that you'll turn back on the trail."

"No, Johnnie. I won't go back on my word to you."

"Hold on," said Johnnie Tanner. "I don't believe a word that you told me about being afraid of Indians. I'll bet that you've never run from any of them, without first letting 'em hear a couple of bullets whizz around their ears or, maybe, come still closer than whizzing."

"Well, Johnnie," said the other, "it looks like I can't persuade you, very well. But I want you to know that caution is worth a lot more than courage any time. And particularly, caution when you've been spotted by a pair of rambunctious snakes like Bending Bow and Red Mane. They'd eat my heart raw. They wouldn't even be asking me for toast with it, I can tell you. They wouldn't even want it boiled three minutes, like a soft egg. They'd eat it raw. And they'd eat yours, too, just because you were here along with me. Come along, Johnnie."

They walked on down the street into the center of the town, and there they found such a roar of traffic, so many lumbering drays, so many rattling buggies, such hosts of patient horses laboring with nodding heads, and so many mounted men darting here and there through the traffic mass, that Johnnie felt, for the moment, that he was back in Manhattan.

It was a different crowd, to be sure. There were several men whom he passed in the crowd who were dressed in deerskins like big Raney. There were others on horseback with the look of Cossacks, or any other wild riders of the plains. And every one was brown-faced and seemed

91

quick and eager, as though at that very moment pursuing something of the greatest importance.

"Hello, hello!" said Johnnie suddenly. "There's the three of them again."

And they saw the three familiar forms of the Pawnees striding through the crowd just ahead of them.

18 · THE THIEF AGAIN

"How did they get there ahead of us? And why doesn't any one pay attention to 'em?" demanded John Tanner.

"Because St. Louis is far enough west to know that Injuns don't like to be stared at. A fine-looking set the three of them are, when you look at 'em from behind. Looking at those three backs and shoulders, you don't see the murder in them so easy. Aye, and there they've met their own kind of a white man. There they've come to the right sort. He'll trim them. He'll bleed them white. If I ain't a liar and a blind man, that's Pawnee Harry come back to his own!"

"Who?" asked the boy, following the three braves with the keenest interest.

"Pawnee Harry," said the other. "The smoothest cheat, the crookedest trader, the most medicine-making liar that ever stole hosses on the plains or married Indian wives. Pawnee Harry—he's got the mind of a fox and the ways of a snake. That's what he has!"

"But which is he?"

"Don't you see that tall, narrow fellow, walking there at the side of Bending Bow? That's the one. He looks thin enough to cut the wind, all right. And now he's going back to the Pawnees, after all. Well, they can forgive and forget a good deal, if they take that low-down rascal back. If he—"

But he was stopped here, by the grip which the boy laid upon his arm. John Tanner had halted and actually turned white with excitement.

"You call him Pawnee Harry but I call him Harry, the thief! That's the man that I'm looking for all the way from New York."

"Hold on," said the other. "It ain't likely, son. It ain't at all likely, and you ought to know that. You can't read him through his back."

"I saw his head turned. There it goes again!"

Pawnee Harry—or Harry, the thief—was in the most earnest conversation with Bending Bow, his head turned to one side as a man will do when making an earnest effort to persuade. It was the unmistakable profile of Harry, the thief, and the boy started and uttered a slight exclamation of rage and of joy.

"That's the man!" said he, fully convinced.

And he ran forward, dodging between two or three groups of leisurely pedestrians.

Big Hank Raney bounded after him and caught him in an instant.

"Look here," he said, as the boy struggled to get on. "Look here, son, there's nothing going to be gained by throwing yourself into the hands of those three. He's got all of them to help him. Look at the way that Bending Bow is listening, as if he were getting wisdom out of a well. Red Mane is cocking his ear, too. There as he turns, you can see him smile. Well, then, those Indians will never let down their partner in a pinch. They'll stick by him. And we need help."

Young John Tanner looked impatiently up at his friend.

"Where'll we get help?" he demanded sharply.

"Where every honest man can get help in a pinch," said the other. "Right here!"

Two uniformed policemen were threading through the sidewalk crowd, and up to them stepped Raney, with a wave of the hand. They stopped.

"Partners," said Raney, "can you tell me where I can find Pawnee Harry, the counterfeiter, thief, and whisky peddler?"

They were an athletic-looking pair, those two young guardians of the law, straight of back and wide of shoulder. They looked at Raney with clear, quiet eyes for a moment, as though wondering why the question had been asked.

"I've never seen Pawnee Harry," said one. "He's never worked St. Louis. He's out where his name shows him to be—out among the Pawnees. That's what I've heard."

"He's not among the Pawnees," said the other young

policeman. "He's had trouble with the tribe and they ran him out. He disappeared. Most likely, he's dead."

Raney pointed.

"He's right up the street there, walking with three Pawnees. You must have seen them when they passed. He's the tall fellow. That's Pawnee Harry—if you want to make an arrest and get a reputation. There's enough against him to make a charge, I reckon!"

The two looked at one another with a sudden flare of light in their eyes. It was almost hatred, that glance which they exchanged, as though each wanted the glory to himself. But then, changing instantly, they smiled at one another.

"You know what you're talking about? You're sure of the man?" said one of them, eying Raney.

"I know him as well as I know myself. So does the boy here. He's followed that crook more hundreds of miles than you'd believe. Go ahead and we'll back you up."

The policemen nodded, and turning up the street, they made their way briskly through the crowd. Behind them came Raney and the boy.

"Oughtn't we to be up there with them?" asked Johnnie Tanner. "If there's trouble—"

"There'll be no trouble," explained Raney. "The farther back that we are, you and me, the less likely it is that trouble will start. If we're on hand, the Injuns will fight. But if they only see the police they won't budge a hand. Uniforms kind of bother them. They think that uniforms mean special chiefs, d'you see? And here they're in what they probably call an enemy village, and they're here under a truce, as you might say. No, they won't bother the police."

"But what about Harry?"

"Oh, the two of them can handle Harry, all right. He may make a move. But he's not likely to try his hand against the pair of them. Besides, he likely will think that they've got nothing against him except some old rumor of a crime with no proof behind it. He'll try his smooth tongue, to talk himself out of danger, most likely. And when they've got him between 'em, then we can come up and supply the charge that'll land him in jail. And, once in jail, he'll never come out again."

He chuckled a little. "Let the law work for you, son, when you have the chance." This reasoning entirely satisfied John Tanner. But he was on tiptoe with a furious excitement.

Through the shiftings of the crowd they drifted on in the wake of the two officers, who were now rapidly overtaking the three Indians and Harry, the thief.

Now they were close behind; now one reached out a hand and tapped Harry on the shoulder.

Harry turned. At once, as Raney had prophesied, the Pawnees drew aside, mantling themselves like nuns in their blankets. Plainly they felt that they must not interfere in this business, whatever its outcome.

Then Harry could be seen speaking with many gesticulations and smiling, as a man does when he is confident of success.

It was at this very moment that a little lane opened through the crowd, leaving no one whatever between the boy and the thief, and down that lane shot the glance of Harry.

His look fixed upon young Johnnie Tanner with recognition and with the most utter bewilderment. So far as he knew, the boy had last seen him when he leaped from the upper deck of the Jersey ferry onto the freight platform. But here he was, transported those hundreds and hundreds of miles to the west, calmly walking up a St. Louis street! Mere talk and supple explanations would never do away with the direct accusation which Johnnie Tanner could bring against him!

It seemed to John that he could see, from the near distance, the flight of all of these emotions across the face of the fugitive, like shadows over a lake.

Then Harry, the thief, acted!

Something twinkled into his hand. There was a deep, short barking explosion, and the nearest of the two policemen lurched sideways to the ground, clutching at his thigh. The other policeman, whipping out a gun, was ready to avenge that fall, but instantly on the heels of the first shot followed the second, and the policeman dropped his own weapon and whirled staggeringly about, gripping a wounded shoulder.

Harry, the thief, in the same instant, bolted.

He did not run down the street. Instead, he darted

95

straight across it under the noses of the leaders of a sixteen-mule team, which hauled a great pair of lumbering freight wagons. In a trice he was out of sight.

Johnnie Tanner struck out in pursuit.

With him went Raney, swearing volubly, but when they had run around the end of the wagon, Mr. Harry was out of sight.

People were streaming toward the place where they had heard the shooting. They came singly and in groups, like iron filings toward a magnet. And in their coming they made unwittingly a moving screen behind which Harry was safely hidden from sight.

Raney stopped and seized Johnnie by the shoulder.

The latter pulled away in a frenzy, but he might as well have tugged at a great sea anchor firmly fixed.

"It's no good," said Raney. "He likely knows this town pretty well. He's gone, and nothing will fetch us to him. He's going to disappear like a greased snake down a hole. You'll never put eyes on him in St. Louis again!"

Johnnie gave up struggling. A great reaction set in which made him tremble. He could have covered his face with his hands and burst into tears, so bitterly did he take the disappointment to heart.

"I've lost him!" said he. "I'll never find him again. This was the last chance, and I've bungled it! I've bungled it! If he hadn't laid eyes on me—"

"Did he see you and know you?" snapped the hunter.

"Aye! He saw me and he knew me. He looked as though he'd been struck by a club. Then he pulled out the revolver."

"That was what saved him then," said Raney. "I never guessed that two shots could follow each other so fast, except out of a two-barreled pistol. It was a neat, quick bit of shooting that. But Pawnee Harry always was a rat. Corner him and he'd show fight. Now let's see what's happened to the two poor devils who were dropped. Aye, and the three Pawnees."

The policemen had been conveyed away to have their wounds attended. Neither was seriously wounded, and the boy wondered if even Harry, the thief, had purposely shot to stop his enemies rather than to kill them. But Raney said it must have been the sheerest chance.

The Pawnees were gone also. No one had marked the direction in which they had disappeared.

"And Harry will turn up where they turn up—out West on the prairies. What do you say, Johnnie? Is this the end of your trail, or do you go straight on out onto the plains?"

"Straight on!" said Johnnie sullenly.

He set his teeth.

"I won't give up," he said, "while I've got the strength to breathe!"

19 · JOHNNIE WRITES HOME

THEY carried their packs to a hotel and ate a meal together. While they ate, Raney made his idea clear. If Harry, the thief, had made his peace with the three Pawnee chiefs, as was apparent from the intimacy of their conversation on the street, then it was equally sure that he would be welcomed by the entire tribe if he cared to return to them.

"Why should he care?" asked the boy.

"Why shouldn't he care?" said Raney. "He's a shiftless, lazy, no-account beggar. He'll pick himself up a couple or three strong young wives to sew and cook, tan skins and do embroidery. He'll set back and go to the feasts and tell yarns every night, and he'll get fatter and easier every day."

"Will Indians let such vermin come and live among them?" asked the boy.

"Why, the Indians don't care who comes and lives among 'em. Besides, the Pawnees have got a respect for this fellow; Long Arrow they call him, and he's long enough as you've seen for yourself! They've got a big respect for him as an adviser to war chiefs about to get onto the warpath. He can work up more foxy schemes than you'd dream of; schemes for stealing horses is his main holt. But he's got other good ideas. He was with Red Mane once, and gave that chief an idea that enabled him to set a trap for fifty Sioux; and the trap was so good that not a single one of those Sioux got outside of the teeth of it.

"No, the Pawnees put a lot of value on him. He's pretty

much of a medicine man, with them. They turned him out because he was such a cheat and a liar, but likely they'll be glad to have him back again. He'll be out there on the plains before long. I'd lay my money that he's starting out there this very day and that he'll meet the three of 'em, and they'll head for the home hunting grounds. The only question is, Have I a right to let you go out there on what looks like a wild-goose chase? Even supposing that I was right, what good would it be for you to know that your friend Harry, the thief, is lodged there among the Pawnees, where a thousand braves would be mighty willing to lift your hair, if he so much as winked at 'em? What good would it do you?"

"I don't know," admitted Johnnie. "Only, I feel that I've got to get there. If I can get close enough to strike at him, I might have an idea good enough to land him like a fish! I don't know about that, but I do know that we've got to get out there close to him and give myself a chance to hit home and hit hard. As long as I've got a hope, I've got to try all that I can!"

The other nodded, looking rather grimly at the boy.

"How many times have you wrote home to your dad?" he asked suddenly.

"Not once."

"What!"

"Not once. I wouldn't write to tell him that I'd failed."

"What's he thinking, then?"

"He thinks that I'm a thief, and that I've run off with what means more to him than anything else."

"Look-a here," said the other, "you go into that room and take a pen and some paper and write him off a good fat letter. You can take a couple of hours to do it. I'll need that time to go out and get our boat ticket up the Missouri to Liberty."

So the boy went to write his letter and, as the words came slowly from his pen, with a struggle, he gradually recalled most vividly the face of the old boarding house, the back yard, the brush and the trees in the vacant lot, Aunt Maggie herself and his father.

But, strangely enough, from this distance and from such a place it seemed to him that everything faded and shrank dim and small, including Aunt Maggie herself. There was only one daylight reality, and that was the face of his father. That face was not dimmed in his memory, the gray-green of the eyes, or the faint, mocking smile.

Words flowed faster and faster from the pen of Johnnie Tanner.

And he told everything that had happened to him, everything he had done and suffered from the first. He did not try to win sympathy. He merely tried to explain his long absence, and how he was working on that trail.

"I feel sometimes," he said, "as though there's a sort of luck about the thing—something that's pulling me along farther and farther west, until it turns on me and swallows me whole. I feel the way that a bird must feel when a snake has looked at it, and yet it can't fly away. But I'm going on until I get what I've lost for you. I'm going to go on until I've got back into my hands the thing that I lost for you. I don't hardly dare to think of really getting it back. I think that I'd burst with joy, if I ever have my hand on the butt of that revolver.

"I've told you some about Hank Raney. I haven't told you that he's teaching me every day how to shoot with a pistol and with a rifle, and he's talking a lot of Cheyenne and Pawnee to me. I write the words down in long lists and try to memorize them. It's very hard to make them stick, because the sound of them is very different from anything that I've ever heard before. Hank says that I do pretty well at it, though. Of course, when once we get out onto the plains, it'll be very useful to talk even a few words of those tongues.

"Our plan is to go straight out among the Cheyennes, because Hank says that he knows those people and likes them, and they know and like him. Once we're among the Cheyennes, we'll do what we can about the Pawnees and the thing that was stolen—that is, if Pawnee Harry, the thief, is really with that tribe again.

"Whatever happens, I won't write to you again until I've got in my hands what was stolen out of them."

He wrote little more, after that, because he felt as he put down these words a glow of almost holy satisfaction and resolve. He would push through to the bitter end. If by some miracle he won, he felt that he would be happy forever.

He had barely sealed that letter when Raney returned. He was brisk and businesslike. He had engaged passage for them up the Missouri on a strong new steamer and, though the current was running with great speed and power at this time of the year, when it took down the newly melted snow waters from the North and the West, yet they ought to make pretty good time against the strength of the stream.

"What would be good time then?" asked the boy.

"Forty or fifty miles a day. You have to tie up at night."

"Forty or fifty miles!" cried the boy. "Why, we could almost walk that fast!"

"Aye," said the other, "but every day you're on the steamer you are forty or fifty miles fresher than when you started out in the morning for your day's hiking."

And by the middle of the afternoon, they were on a Missouri steamer, dragging painfully against the ever-downward tide.

The Ohio had been beautiful from first to last. The Mississippi had been disappointing. The Missouri, however, filled the mind of the boy with awe.

Yellow, brown or red with mud, wild and powerful, the raw banks on either side showed the force with which the currents could rage. In the calmer and more evenly flowing places, the rate was no more than four miles an hour; but over the sand banks and the bars, sometimes it shot along at a rate of eight or ten.

What a river, indeed!

As for its wildness, it seemed to speak of the lawless plains from which it descended. As for its size, they passed before long an island eight miles long, and a mile in breadth, heavily wooded, but with cleared places, here and there, under cultivation. A sea might contain such an island, but who would expect to find it in a river bed?

The very climate was wild and violent in its strength and in its changes.

They were five days from St. Louis when, after a sultry day, the night instead of bringing coolness appeared to become yet hotter. People could not sleep. There was on the steamer a woman and her child, bound for Fort Leavenworth; and those who walked the deck continually heard the delirious moans of the little one. Men did not talk. They merely grumbled. And young Johnnie Tanner continually felt tremors of nervousness sweep over his body and a ringing came into his head.

That was at midnight.

Two hours later, people had huddled into their beds, piled on extra blankets, and great coats over the top of these, and even then were shuddering with cold beneath the pile!

Two hours had been enough for a changing wind to blow up such a drop in the thermometer. The very air had altered completely. It had been at first a heavy, hanging mist, disagreeable to breathe and hardly refreshing. The wheezing of a man who suffered from some lung trouble and his agonized gaspings had alarmed and irritated all of the passengers. But now the air cut clean and clear as the polished edge of a knife. One taste of it was enough to dry the throat and set the nerves on edge.

How could human beings stand such bludgeoning changes, wondered Johnnie Tanner. And what was there that could make a land capable of such alterations worth living in?

That was his thought during the suffering of this night, but in the day, it was a different matter. Then he had his hours of schooling from his friend, big Hank Raney; and he had his hours when he studied and rehearsed and struggled over the miseries of two Indian vocabularies. But his ear was growing more accustomed to the sounds, and when he was with Raney, which was most of the time, he was never allowed to express himself except as a Pawnee or a Cheyenne.

His mind was quick, his ear keen, his enthusiasm boundless. And so he made unmeasured strides, though from day to day it seemed to him that he was standing still. And there were the people of the boat to watch during the day and chat with a little now and then. There were half-breeds, two Negroes, several traders, with their equipment loaded onto the boat, a few soldiers going up to take their distant post at Leavenworth on the rim of the wilderness and, in addition, there were two or three trappers, one of them a quiet little man who seemed ready to creep into his grave, one a sardonic, lean-faced Yankee, one a chattering French-Canadian.

All of these types were new to the boy. His friend supplied him with a key to their characters, as it were; and he studied them cautiously and carefully from day to day.

Twice they were turned out of their chosen channels by piled masses of driftwood. Three times paddle wheels were disabled by the smashing blows which the shooting drift logs delivered. And once a paddle box itself was so damaged that they were tied up for two days repairing it.

At that rate of progress, it seemed very likely that the Pawnees and Harry, the thief, if in fact they were heading westerly from St. Louis, would reach the Indian camps before the steamboat passengers could possibly arrive.

20 · A RIDING LESSON

THEY reached the town of Liberty. It seemed like the ultimate outpost. It was not so much a stronghold of civilization; it was rather a tentacle through whose pores the wilderness seeped. At a step, Johnnie Tanner passed from the region where home-spun or other cloth predominated and found himself in the region of deerskin garments. These no longer appeared outlandish. They were the natural garb; in a day or two, they appeared the only graceful fashion.

But they were very busy outfitting here. They bought three horses, and they had three small packs for them, since Raney, from the first, frankly declared that he did not intend to load himself down like a freighter. They would do without most of the usual cooking utensils, et cetera, which give ponderousness and bulk to a pack.

"If we're going to try to deal with Harry, the thief," said Raney, "we've gotta be able to handle real Injuns, and they don't move like the whites. They fly over the prairie the way that birds fly through the sky. Well, whites can do it, too. But they have to change their style. Parched corn meal, jerked beef—those two things, they don't cost nothing hardly. And they'll last you a long time, and they're little in weight and in bulk."

He added: "We've got one luxury: a kettle and some tea for it. But if we're ever in a pinch to make speed, we chuck it all away. Ammunition, salt and rifles, is all that a man needs really. It's all that the Injuns need, and we've gotta be as strong as they are!"

The boy listened, but his heart sank when he saw the smallness of the packs, at least, when he considered the small proportion of weight and bulk assigned to their necessities and luxuries combined.

The greatest portion of the packs were composed of beads, hatchets, fine steel knives, etc. These were, as Raney called them, "Indian money." And a good knife was worth a great deal more than its weight in gold, when one had to deal with a plains Indian.

However, they were equipped at last.

And Johnnie Tanner found himself on the back of a wild-eyed little mustang with a scraggy mane and not much of a tail, a ewe-neck, and an awkward gait. But it was a true mustang, and he had heard enough of the breed to fear and respect it.

He possessed, also, a fine new rifle, ammunition for it, a good double-barreled pistol and a single-shot pistol of still better and heavier make. He had a hand ax, a perfectly balanced knife, a packet of needles, stout thread, wax, and other essentials. He carried with him a package of tea, some parched corn, which tasted like nothing but sawdust from a very hard wood when he sampled it, and jerked venison, which was possessed of an odd smell but rather a good taste.

There were a great many suggestions which he would have liked to make before the start. But when, at last, he had fitted his toes comfortably into his stirrups, he felt himself very much the cavalier of the plains, ready for all manner of wild adventures.

So they rode out of Liberty and started for Fort Leavenworth, a good long march, but one which they could cover in a single day by pressing on a little.

"But where's the black horse? Where's Midnight?" asked Johnnie of his friend. "I thought that Midnight was really the thing that started you back for the West?"

"Midnight? Oh, he'll turn up while we're along the way," said Raney, rather mysteriously. "Now you keep a rein on that mustang of yours. Have him gathered into your hand, and always act as though he was covered with grease and you about to slide off. He's got a mean eye. He's likely to teach you a lot about riding in a mighty short time. Some hosses, they don't know how to teach. Other hosses, it's like throwing a boy into a river. He learns to swim or he drowns. I reckon that that mustang is that-a-way. If he starts anything, you turn in your toes a little to give your knees a grip, and keep thinkin'!"

Johnnie Tanner swallowed the faint beginnings of a smile. For every moment he was in that saddle, he felt bigger and stronger, and the horse seemed smaller and weaker beneath his saddle.

And then, as they reached a clearing in the woods and as they were passing a bald lightning blaze, where a bolt had stripped away the whole side of a tree, the mustang departed suddenly from beneath John Tanner.

It was a very strange thing. At one moment he was riding along very securely, quite the master of everything he surveyed. The next instant, as though a spring door had been jerked away beneath him, he was falling sheer down.

He landed in a sitting posture and with such a jar that his head was driven down heavily upon his shoulders, and a shower of sparks leaped from his brain and went crackling off into space.

His eyes remained clear enough to see the little pony darting away, and a long, snaky shadow leaping from the hand of Raney. The snaky shadow looped over the neck of the horse, stopped it suddenly, and then brought it wheeling back, snorting and shaking its head.

"He's got a neat side-step," was Raney's critical comment. "I ain't seen what he can do in the air, but he's got the makings of a jim-dandy, I'd say."

Johnnie eyed the pony with a profound emotion as he got to his feet again.

"That horse hasn't been trained at all!" he exclaimed.

"Trained? Say, how could he've learned to jump sidewise like that without trainin'?" said the other, grinning faintly. "Yeah. He's a trained horse, all right. He's been gentled a lot, too, I reckon. Climb back on top of him, sonny."

Johnnie bit his lip, but he obeyed. He distrusted that mustang mightily. He wished with all his heart that Raney would change horses with him, but he had altogether too much pride to suggest the thing.

They went on. They came to a dusky lane among the trees, and suddenly the gray mustang which the boy was backing mounted as from strings into the air, leaped up, and up, and then dropped sheer down, with a humped back and head stretching far forward. It was as though the agile and stubborn little beast intended to land on the point of its nose. But at the last moment, one black hoof shot down and received the whole impact of the blow.

So Johnnie felt a downward jar and a side-snap at the same moment; and he was flicked neatly, cleanly out of the saddle.

His fall had been heavy before. This time it was stunning.

He lay for a long moment, before he found that he was stretched flat on his back, gazing toward a sky which gradually became a clear blue.

He gathered himself. He sat up.

And there was his friend, Raney, busily lighting a short-stemmed pipe.

"How are you, son?" asked Raney with a bright indifference.

Suddenly John Tanner hated this man. Suddenly he knew that from the first there had been unmistakable signs of bully, brute and fool all commingled in the fellow.

"I'm still in one piece, I guess," said the boy gloomily. And he dragged himself back to his feet once more.

"Try to stick with it a little longer the next time," said Raney, without offering the slightest word of sympathy. "Stick with it a little longer, and you'll learn something. But you can't learn much unless you stay with the game a few licks at a time. That's a mighty handy hoss. Good on the ground and good on the air. Keeps himself all together and never stops thinking—the way that you did, that time."

Fury drove the fear from the boy's mind. Resolutely he mounted the gray mustang. He wished that he never had heard of the great West, never seen a man clad in deerskins, never, above all, seen the face of the scoundrel, Raney.

"What should I have done?" he asked coldly.

"Why, when you seen which end of him was coming down first, you should've leaned back against the slope of him and pulled up his head and cracked him with that quirt you've got just before he landed. When you whang a horse in the middle of the air, sometimes it makes him nervous and he forgets his system of footwork, I've often noticed."

"I did pull on the bridle," said the boy. "But his mouth is iron."

"Oh, no, it ain't," said Raney, with the same detestable cheerfulness. "It's just the same as any other mouth. You didn't pull on it the right way. A kid of eight years, that knows the trick, will keep the chin of a hoss closer to his chest than you did that time."

The rage of the boy choked him, and he dared not trust his tongue to answer. They went on. He was still half stunned, and the bruises were beginning to ache.

They came into an open space that might be five or six miles long, the woods running a dim, green border all around it. "There's the prairies beginning," said Raney.

The boy looked. The ground undulated softly; the bright feet of the wind ran twinkling over the grass; and suddenly there seemed a new sky above them, and a new life in the air.

He forgot that he hated his friend, Raney, and looked askance at him with a smile.

"I suppose," said the boy, "compared with the big prairies, it's like a pond to the ocean?"

"Yeah. Just about," said Raney, smiling back.

And at that moment the gray demon in the mustang moved again—moved as a jagged lightning flash moves, forward, sideways, jerking and darting here and there, and making short bucks that jarred like the strokes of a giant's fist.

But there had been a single preliminary tremor, and that was enough for the boy. He forgot all his bruises and aches. A terror so complete that it was almost a ferocity mastered him. He became compact of nerves and attention.

And so he stuck to the saddle.

He was jerked here and there. Sometimes he cruelly rode the pommel. Sometimes he sat on the cantle. Sometimes he was without one stirrup. And once both stirrups were flying upward almost as high as his head. But luck, desperate attention, a quick, fighting eye saved him.

The pony began to repeat its second maneuver of the day, vaulting high and landing on one foot. It was a cruel beating that the boy received, but now it was no longer a mere torment. It was also a fight, a fight in which he seemed to have a chance.

He remembered what he had been told. He kept a good pull on the reins and, slanting his body back against the pitch of the down-dropping horse, he slashed it thoroughly with the quirt, just before it landed.

Something seemed to happen to the spirit of the pony or to its designs, for it landed far more softly, and he kept his place easily.

He had both feet in the stirrups, a savage triumph was rising in his breast, and then the pony began to spin like a top. He gripped the top of the pommel, but his grip failed to hold. Suddenly he was streaming out in the air like a flag; a second later he shot outward into space.

21 · MIDNIGHT

HE flew like a stone, and he told himself that this time he would surely have a broken neck. But the other two impacts had been solid whacks, and this was only a rolling fall. He spun over and over, like a top, but he got up little the worse for wear.

He heard his friend saying: "Why, that's a dog-gone little dancing fool, that hoss is. I'll try my own long legs on the sides of him. He needs a lesson. Or maybe I'll get the teaching!"

He prepared to dismount, but the boy ran forward eagerly.

"He'll never get me off again that way," said he. "I didn't think right. I was a fool. I should have got my balance sooner. No, sir. You don't get into this saddle. It's my horse. And I'm going to ride him, or else he'll ride me!"

He swung back into the saddle. He cut the mustang with a mighty blow of his quirt.

But, behold! The gray merely humped its back a little, flicked its tail up and down, and then cantered away as smoothly as flowing water.

"Oh, look, look!" shouted young Johnnie triumphantly. "He's had his lesson already!"

"He's had his lesson for to-day," said Raney. "But he'll take about that much warming every day, I reckon. However, you're learning fine. I'm right about it. Throw the kids in, and they swim before they'll drown. I hope that he didn't hurt you none too much?"

"Hurt me?" laughed the boy. "Of course he didn't hurt me. I don't feel a thing."

"You will soon," grinned Raney. "You'll feel plenty before the end of the day, and you'll be an old man to-morrow morning."

They pushed straight on. The spirits of the boy were high now. They ferried the Platte. They struck on through the Missouri bottom lands, where the mosquitoes arose in air-darkening swarms and tortured beast and man.

But at last they climbed, about the end of the day, out of the woodland and in the sight of Fort Leavenworth, which stood on a strong bluff, around which the river swung in a mighty bend.

Raney was not a man given to using impressive words or gestures. But now he halted his horse and extended his arm in a rather grand attitude.

"There we are," said he, "and I take it that we're at the beginning of something that may take a lot of finishing, son. But, you and me together, we'll work till we drop, and if one of us drops, the other one will work down the trail. You wait out here. There's nothing for you to gain at Fort Leavenworth. But there's something for me to pick up there. You stay with the horses."

He dismounted, and walked away through the warmth of the late afternoon, leaving the boy alone.

But he was not really alone. He never could be alone while he had those dull but important word lists to con over. And when he had spent an hour memorizing, then he changed his attention to his fine new rifle. He did not fire it, but he tried a thing that his friend had shown to him, drawing a careful bead with an empty magazine, taking the target dead in the center, and closing the hand with a slow grip.

"You can shoot things dead with your wits only," the hunter was fond of saying.

But his favorite way of disciplining the eye of the lad was as they rode along through the country, picking out distant objects, up to half a mile, and making Johnnie

Tanner estimate the yardage. After the estimate was made, Raney gave his own guess, and then they counted the steps of the gray mustang, which went with a very even gait that they had measured carefully beforehand.

Invariably Raney was closer to the truth. He pointed out various methods of helping the eye to get nearer to the fact. Formations of the ground in the distance were apt to be of the same sort as those near at hand. How much smaller did they look? Or how much mist was there in the air, a thing to be dimly judged by the smallness of the horizon?

Then there were maxims of many kinds to be memorized. "Left and low" was the favorite chant of Raney.

He taught these things seriously, and he grounded the need of seriousness upon very important considerations.

"Now, look here," he would say. "You're going to be out in a country where they ain't any Sunday school; but they's scalping knives. They ain't any regular school of any kind; but they's rifles. Your rifle is your Bible, and your horse is your pa and ma and old-maid aunt, all rolled into one. Your knife is your brother; your pistols is all your friends and distant relations. Look what I'm telling you. The time'll come when you'll love your rifle because it shoots straight. The time'll come when you'll trust it more than you ever trusted any living thing in your born days!"

And Johnnie believed him.

So seriously, patiently, he did his best to learn how to judge distances and, while he did not burn up much powder, he was constantly learning the feel of the gun butt in the hollow of his shoulder and the balance of the long and heavy barrel which his hand and arm got to endure without the slightest tremor. He learned the sights. And habitually he followed the advice of Raney and took everything exceedingly low and to the left.

Most people make a vast error. They practice only with powder and ball, and they shoot only at easy targets. The groundwork of good marksmanship, outside of marked rifle ranges, is a hand like a rock, a clear, keen, practiced eye and the ability to judge distances. Practice with a silent rifle is as good as practice with a loaded one, except that a few rounds must be fired every day, of course.

At least, this was the system which Raney used with

John Tanner, both on this day and the many which were to follow. And the astonishing results which he achieved we shall see in more detail later on.

Time killing had been accomplished with vocabulary lists and with gun sighting. Then, through the soft mist of the early evening, Hank Raney rode down from the fort.

He looked like a stranger to the boy at first. He had gone up on foot, and he came back riding on a shining wind.

It was Midnight.

He guessed from the distance, not alone by the color, but by something imperial in the bearing of the animal, that this must be the great stallion for whose sake Raney had to return to the West. And, from the first glance, he understood perfectly why Raney had found the lure irresistible.

For Midnight did not gallop; he flowed over the ground. And Midnight did not trot; he floated, suspended in the air. He seemed hardly flesh and bone. He seemed a splendid, shining javelin, fitted to the hand of a god and ready to be launched into immensity of distance. And when Raney came sweeping up to the boy, he could not refrain from showing off the fine points of his animal like a child —or a savage!

Around and around in flashing circles he sent the stallion at full speed, while Raney himself went through all manner of evolutions to the delight of the boy.

Now he disappeared over the side of the horse and aimed a pistol under the throat of the stallion; now he threatened to ride down Johnnie Tanner under the powerful hoofs of the black; but at the last instant he would swerve away, side-stepping like a boxer. Last of all, he brought the stallion to a halt with a single bound and smiting of his hoofs deep into the soft turf. There he stood shimmering in the soft evening light, aflow and aglow with running sweat, while his master sprang down to the ground and stripped off bridle and saddle. Only the light headstall and trailing rawhide rope remained on him.

"There you are," said Hank Raney. "There's the hoss for you to look at. They's been hosses and hosses. But they's never been one like Midnight. Look him over. Fault him if you can. There never was bone before the bone of Midnight was seen. There never was shoulders framed like his and set on at such a slope. Look at the back of him. There's only just enough for a short saddle to cover. The rest of him is all sinews and running muscle. He goes under you like a wave goes on the sea. He goes like a sail in the wind. I tell you, son, that hoss is hitched to something, and he's always spinning along downhill.

"Look at him. Don't just stand and look at his head, but walk around him. See that barrel, for instance. He's got room for heart and wind both, inside of that. He's got some belly, too. You have to have bottom on a prairie cruiser. He's got stomach, but no bulge to it. Feel the muscles of that stomach, as hard as iron. That's a keel for you, that you can build on.

"A two-day gallop without food and water won't gaunt that horse. Look at the quarters, now—square as a door and deep. They'll carry your weight; they'll shove you uphill. And here's the hocks under them. Get your thumb and forefinger on that tendon. That's the mainspring of the watch. Look at it! There's plenty of it, but it's soaked and pretty near swallowed up by the muscles.

"Now you can come back to his head and have a look at that, because there's the whole of the horse, really, what you can take in the spread of your two hands. Stand there and look him in the eye, because he's a king!"

So Johnnie Tanner stood in front of the stallion and gazed into the steady, brave, joyous eyes. They took highlights from the gleaming western sky, but they also had an inward light of their own unlike that which the boy ever had seen in any other animal.

"He's a beauty!" said Johnnie with a sigh. "I don't blame you for coming back West for him. I only wonder that you ever could have left him."

"I was going to sell him if I could," replied the other, with a laugh. "I told the fellow that I'd go away, and if I stayed for six months, he could send me the money. A thousand dollars is what he offered me. I thought it was a fortune, but I been pricing hosses back East, and a thousand ain't so much. A thousand is dirt, for a hoss like that. Well, if I could've stayed away from Midnight for six months, I would've had the thousand, and the colonel would've had the hoss. But I couldn't stay, and here I am back ag'in!"

His laughter rang out joyously across the plain.

"There's only one thing," said the boy. "It seems to be as though there's a sort of a sad look about his eyes."

"Aye," said Raney, "I think that there is, and whether it is mourning for his first master, or waitin' and hopin' for a real man to come over the edge of the world and be his boss, I can't say. But I can tell you another thing that I've heard at Leavenworth."

"It's about the thief; it's about Harry!" exclaimed the boy.

"That's just what it is," replied Raney. "He's come across the country like the wind. He's out there with the Pawnees again, and he's getting a great reception from them. They say that Long Arrow, as they call him, shoots six arrows at a time from his bow, and I suppose that's the revolver—and the revolver is big medicine; and there's Pawnee Harry started on his crooked way again, and sitting out here in the middle of the plains like a king!"

22 · BUFFALO

THEY sank into the wild green sea of the desert. Like mariners in the old uncharted days of travel, they wandered for weeks of sunburn, hard riding, hunting, continual labor, precarious food, and sleep which was like the sleep of the dead.

During the first week, between lessons in horsemanship —generally given mutely by a wickedly bucking mustang —constant work at the two Indian dialects, infinite hours in the saddle, furious hunts, cooking, skinning, trailing, stalking, it seemed to the boy that his body would be fairly unjointed by these devastating labors, and that he would sink from the saddle, falling into the waves of the long green grass, and would lie there and wait for death gladly. Anything was preferable, it appeared, to the agony of the long effort.

That first physical despair passed off a little. Its place was taken by a great nostalgia. For his companion, the moment Fort Leavenworth sank from sight behind them, became a changed man. He spoke little, except in giving instructions, lessons, and the like. His way at all times was crisp, blunt, stern. He offered no sympathy and never attempted to while away the time with pleasant conversation. He could speak in rebuke in such a manner that his words stung like a whipstroke. And this harshness of manner, together with the infinite loneliness of the inland sea, made the boy look back toward his home with a weakening of the nerves and with tears in his eyes. It filled his night with dreams of the most tender sweetness, and when he wakened in the morning, the vast and unbroken level of the green plains oppressed him with a bitterness like death.

Even this emotion changed. They had been out for two weeks. In that time they had not seen a human being. The boy had grown brown, lean and hard. Bucking horses, every day, had taught him, as his companion had promised, how to sit the saddle. Every hour on the backs of those tigerish and treacherous mustangs was an hour of danger and dread until, at last, he had both a powerful leg grip and a sure sense of balance. He was not an accomplished horseman in the manner of the plainsmen who have been born to the saddle; but he knew more after that fortnight's battle than a man can learn in ten years of pleasant hacking along park paths.

They had had shooting at deer, at antelope. Their bag consisted of exactly one of each! Both had fallen to the rifle of his older companion, and poor young Johnnie Tanner began to feel that he never would have the good fortune to bring down game. And then, on that glorious day, came an event which altered his mind, changed his soul, filled up his very heart with triumph.

In the full of the moon, on a bright night which was verging toward the dawn, he heard a confused sound which was very much like the rolling of great and tumultuous waters in the distance.

He sat up and saw that big Hank Raney already was up, leaning on his rifle.

"What is it, Hank?" he asked.

"Buffalo!" said Raney.

The boy did not wait for the command. He rolled out of his blankets and built his pack like lightning, a thing which he had learned to do with very skillful expedition whether by day or by dark.

113

He saddled the gray mustang, which tried to kick off his head as soon as the hobbling rope was untied, and then, mounting, he was ready to join with Raney.

With the led horses behind them, they cut straight for the cataract of noise, which rose rapidly out of the night. In the death of the moonshine, with the gray morning rising in the east, with the prairie beginning to turn from glistening black to green, at last the boy saw what Raney had often told him of and what he had read of in books.

It was like the flow of a river seen from a distant bank. All the farther half of the prairie was alive, and all of that stream of life was composed of masses and masses, armies and still more armies, of huge bison and calves. The clacking of the big hoofs, the roar of constant lowing made the air tremble. The wind blew across the host toward the hunters, and a distinctly pungent, disagreeable odor reached them.

Going a little nearer, they hobbled the led horses securely, loaded their rifles, then approached the flank of the solid, living mass.

It moved slowly. An hour went by; the sun was now shining brightly; and yet the mobs of the buffalo flowed along steadily. And, since the hunters sat motionless and had grown out of the night rather than having suddenly been seen to approach, the buffalo did not bolt. Only, as the flanking swarms saw the two strange apparitions, they swayed to the right and kept pressing in until they had formed a deep indentation, a sort of eddy which marked out the position of the hunters. This indentation never filled. The fresh onrushing hordes followed, exactly, the footsteps of those who had gone before.

As the huge army marched out of the darkness and into the dawn, Johnnie Tanner felt that he had been plunged into a fairy tale—no silly matter of princes and princesses and enchanted castles; no oddity of gnomes and elves and mysterious woods; but it seemed to him as though the fertile face of the earth had converted its rocks into bones, and its soil into flesh which was here breathing and moving before him.

The size of the bulls and the strange shape of them, mountainous and shaggy, amazed him. Now and then, one of them turned his bearded face toward the hunters and shook his ponderous, curved horns, as though in a challenge. Now and again, one of them would halt a moment to paw at the grass and to bring out a thunderous bellowing with his nose held close to the trodden ground. Always, when that bellowing ended, from the center, from ahead, from the far flanks of that army came back similar trumpeting, huge and vague, like indistinct echoes across a great valley.

A sort of fire burned up in the boy, he looked repeatedly to his companion; but it was not until the rear of the host had passed that Raney said quietly: "We'll take two young cows. That one, yonder—do you see, with the broken horn? That one is yours. Ride right up alongside of it and give it a bullet just behind the shoulder. And don't miss. Now—at 'em!"

At the same instant, he sent the black stallion forward in a gleaming streak that left the gray of Johnnie Tanner far behind.

But the boy, rifle ready in his right hand, his left on the reins, swept straight on for the young cow with the broken horn.

She saw him, it seemed, before any of the other animals around her were aware of the flying danger. She saw, and she bolted into the midst of the bison ahead of her. She was young; for that very reason, she was lithe and almost as fast as a deer. But the ugly gray mustang proved his worth at that moment. He must have been used on buffalo before. With his ears flattened out and his head stretched out in a straight line, he flew through the galloping press of the bison, dodging this way and that through the living current of flesh.

And the boy saw shaggy heads and red, flashing eyes about him. A spume of hot breath, of foam, of dust flew up in his face. He saw the powerful tossing of the horns and told himself that he was lost.

And then he saw the cow with the broken horn just beside him.

Fear left Johnnie Tanner; he abandoned the reins, merely closing his knees in a harder grip against the sides of his pony. And swinging to the side, he leveled the rifle and curled his finger around the trigger.

But even at this close range it was not such an easy shot. The horse bobbed up and down in one rhythm, and

115

the young cow in another. Now in the sights he caught a part of the flying cow; now he lost her entirely.

And then the will of John Tanner grew stronger and firmer. He straightened himself with a savage determination. It seemed to him that something flowed down from his brain into his arm, and settled with sure power in the tip of his trigger finger.

That instant he caught the desired spot well within the sights and fired. The buffalo went down and turned a complete somersault. Victory was his!

He pulled up the pony.

All around him rushed the rear-most remnants of the bison herd, stamping and bellowing, and the whole earth seemed to be trembling as the panic reached the heart of the army and set them all flying. The last of them fled past him. He looked back, and there in the distance he saw Hank Raney had dismounted and was calmly going about the work of cutting up his quarry.

And Johnnie Tanner dismounted in turn and walked slowly around and around his kill.

It was the first living thing which had fallen to his hand. And what a monster! The open eyes seemed as bright and wild as ever. The wind, ruffling in the hair of the cow, made it seem to breathe and to stir with life. But it was not living. The stain of blood that issued from about the mouth told its story. It was dead, and he, John Tanner, was the victor in the battle.

Next to creation, there is only one fully satisfying work for man, and that is destruction. Now John Tanner had destroyed. And what a prey!

He mastered himself and mounted again.

That is to say, he mastered himself in so far as he became able to control his facial expression, but inside there was music in his soul. He could have laughed and danced like a madman. But he went back to the waiting hobbled horses and he brought them up as his friend finished working on his kill.

It was a shameful waste. They took part of the hump from which good steaks could be cut, and they took the big tongue out by the roots. When this had been rolled in a portion of the skin, they went on to the kill of the boy.

He waited for a word, but it seemed that it would

116

never come. The bearing of Hank Raney was that of one who merely considers that the most ordinary item in the day's work has been performed and has neither praise nor blame to distribute.

He stood by, giving directions, while the boy performed the cutting up which was necessary, and while the meat was wrapped in more skin.

"We'll get to brush if we find any handy," said Raney then. "After that, we'll have a real fire and some real roast meat. Come along."

Rather downhearted, Johnnie Tanner mounted.

Said Raney: "If you'd hunted 'em for ten years, every day in the year, you couldn't've done a better job, son!"

That was all; but that was enough. In some way, the boy told himself that he knew he had passed his apprenticeship; that he was no longer a child; that he had become a plainsman in very fact!

23 · THE CHEYENNE

THE prairie had changed, in the estimation of the boy. It had become, instead of a green desert, a great and wonderful playground, filled with adventure. Though his companion talked very little, the sternness of his manner had relaxed. It seemed that he had looked upon himself as a schoolmaster who had to be somewhat grim if he expected that the lessons would be learned. As though to celebrate the initiation of Johnnie Tanner through the killing of the first buffalo, Hank Raney suggested that they should camp for some time in that place where they had found the brush. After the steady traveling all the horses, except the indomitable black, needed a rest. Besides, they had here water from a little meandering stream that ran close by, the brush gave shelter and plenty of firewood, and in every respect the place was, in the eye of Hank Raney, an ideal site.

So they maintained the camp, and every day they went out hunting. They were always in luck now. The long famine was distinctly and suddenly ended. The very first morning, they had not gone two miles from the camp before they saw the flashing disks of antelope on the green breast of the prairie.

The antelope were off at a speed which no horse could follow. But the two hunters made a long detour down wind, and came up in the middle of the day with the herd. Then, leaving their horses at a distance, they wormed their way through the grass, often on hands and knees, taking advantage of random depressions, until they came close enough to the herd to open fire.

Never would Johnnie Tanner forget the moment when he parted the thick tufts of the grass and saw before him, not thirty feet away, a fine little pronghorn buck with his head raised, his big eyes flashing, his whole body tense with alertness and ready to leap off at full speed.

A tremor ran through the hand of John Tanner. His rifle shook as he raised it, and then, glancing confusedly down the sights, he saw others of the herd scattered here and there, standing knee-deep in the rich grass. At the same moment, the tail disk of one of them in the near distance flashed like a metal sheet in the sun, and in an instant the whole herd was in motion.

They started like jack rabbits, with a suddenness which took the breath, so that the fine buck which had been standing near him fairly jerked itself out of the circle of the sights at the first bound. He caught it again. And then that feeling of savage certainty came over him once more, exactly as he had felt it the day before in shooting at the buffalo cow. He caught that little racing streak in the sights, he followed the course over a small arc, and then fired.

The antelope fell, spinning over and over in the long grass, then disappearing into it. The boy hardly watched the fall. He was jamming a new load into his rifle, but, before he could complete the task, he had heard the report of Raney's rifle on the left, and the antelope had faded out of range completely. They were gone as a cloud of dust, vanished on the wings of a powerful blast of wind.

Then the boy stood up, saw Raney rising at the same time and heard the hunter cursing softly, steadily, through his teeth.

And Johnnie knew that Raney had missed his mark!

"Hank," he called out nervously, "did I shoot too soon? Was that what the trouble was?"

Hank Raney turned a dark look on him, a look that made young John Tanner quake in his boots. But Raney said merely: "You didn't fire too soon. You didn't shoot till they was running. It was just me that fired too late, and curse my hide for it!"

He strode off in the lead to the place where the antelope had fallen under the boy's shot, waving John Tanner back to get up the horses. When Johnnie returned, Raney's good humor had returned too. He looked up from the work of skinning the little deer with a broad grin that made his whiskers bristle tremendously.

"Son," said he, "I thought that I was getting along. I thought that I was old enough to be a man, but I reckon that I ain't. I can be jealous of the very kid that I'd taught how to shoot."

And, with this, he broke out into hearty laughter.

John Tanner was much relieved, and his pride made his very heart leap as he looked down on the slender body of the antelope.

Morning and evening, after that, they were constantly afield. Apparently, they were collecting meat, and a great quantity of it was, to be sure, cut up in thin strips to dry on racks either over slow fires or in the heat of the sun. But, in reality, it was chiefly for the sport that they hunted. They cut only the choice portions of each kill.

They found antelope again on the second afternoon of their hunting, and this time they actually got three specimens, because Hank Raney brought down the first with a fine pistol shot, and dropped a second at a more distant range with a rifle bullet, while the boy did his part by sending an ounce of lead through the head of a handsome buck.

They had finished skinning and cutting up when something made Raney spring to his feet.

He left the spoils lying in the grass. He did not even pause to wash the red from his hands, but leaped into the saddle and waved to Tanner to do the same. The moment that Johnnie was mounted he could make out the cause for the excitement. In the distance a single horseman was coming toward them, still so far away that

119

sometimes to the straining eyes of the boy it seemed like two forms, riding closely, shoulder to shoulder.

As the rider approached nearer, though still almost indistinguishable to Johnnie, Raney pronounced it to be an Indian. A little later, squinting under one hand, which shaded his eyes from the sun, he exclaimed: "I think that I've got luck! I think that I've got the best luck—and it's a Pawnee!"

"I thought you weren't friends with the Pawnees?" said the boy.

"Friends? I hate their hearts and livers!" said Hank Raney.

He gathered his reins as he spoke.

"There may be one less Pawnee thief on the plains, when that sun goes down," he added, through his teeth. The boy looked at him with a peculiar interest.

"I thought you always ran away from any Indian, Hank?" he queried.

"Never mind about that!" snapped Hank Raney. "You stay here—get the meat packed."

"Stay here? No; I'll go along with you and help if I can—"

He was interrupted by a roar of impatient anger.

"When I've got this chance before me, am I gunna be stopped to argufy with a half-baked fool of a kid like you?" demanded Hank Raney, his temper completely out of hand. "Suppose that he picked out you for his first shot—and suppose that his shot landed on the spot! What would I feel like then? No, you stay back here."

A strange smile came on the lips of the boy.

"But suppose that he downs you, Hank. Then what would become of me?"

"You turn your horse and ride like the devil."

"How could I get away, with him on the back of Midnight then?"

The other glowered at him, then snapped:

"There's nothing for you to worry about. No Pawnee this side of the next world will ever put me down!"

"I wasn't worrying," said the boy. "I was just thinking that I'd better stay close enough to be on hand."

Hank Raney no longer glowered.

"All right, son," said he. "If you got it in you, I can't

120

talk it out. Only—I want to tell you that Pawnees is tougher meat than antelope, and harder shooting, too!"

He turned to examine the approaching horseman again. The man was quite close now, so close that they could see the gleam of feathers above his head, and then Raney exclaimed, with an accent of bitterest disappointment: "No, it's not a Pawnee, after all!"

"How can you tell?" asked the boy, amazed.

"Look at the shadow round about his head. No Pawnee ever had as much hair as that, I reckon."

"What could it be then?"

"A Cheyenne. Or maybe a Crow, though it's pretty far away from the Crow stamping grounds."

Then he gave quick directions.

"Get over there ten yards to my right. Watch that fellow like a hawk. Have your rifle ready. In a pinch, do your thinking with your hands. Your forefinger on a gun trigger is likely to be worth more than a whole Bible to you, when the time comes."

The Indian, riding slowly over the prairie, had now come so close that they could see the shadowy line of his long lance, and the fiery gleam of its steel point, well above his head. They could see the oval of the shield, also, and certain brightly painted markings upon it.

"A Cheyenne, a Cheyenne!" muttered Raney, still disappointed.

"Well, he's a friend, then," suggested the boy.

"Oh, if he ain't too scalp-hungry," said Raney. "Don't trust anything. There ain't a thing on the prairies that can be trusted except—except—hold on! I've seen the paintings on that shield before."

The warrior came on, his naked shoulders gleaming like bronze, and a long-barreled rifle thrusting up at a sharp angle behind the shield. Now he paused, and raised a single hand in the air, high above his head.

A sudden wild whoop broke from the throat of big Hank Raney. The sound of it went knifelike through the brain of Tanner. He was amazed to see his friend spur Midnight forward with a bound, while Raney shouted rapidly in the Cheyenne tongue.

So much the boy could distinguish, though he was too bewildered at the moment to make out any of the individual words. But he saw the other suddenly put aside

121

rifle and shield. The long lance was already swinging behind his back. He, also, urged his horse forward. At full
gallop they met, checked their mounts until the horses
slid through the grass to a dead halt that brought them
side by side and then, behold! The Indian and the white
man were closely clasping hands, laughing, shouting, chattering together for all the world, thought the boy, like two
friendly women.

But there was more meaning behind this.

He swept his eye around the vast and circling skyline
of the prairie, and it seemed to him that here, where the
heavens were wider, the hearts of men were greater also.
Their passions were more important. Hatred was more
than human; it was devilish. And in friendship there was
something divine.

He waited. He thought that the two would never have
done speaking with one another, but at last they turned
their horses toward him and came on.

They made a grand picture, riding side by side. The
glory of Midnight quite eclipsed the Indian's horse but,
on the other hand, the bare, brawny shoulders, the sweeping black hair, the brightly stained feathers in the head of
the Cheyenne made him more imposing than his white
companion.

As they approached, it was plain from the bearing and
the gestures of Hank Raney that he was explaining the
boy to his companion. And a pang started suddenly in the
soul of Johnnie Tanner. The moment before, he had felt
that Hank Raney and he were the closest of old and dear
companions. Now, in a trice, he was excluded and thrust
away to a distance. With a cold and bitter jealousy he
examined the approaching brave.

24 · INDIAN GULLET

HE was a man of middle age, his great body set off
with masses of muscles which were forever casting new
gleams as they stirred under the brightness of the sun. He
gave an impression of inhuman fierceness, for he had the
nose of a bird of prey, frowning brows from under whose

shadows his eyes gleamed. His jaw seemed set in a passion, and his nostrils quivered. He had the look of a man whose last patience is gone and who is about to fling himself headlong into battle.

If he was cruel, he had not only the physical strength, but the accouterment to execute his purpose. He carried not only the long-barreled rifle, but also a hatchet sheathed beside the bow of his saddle, a long knife at his hip, with a sheath of white skin, beautifully beaded in a small pattern; he had besides the long war lance, whose shaft arose like a ghostly, shadowy finger, pointing above his shoulder. This was not all. A strong war bow, strung for action, was hung on one side of the saddle. A quiver closely packed with arrows was on the other. The boy had heard Raney tell what a practiced warrior could do with bow and arrows at close range. The feathered shower might be more deadly than bullets from a rifle. Raney had told him that a strong hunter had been known to drive his arrow clean through the body of a buffalo.

So he looked with respect upon this equipment. It would have been too much for an ordinary man, even for a cunning plains Indian. But everything seemed natural, useful, and in place with this rider.

His clothes were as plain as could be. Naked to the waist, he was clad in the usual loin cloth and deerskin leggings. The only two points upon which the eye would be drawn to rest were the beaded sheath for the heavy hunting knife and the highly ornamented moccasins. His face was made still more hideous with daubs of black and crimson war paint.

When he came up to the boy, he rode straight in upon him with the expression of one about to strike a blow, but when he was close enough he checked his war pony and extended his hand with a gruff "How!"

No one has ever been able to pronounce that word exactly as the Indians did. It was partly nasal. It was partly guttural. It was partly a cry and partly a grunt. It could be spelled "How!" or "Ough" or "Ugh" and has been given all of those meanings. But the strangeness of pronunciation was not troubling the boy at that moment. He was too busy enlarging his mind to take in the portrait of this powerful warrior. He replied to the greeting in the same kind. When his hand was in that of the brave, he half expected a pressure that would shatter his bones to the wrist, but, instead, there was merely a mild and steady grip.

Then the Cheyenne turned to Raney and said in a voice very deep but not unmusical: "Brother, only an unlucky man goes on the warpath with children that have to be carried!"

Said Raney, quickly: "Be more careful. My friend understands your own tongue!"

The Cheyenne, at this, turned to the boy with an air perfectly undisturbed. Young Johnnie Tanner was crimson to the eyes. His breast was heaving.

"Well," said the Cheyenne quietly, "chance blows strike us in the dark. But they should hurt the skin more than the spirit."

"That's an apology," said Raney, watching the boy curiously.

Johnnie Tanner was more angry than ever. He felt that Raney, as a true friend, should have interfered more strongly on his behalf. There were certain things he might have said that would have convinced the Indian chief that he, though a boy, could in some cases do what men would have been proud to accomplish. But Raney did not offer any praise or any explanation.

So Johnnie Tanner turned a little in the saddle and, meeting the glance of the Cheyenne, he made his eye like stone. Equally hard and bright was the look of the chief.

"Come, come," said Raney. "We'll start back for the camp as soon as we've packed up the meat."

"Go on—with your friend," said the boy. "I'll pack the meat. You'll have a good many things to talk about, I suppose."

"That's not a bad idea either," replied Raney, too readily for the inward comfort of Tanner. "We'll ride on. You know the way, by this time."

With a sullenly aching heart, John Tanner dismounted again and set to work packing the antelope meat in its own hide. His bitterness increased, as he saw the two riding off together. A sort of blindness came over him. Through the dark of his mind he wished, furiously, that he could find a means of leaving Raney now, at once and forever. He had been insulted by a stranger, a barbarous red man; and Raney had stood by and permitted the thing.

He wished to be revenged upon Raney. He wished to stand in fight against the Cheyenne. Then, let them see whose rifle could shoot the closest to a human mark! No matter for lance, bow, arrows, and the rest. One well-placed ounce of lead would settle all the argument!

He finished the packing of the meat, and, standing up beside the horse again, with a sigh he told himself that he was acting like a sulky child. He should forget it. No, he couldn't forget, but he must endure.

What was he to Raney?

As for the Cheyenne chief, of course, from a trader's viewpoint, his friendship was worth a great deal more than the companionship of any half helpless tenderfoot on the prairies!

But still there was a cold iron in the heart of Johnnie as he mounted and started off in the direction toward which the two forms were disappearing. In the faint swales and through the long grass, sometimes they sank almost from sight; sometimes they grew closer and larger again.

The pony knew the way. He plodded along stolidly—the same gray which had been such a fierce burden-bearer during the first part of the journey. Well, he was not tamed now, either. He was liable to pitch and buck, jump and try to dive into the blue of the sky as into the blue of the water. But he despaired of shaking off his young rider now.

And Johnnie Tanner, with a sort of fierce scorn, rode on with the loosened rein, inviting the contest. Fighting of any sort, even against a dumb beast, would be pleasant to him just now!

But the mustang did not start trouble. Sometimes, flicking one ear forward and the other back, it would turn its head a little, so that Johnnie could see the ugly glint in the corner of its eye. But the actual fight it would not begin. For one thing, it knew the cruel, cutting whiplash which Johnnie had learned to use on the most tender pieces of flank and shoulder and belly.

So they came into the camp.

He found the two men seated, smoking pipes. Their horses were not even unsaddled, but bit at the grass near the masters. And big Raney nodded to the boy and waved toward the horses without a word.

At this the heart of the boy swelled so big that it well-nigh burst. He had always been willing enough to perform every commission which was assigned to him when he and Raney were alone in the camp. For that matter, Raney always did more than one share. But now, to be commanded silently, with a gesture, as though he were a slave or a squaw!

He bit his lip, but he obeyed.

He would not give the Indian the satisfaction of seeing the two white men quarrel in his presence. Besides, he was so hurt that he might be unmanly in his outburst of rage. Therefore, he kept his peace and went about the unsaddling and the hobbling of the horses. He was very sick at heart. Never since he left his father's house had he been in such a deep well of hopeless darkness.

To-morrow, when the occasion served, he would tell Raney that he would not accept his company any longer. He would go on by himself and let Raney carry on with his preferred barbarian, his Cheyenne.

And how madly futile the whole affair had been. Was he, in fact, in the possession of his right senses, that he should have left New York and run halfway across the continent for the sake of hunting down a thief who had a revolver with a pearl in it? Even suppose that he should come to grips with the thief, what could he accomplish?

Grief, homesickness, despair overcame the boy.

But he kept his head high and went patiently, slowly about the camp work.

Once he heard the Cheyenne say: "A young boy learning the ways of the warpath should have the foot of a rabbit and the quick hand of a wildcat!"

"And the claws in your throat, copper face!" said the boy, understanding perfectly that the allusion was to his slowness in the work of the camp.

Even this he had to endure, though it made him see black.

Passion that is restrained is likely to turn into the fiercest, the most violent of action. The rage which is kept within hand will find the hand a weapon, when the time comes.

So the anger of Johnnie Tanner grew harder and colder as the moments went by. He finished the work with the horses. He saw that they were grazing peacefully. He built up the low fire, making it of the driest, deadest wood, so that the smoke would be dispersed by the wind before it could rise into a tall column to be observed from afar.

Then he carved antelope venison into square lumps, of a convenient size, and he pierced these with tough, clean splinters of wood and put them near the blaze to roast. It needed most careful work in the tending of these bits of meat, so that they should not burn on one side or remain underdone on the other.

He was in the midst of this, when the great hand of the Cheyenne was extended.

"Give me!" said the chief.

And young John Tanner lifted his eyes from the hand, and looked along the vast, supple muscles of the arm up the shoulder to the brutal strength of the neck and jaw.

He smiled. His detestation of the creature was complete and, therefore, he smiled as men do in their most infinite disgust. Then he handed several of the meat morsels to the Cheyenne on the splinters which held them. The Indian picked off the meat in chunks. Of each chunk he made a single mouthful. There did not seem to be any chewing. With the incredible gullet of a lion, he swallowed each chunk as it came from the toasting wood. The naked splinters he threw back into the fire, without enough forethought to put them aside, that they might be used again. No, he simply cast the splinters back into the fire, without looking at the boy, continuing his talk with Raney at the same moment and stretching out his ponderous hand for a fresh supply!

25 · BROKEN KNIFE'S STORY

NINE-TENTHS of Johnnie Tanner's enthusiasm for the wild western life and for the great red man in his native habitat disappeared that instant. But, more profound than his disgust for the Cheyenne, was the disgust that he felt for his companion Raney. The latter accepted these conditions with perfect sang-froid. He did not lift a hand to assist in the cookery, but took his own share from the hands of the boy, who was kept busy supplying them both. It was not until both their large appetites were pacified that

Johnnie could roast meat for himself, and then his anger made it as tasteless as wood.

In the meantime, he had been listening to an animated discussion of old times, between the two. The name of this Cheyenne was Broken Knife, and it seemed to the boy that the name fitted perfectly with his abrupt and harsh manner. However, it was plain that he respected Hank Raney immensely. He told him the news of the tribe, how they had wintered, the names of young braves who had lately distinguished themselves, recounted several marriages, and poured forth a flow of tidings of all sorts. He did not pause until Raney asked him what brought him out singly on the warpath. Was it to steal horses, to lift a scalp, or simply to cruise in search of random adventures?

The Cheyenne paused, as though deep in the consideration of these questions, before he answered:

"Brother, I have made a prayer and made a vow. Then I have sent a message to the Pawnees. I sent it to Talking Wolf."

"I know him," said Raney. "I remember seeing him at Fort Leavenworth. He's a big man and a great fighter, I think. What message did you send to him?"

"Only this: that I was to leave the Cheyennes and ride across the open land. I told him what line I would ride along. Somewhere between the two nations, I told him that I hoped to meet him."

"To fight him, Broken Knife?"

The chief stiffened a little.

"You remember that in my tepee there were four children, and three of them were girls?"

"And I remember the fourth," said Raney, nodding. "He only had a play name, then. But he was as fine a boy as ever forked a horse."

"He won a name when he first went on the warpath. When he came back, he was called Hawk-that-rises. All of the old men spoke of him. All the braves looked at him. The chiefs wanted to give him their daughters as wives. He had killed two men, and taken a scalp, and counted four coups, all in one great battle."

"He looked it," said Raney, smiling a little, as if with pleasure. "He looked like the kind of boy who becomes a

128

man at one step. And once a man—well, he's your son, of course!"

The flattery did not touch Broken Knife.

"He is dead," said the Cheyenne. "He went again on the warpath. The Pawnees set a trap, and the young man rode into it. Perhaps they all would have got away, because they had fast horses, but an arrow hurt the best friend of Hawk-that-rises. He fell from the back of his horse and my son stopped and got down to fight for him.

"He killed his own horse and that of his friend. He lay with the wounded man between the two bodies and they fought as if from a fort. Finally so much blood ran out of the body of the friend that he knew he was about to die. So he stood up and sang his death song, and the Pawnees shot him full of arrows and bullets, so that he fell back upon the ground dead."

Johnnie Tanner had forgotten his wounded pride, his sense of many wrongs. He listened, enchanted, to that story, and saw in his mind's eye the young Cheyenne singing his death chant and waiting for the Pawnee arrows which would end his fading life. It was a picture such as one would take into the mind and keep there among the few unforgettable pictures.

He stared at the Cheyenne chief with a new emotion. The man had lost a son whom he loved. Something in the way of manners could be forgiven to him.

Broken Knife went on:

"Then the Pawnees crawled up closer through the grass and called out to my son to surrender, but he laughed at them. I know all of these things from a Pawnee who was with the war party, but he deserted and came off and joined our people, because he wanted one of the chief's wives, and ran away with her. He said that the Pawnees kept calling to my son, and my son laughed. Finally he saw a chance, and sent a good war arrow through the shoulder of one of the Pawnees.

"They were very angry. They filled the air with arrows. But as they fired their guns and shot off their arrows, still they could hear my son singing."

"Aye," said Hank Raney. "He surely had the look of that sort of a man."

"Let me fill my pipe and smoke it, and talk a little

129

through the smoke," said the Cheyenne. "There is not much left of his life!"

Then he resumed, after he had lighted the pipe, with his forehead puckered, his eyes almost closed, the look of one who sees and interprets dreams. He even smiled a little as he talked slowly on.

"In the middle of his song of defiance, all the singing ended suddenly. The Pawnees listened. They fired again, many shots, but there was no sound. Then they thought that they had killed my boy with a bullet, or that they had struck him with one of the arrows which they were arching up into the air so that they would fall straight down. They thought that one of these arrows might have dropped down through his heart, or broken his backbone.

"After they had listened a while, they crept in close. They came out of the taller grass. They began to slip closer. Finally, two young braves leaped up and ran toward the place where the two horses were. And then an arrow string twanged twice, and one of the young Pawnees fell on his face, and the other screamed and ran back for the longer grass, but a third arrow struck him in the middle of the back. The next day he died."

"Hai! He was a man, that son of yours," shouted Raney. "He was a man, my friend. That was a good trick to play the Pawnee wolves, may the curse come on them all! I should have liked to see those arrows go home, I can tell you! Then what happened?"

"You shall hear," said Broken Knife. "For two days the Pawnees lay around the place where my son was fighting. The sun was very hot. He had no water. The sun burned him as fire chars wood, but still they could hear him singing. Twice they came closer, when his singing ended toward the end of the second day. But his arrows drove them back. They wanted to rush on him at night, but the moon was bright and they feared him as much under the light of the moon as under the light of the sun."

"A brave man is feared by night and day," agreed Raney, rather sententiously.

"And when the morning of the third day came, the Pawnees began to worry a little," went on the Cheyenne. "They remembered how long they had been there because their bellies were empty. They had only a little water from a muddy pool, and that water was sour and harsh as ashes in their throats. Their lips began to crack and to grin. Also, they felt that the young Cheyennes who had escaped from them might soon be back with many warriors from the Cheyenne camp. So the Pawnees were about to give up and go away. But among the Pawnees there was a great chief, and his name was Talking Wolf."

"Ah?" said Raney.

"They called him Talking Wolf because, though he was a good fighter, he was better when he talked. All the tribe listened to him. Now he told his men that he would make one more attempt on my son. And he asked them to listen to him, because he would surely conquer, and he would conquer without weapons.

"They all sat about and nodded their heads at him, wondering how he could do such a thing. Well, he stood up from the long grass and shouted, making signs for a truce, and when he stood up, my son stood up, also. It showed that he trusted in the Pawnee truce, and it showed also that he still had strength and that he laughed at the need of sleep and food and water. He stood up and made the sign of truce back again—"

"And then the Pawnee dogs shot him through the back?" asked Raney savagely.

"No," said the chief. "He was only fifteen, but he was a man, and the Pawnees, even, tremble before they shoot a young chief. They had seen him kill two of their band and wound two more. They wanted his blood very terribly, but they were afraid to shoot until their leader told them to.

"My son walked out from the dead horses and stood before Talking Wolf.

"And Talking Wolf said: 'If you were not a Cheyenne, I wish that you could be my son. I have never seen a young man so brave. Come back with me, and live in my lodge like one of my family. There is enough of this thing. You see that we cannot leave you, with honor, lying out here among the dead, and it makes my heart small to think of you dying of thirst, like a mad dog.' "

"I understand where he got his name!" said Raney.

"Yes," said the Cheyenne. "Listen to every word that he uttered and mark it down in your mind. He talked like a snake, and my boy listened. He was flattered when such a great warrior spoke to him as chief to chief.

"Said Talking Wolf: 'Listen to me again. You see that we cannot leave you while you are alive. But enough men have died here. We are willing to forget the dead men we have lost to-day. But both of them have widows and children. Now, then, we must have something to give to the widows and the children to make up for the loss of their hunters. What is it to be? Well, your father can decide that. He will send a few horses, some robes, and perhaps a gun. When these things come, they will be given to the families of the dead men, and you will be sent back to your father's tepee. Otherwise, you must understand that I cannot keep my honor, if I return to my people with two dead and two men wounded, and nothing but one dead Cheyenne left behind us on the trail.'

"That was the way he talked, and my son stood up straight and looked into his eyes. But the eyes of a liar are dim and bright by turns and no man can see to the bottom of a liar's soul. It is a well filled with dead leaves and with slime. So my son thought he saw the truth, but he was seeing only his own honest soul. He said that he would go with the Pawnees, and there he would wait there until his father sent a ransom for him."

Raney groaned heavily.

Johnnie Tanner was so moved that he could hardly breathe.

"Then they killed him?" whispered Raney.

"No, but then they took him to their tribe. They left him free all the way, trusting his word not to escape. He rode and he hunted with them, all the way, but before they rode into the Pawnee city, they tied him with lariats and brought him into the town, and all the Pawnees tortured him, like devils!"

132

RAGE, pity, horror, disgust so filled Johnnie Tanner that he was turned to stone. His eyes and his ears were wide open to drink in the frightful story, but he could have been burned with fire without feeling it.

He began to loathe all Pawnees with a mighty loathing.

As for Raney, the story had now reached a point when he could not endure it. Straightway, he jumped up to his feet and began rapidly to pace backward and forward with long strides.

But the narrator, unmoved and unmovable, looked into the circlewise puffs of smoke which, issuing from his lips, rose gradually, expanded, became a silver dimness in the sunlight, and then disappeared. His eyes remained half closed, squinting, and his lips were half pursed, half smiling. He had the look of a Chinese idol, hideously carved. And yet there was a certain peace in his expression. The boy guessed what it was. It was the rigid stillness that springs out of a great hate.

Then Raney sat down, suddenly, without having spoken, and the speaker went on:

"They brought him to their feast. They tied him to a post. They gave whips to the children and the women. They flogged him until he was crimson from head to foot. He was dripping and running with blood. But he only stood against the post without struggling and sang. They lashed him across his singing mouth. But still he sang, with ragged lips. He showed that he was a man," said Broken Knife.

He maintained a long silence, which the other two religiously respected.

He no longer seemed, in the eyes of Johnnie Tanner, a mere brutal savage. He was something more. He began to fill the eye of his mind more than any man he ever had looked at before this hour.

Then the Cheyenne resumed his narrative in the following manner, his face and his voice and his attitude still unchanged:

"You could guess that the Pawnees, when they saw what

my son was, did not wish to have him die immediately. He was so much of a man that they wished to torment him for a long time. So they took him away from the post and a squaw washed his wounds. They kept him for many days until he no longer raved from the fever. Then his eye and his brain were open and clear once more, and he saw the truth.

"He saw that he had been a fool, because he had trusted a Pawnee's word. But he made no complaint.

"When he was healed, they took him out again and strove to break his spirit. In order to accomplish this, they loosed the squaws at him, with knives and with splinters. And then they charged him with mounted young warriors. And, last of all, they tied him to a stake and piled the wood all around to burn him alive."

Here Johnnie closed his eyes.

He heard the voice continuing:

"They lighted the fire and, as they lighted it, the voice of my son was heard rising in a great death chant, and he told how he had killed four Pawnee wolves and, because of that glory, how his soul would go to the happy hunting grounds. But, as the flames began to rise, before they touched his body, then they cut his bonds and quickly took him away from the fire once more."

"That doesn't sound like Pawnee devilishness!" exclaimed Raney.

"Do you see, my friend," said the warrior. "The great medicine man watched the fires rising, and heard my son singing through the smoke, and he said that Hawk-that-rises should be kept for some great moment, when the Pawnees were in need, and then he should be honorably sacrificed in order to change their fortune.

"So, since that moment, he has been kept as a close captive, and treated very well. They are waiting for the great moment to come when they shall need his life. Perhaps he is already dead. At any rate, he is as good as dead. And therefore I, not long ago, sent in a message to the Pawnees by a white trader who visits both of our tribes. His name is Long Arrow, and he is, above all, a great man among the Pawnees. By him I sent the challenge, and I said that I would leave the Cheyenne village and ride toward the Pawnees, and that if Talking Wolf is a man he will ride out and meet me on the way. That

134

is all. Somewhere across the land I shall find him. Somewhere I shall meet him and strike him down, and spit his heart on my spear point, and roast it over a fire of buffalo dung. That is all!"

He spoke, finished smoking, knocked out the ember from the pipe bowl and, slowly rising, walked away across the prairie.

Big Hank Raney, without a word to Johnnie Tanner, arose also, and went along with his red-skinned friend, leaving John Tanner alone in the camp in a very changed and thoughtful mood; for he no longer wondered at the affection which his friend showed for the Indian. He only wondered that either of them would bestow a single glance on such an insignificant person as himself, a mere boy.

But his thoughts soon left both Raney and the Cheyenne.

He centered his attention upon the story of young Hawk-that-rises. The boy was barely fifteen. So was Johnnie Tanner.

But the young Cheyenne had killed four men in honorable and open battle, and what had young Tanner done, except to become the stupid victim of a thief, and then chase the criminal and involve a friend in the same effort?

He thought of the boy as a careless and yet dignified, laughing but formidable lad. He thought of him with a leap of the heart and a smile on his lips.

Some day, perhaps, he might himself roam the prairie, and perhaps grown men would speak of him, reverently, as they spoke of young Hawk-that-rises.

The dusk was coming on. A hoot owl skimmed above the grass, and then stooped out of view, like a shadow gone out on a wall. It had dropped, probably, to capture a prairie dog or some other rodent.

Johnnie took up his rifle. It needed cleaning, after the day's hunting, and he cleaned it according to the good teaching of Raney. He cleaned and oiled it, and then, putting the butt of it between his knees, he sat cross-legged and worked with ashes to remove from the cheek of the lock piece some imaginary dimness. He worked the metal over the water and ashes, and then he scrubbed and polished until the steel shone bright as the blade of a good sword. Still he worked on and on, vigorously.

His mind was only half on its work. The rest of his

135

thought was off there in the dim distance of the imagination, seeing the Cheyenne boy ringed around with enemies, but with his laughter and his singing still going up like a cloud of fire to the sky.

That was to be glorious, to be heroic!

But, still more marvelous, to be tied to a post and lashed until covered with blood, and still to shout a death chant, filled with tales of his own achievements; to give not a moment of triumph to the treacherous victors—indeed, that was far greater.

A small and fierce smile trembled on his lips. With vacant eyes he raised the rifle before him, to squint at the gleam of the polished metal. How it would shine the next day when they rode out, and the full glance of the sun was reflected from it!

He thought of this—and then his thoughts went out!

The metal was bright enough. It was so very bright that it showed, behind him, the glint of the green prairie, now darkening with the evening, in the hollows. And it showed, above all else, something close at hand and immediately behind him—a wild face that peered out from the tall prairie grass, and a rifle leveled straight into the mirroring steel itself.

No, not into the steel. The truth staggered him. Some one was lying there securely behind him and, looking through the parting grass, was drawing a bead to fire a bullet into him. This very instant, no doubt, the forefinger of the enemy was contracting!

The horror of it froze him to a statue, as it seemed to him, for long hours. In reality, in the tenth part of a second he had acted.

He threw the rifle blindly over his head, backward, and at the same time he snatched for the pistol at his belt and cast himself sidewise toward the ground.

He had not struck it. He was still in full momentum when the rifle roared like a waterfall's thunder behind him. The sound went through him like the invisible glance of death. But he was not struck!

He knew that he had escaped even as he rolled from his back to his face, with the pistol thrust out before him at arm's length.

A copper-skinned monster was rising from the grass.

Like the Cheyenne, he was naked to the waist. Like the Cheyenne, he wore feathers in his hair, but this was a mere scalp lock that ran backward and forward along the center of his head, much like a horse's mane.

It was a Pawnee. And the word shocked his mind like the blow of a fist. He had heard enough about Pawnees and their methods in the last hour from the lips of great Broken Knife.

This giant, as he sprang out from the grass, raised a hand from which dripped something like water—it was the gleam of a long, curved hunting knife, at the center of the Indian's body.

He knew that the bullet had struck. He knew it because the Pawnee swerved to the side with a short, deep grunt, and then, recovering, bounded straight in.

Johnnie Tanner fired again.

There was only the hollow, flat sound of the hammer striking, to no avail. The cap had failed him!

He had not time to get to his feet. But he struggled to his knees and hurled the heavy pistol with all his might at the head of the enemy. That stroke did not go home, but even a glancing blow along the side of the red man's skull was enough to stop and stagger him.

Johnnie Tanner came lurching to his feet, pulling his own hunting knife as he rose.

Far in the distance, he heard voices shouting. They would be coming now, both his friend, Raney, and the Cheyenne. But the promise of their aid was not enough. All they could do for him would be as far off and ineffectual as something seen in a dream. For he could see the red splotch on the center of the Pawnee's body. He knew from the contorted face of the savage that the latter felt he had received his death wound. He would make a last, tigerish attempt to kill one enemy before he died.

That was what Johnnie Tanner was sure of as he confronted the big man. Then, savagely, he determined that he would not wait to be attacked.

He could see the contempt and rage in the glance with which the Indian measured him. He could see the frightful power of the naked, bulky arm, as it raised the knife a little higher, preparatory to springing in and finishing the fight at a single stroke.

That instant, Johnnie leaped, and not away. He ducked, drove straight under the impending arm, and struck hard, upward, into the body of the man. At the same time a powerful blow flattened him to the ground.

27 · SPOILS TO THE VICTOR

HE got up in haste, whirling to meet the Pawnee's second stroke. The first one had been a blow of the arm, rather than of the knife, for Johnnie knew that he was badly shaken, but not touched by a steel blade.

As he rose and whirled, and as the shouting of the Cheyenne and of Hank Raney rushed in upon him from the side, he saw his gigantic antagonist lying writhing upon the ground, twisting his knees up to his chin and then kicking out convulsively again, the force of the strokes turning his body around and around upon the ground.

It was a horrible sight. As he moved, bright crimson blood spurted out on the grass. It was like looking at the hideous, foolish struggles of a chicken whose head has been wrung off, seeing it hop and twist upon the ground.

So it was with the Pawnee, whose head was strained far back between his shoulders, so that the throat muscles pulled the lower jaw down. The eyes rolled back in his head. He looked as though he were about to shriek; but only a bubbling, gasping sound came from his lips.

Johnnie Tanner looked down with a strange mixture of emotions on the picture. It was a man, and a man in the last agonies of death, he knew. But it was an enemy, a cruel savage, a stalking wild beast which had attempted to kill him from behind.

Therefore, while his cheek grew cold and white, his lips remained firmly compressed. Whatever he blamed himself for, he never would blame himself for this. It was justice. He could claim it as absolute justice, even though it were dispensed from his own hand.

The last fierce struggle tied that great, muscular body in a knot. Then, twisting over on his back, the Pawnee cast wide his arms. His chest heaved once. He was dead, and looking, with his sightless eyes, steadily upward toward the heart of the rosy, evening sky.

The boy heard the running footsteps.

He glanced aside and there he saw Hank Raney coming at full speed, his face desperate, his drawn pistol ready in his hand, his hair blown back behind him.

Hank Raney was celebrated for his speed of foot. He was famous for it, in fact. And yet far before him ran the ponderous Cheyenne, Broken Knife, and with each step he put greater distance between himself and the companion who ran to help.

It was Broken Knife who bounded into the narrow circle of the campfire and, checking himself as he saw death on the face of the fallen brave, he exclaimed, with a panting, broken voice:

"Talking Wolf!"

Talking Wolf!

That story which Johnnie Tanner had heard had been grim and real enough. But it was the dreamiest of fairy tales, compared with the knife thrust of this fact. For Talking Wolf lay there dead before him, the ingenious and the cruel devil who had captured the Cheyenne lad by cunning, where force of hand was not enough, who had used wit to supplement courage.

If there had been some pity in him for the stranger, it was extinguished at that instant. The Cheyenne, his arms folded over his panting breast, looked down upon the dead man. Up beside him rushed Raney, gave the fallen body one glance, and then gripped the boy with gigantic hands.

"You ain't hurt, partner?" he gasped.

"Me? I'm not even scratched," said the other.

Raney stepped to the dead.

"Talking Wolf," said the Cheyenne, in a growling, low voice.

Then he dropped to one knee, touched the dead breast with two fingers of one hand and muttered a word which the boy did not understand.

"He's counting coup!" whispered Raney.

The Cheyenne rose.

First, he glanced keenly around him. Then he stepped to the very spot on which the Pawnee had lain and beside which was his rifle. That rifle he picked up, examined, and nodded his head over, as much as to say that the thing spoke for itself. He pointed to the spot; he pointed next to the boy.

"Did he stalk you, son?" asked Raney, much moved.

"By thunder, he did! And there's the sign of him. Follow the back track, Broken Knife, and see if the trail don't run you to a hoss."

But Broken Knife was already springing through the grass with a matchless stride.

The white hunter looked after him with an eye that burned with admiration.

"Look at him!" he said to the boy. "There's one that could break me in two with one hand, though I ain't a child's toy or an imitation man, either. But, for all the size of him, see the way that he runs, like a boy sprintin' for the swimming pool. And he could keep that up, mind you, long enough to fag you or me in five minutes, and still he'd go on for an hour!"

Johnnie Tanner looked on and watched with admiration also.

He felt somewhat detached from everything, now that the great shock of that effort was ended.

As for Raney, he asked not a single question at first. He examined the place carefully and spoke quietly.

"Here's where he sneaked up. Here you were sitting. Here he pushed his rifle through the grass. Here's the rag you were polishing your rifle with. But——how could he've missed, close as he was?"

He turned on the boy with that final question.

"I lifted up the rifle and the cheek piece was bright enough to be a mirror. I saw him in it, and rolled over sideways. That must have spoiled his aim, I suppose."

"And then?"

"He came in. I shot him with the pistol. The second barrel of the gun wouldn't go off. I got to a knee and whanged it at him, and it hit him a glancing blow and stopped him again. So I had time to stand up and get out my knife."

"And I seen the rest," said Raney.

He began to frown. "You oughta look to your pistols," he said gloomily. "I've noticed it before, and I wanted to speak of it, but it got out of my mind. You've gotta

140

keep looking to pistols. Mind you, this might be a lesson for you."

"Yes," said Johnnie, "it'll be a lesson that I'll never forget."

Suddenly Raney smiled.

"It was grand, son," said he. "It was the grandest thing that I ever seen—the big copper bulk of him, and you like a little white terrier jumping in at him! Jumping in under that big arm of his—I'll never forget it. People are gunna hear about it, and people are then gunna do their share of the talking."

So it proved, before the end, and to such a degree as Johnnie Tanner could never have dreamed of. For, on that day, all the fame of Talking Wolf, wherever men gathered on the frontier of the prairie, was transferred to a young white lad who had barely appeared in the West. But none of this could Johnnie know at the moment.

All he was aware of was the gradual relaxation of his nerves. There was a sort of snapping in his brain.

Finally, the chief returned.

He came riding upon a magnificent bay stallion that went with a lofty lifting of the feet and a gallant carriage of the head. He carried, also, the rest of the Pawnee's war equipment, which the latter had abandoned at a little distance when he spotted the faint smoke of the campfire and went forward on foot to reconnoiter.

When he reached the camp, the Cheyenne dismounted and, looking at Johnnie, he waved his hand.

"He's saying that it's all yours, Johnnie," said Raney. "And you've mighty well earned it. There's a beauty for you. You walk around and take a look at it. I didn't know that the Pawnees had hosses like that. Walk around and take a look at it."

"It's a beauty!" exclaimed the boy. "It's a wonder. But—it's no Midnight."

"No," said Raney complacently. "It's no Midnight. It ain't one in a million, but it's one in ten thousand. That hoss will never say 'No' to you."

"How do horses like that come about?" said the boy. "They're not the same blood as the other mustangs, surely?"

They stood back, while the Cheyenne chief stood again with folded arms, looking down at the dead body of the enemy who had come out to meet him and who had fallen by another hand upon the way.

"I've heard it explained by a mighty wise man that knew a lot," said Hank Raney. "These here plains hosses, they come from the stock that the Conquistadores rode.

"Mind you, those Conquistadores was Spaniards with a real man strain in 'em. Yes, sir! They was the real sort of thing in men. And the hosses that they brought with 'em across the sea was straight out of the old Arab and Barb strain that the Arabs had with 'em when they conquered Spain, away back in the beginning of things. Because that's what seems to've happened. And when those fellows come across the water, they took their favorite hosses with them, and some of those hosses got loose and run astray. And they wander. And they drift up north through Mexico. And De Soto, I guess his gang turned some loose. And they get out here on the plains."

"But, look at the lumpy heads of most of the mustangs," said the boy, "and then look at Midnight and this bay stallion? They're different!"

"They've just throwed back," said Raney. "They've throwed back to the old strain. These here hard winters, and no stables, and catch as catch can for food, after the snow comes, it changed that stock a good deal. It made 'em all iron. The soft stuff died. What was left got pot-bellied, to hold plenty of fodder, and mean as wildcats, and big-headed, and ewe-necked, a good deal of 'em.

"But, now and then, along comes a picture hoss, and he's a throwback to the same stuff that the Spaniards rode. The blood is still pure. The strain is there. Only, these here picture mustangs, they've got a harder kind of steel in 'em than any other hosses in the world. Maybe they ain't got quite the foot to sprint a mile. But they'll kill anything else on four feet when it comes to running twenty. And that bay, there, is the best pony in Talking Wolf's string. And now it's yours! Get on it, and try its paces!"

So the boy stripped off the Indian saddle, put on his own, and mounted. The few terms of Pawnee necessary to manage a horse were repeated to him by Raney, and off he went across the prairie at a round gallop.

It was perfectly simple. The horse swerved and swayed at the least touch, the least swing of the body. It was a perfectly trained war horse, skilled in obeying commands which were transmitted by a pressure of the knees, alone, and young Johnnie Tanner, as the stallion bounded forward felt that he was mounted on the back of a bird, the stroke of whose wings could take him from horizon to horizon.

28 · THE WET SCALP

WITH dancing, shining eyes, he returned to the camp. But he did not quite reach it. He had been gone longer than he guessed and, while he was away, big Raney and the Indian, or Raney alone, had hastily bundled the meager equipment upon the backs of the horses. It was Raney who now rode out to meet him, the train of the rest behind him. Big Broken Knife remained behind in the camp, his arms folded across his breast, as the boy had seen him stand before.

Raney was not mounted upon Midnight. As usual, he preferred to keep the stallion fresh from the ordinary weariness of travel and reserve it for the sudden efforts of the chase, or the possible rigors of battle, escape, or pursuit. He was mounted, now, upon an ugly, piebald mare, and this he ranged alongside the dancing bay.

"Tell me, son," said he, "how it feels?"

"It feels," said the boy, "like heaven."

"Aye, aye," said Raney warmly. "That's what it mostly feels like. I guess there ain't anything finer than to have under you the right kind of a hoss. I never had nothing as good as that bay. Not till I laid my hands on the Midnight here. But what's there in the world like having under you a hoss that can move like a bird and an open place to fly it in? Here we got room for the flying. Here's the place for a man to live his life. Cities? Towns? Why, blast 'em all, I'm sick of 'em. I don't see how folks get the right room breathing inside of the walls of a street, such as they have nowadays!"

The boy nodded. He would have agreed with almost anything that praised horseflesh at that moment.

"But," he demanded, "why are you breaking camp, Hank? What's the use, till we've collected a lot more meat to dry? I thought you said that you wanted another day's hunting."

"We did," said Raney. "But we don't now."

"How does that come?"

"Why, I'll tell you. We're bound, now, and in two days we'll get to a place where you can pick up all the dried meat that you want for nothing. You're comin' to a place where you can have jerked buffalo meat, or pemmican, or fresh venison for that matter, as cheap as the asking, and I guess that it's better to spend a little breath than it is to spend this here lead and powder that we're packing along with us?"

"Of course it is," said the boy.

Then he shook his head.

"You seem to be smiling at me, Hank," said he.

"Am I, a mite?" said Hank Raney. "Well, son, I'm one of the few men out here on the prairies that'll ever smile at you ag'in."

"What do you mean by that?"

"I mean that the rest of 'em will be too dog-gone well scared to do any smiling. You'll meet some mighty rough gents that'll back up when they know that you're the lad that sent Talking Wolf all of the way home. But me, I take my hat off to you, Johnnie, but I pretend to be kind of familiar still."

He laughed, and the boy laughed with him. "I don't mind if you make fun of me, Hank," he admitted. "Only, I'd sort of like to know what the fun is about. I'd like to know, too, what the land is where we'll have all the food that we want for the asking."

"Did I only mention food?" said the other.

"Yes. Is there something else that's given away in that wonderful place we're coming to?"

"Why, yes," said Hank Raney. "There's also a good comfortable home that we can have for the asking and clothes, and guns, and powder and shot, and knives, and fishing tackle and about all that a man would ever want to have, in this part of the world. And horses, too, though not many as good as your bay, or Midnight!"

The boy stared at him in amazement that was round-eyed.

"I wish that you'd explain yourself Hank," he begged.

"I mean the land that I'm talking about is whatever

144

land that the Cheyennes are living on and hunting over. Their land is our land from this time on."

Johnnie was silenced. He still could not understand.

Then the other went on: "This Talking Wolf, mind you, was likely to capture a poor trustin' fool of a Cheyenne boy by lies and promises. But that ain't all the harm that he's done. When it come to hoss lifting, he's taken scores of the Cheyenne best. And when it come to lifting hair, he wasn't a mite backward about that, either. No, sir, it's said that he's wore the hair of seven Cheyenne braves in his day, and the number of coups that he's counted on Cheyenne hide, dead and living, it would take a book to fill 'em all in! You ain't just happened to kill a sneakin' Pawnee wolf. No, sir! You're a dog-gone national benefactor of the Cheyennes. And when they have a chance to show you, they'll show you plenty how they feel about it!"

"But," said the boy, "you don't mean that we're going to ride into a Cheyenne camp now, and take advantage of their friendly feeling, and sun ourselves in their hospitality?"

"You don't want to," said the other, "but they want us to. They want nothing better. Every chief in the tribe, he's got a personal hankering to see you, the size of you, and the look in your eyes. And whatever size you got, and whatever look you got, you can be bang-up sure that it'd be the right size and the right look, so far as the Cheyennes go. Why, there ain't a Cheyenne in the tribe that wouldn't ride a hundred mile just for the pleasure of sayin' 'How!' to you. And that goes for the women and the kids, too!"

Johnnie Tanner blushed.

"But I couldn't do it, Hank," said he. "I just couldn't go in there and take advantage——"

"Advantage your foot!" said Hank, somewhat impatiently. "But I'll tell you what, if you don't want to, I do! I won't mind sitting around at a few feasts and hearing the old braves swap lies, excepting that lies is what they don't swap! They tell the truth, and some of the truth that they tell, it's enough to raise the hair, along your spine, old war cat!

"No, sir, I'm gunna go in with you. Speakin' of sunnin' yourself, I'm goin' to sun myself. I'm a great man with the Cheyennes, too, right now. Not only because I've always been their friend. But because they know that I brung you clean out here on the plains with me, and it'll look to them like I done it special so that you could kill off Talking Wolf!"

He laughed long and loudly, as he said this, and the boy, with a faint smile, nodded as he listened to the laughter. He could not deny that his nerves jumped a little at the thought of being among the red men and considered a person of some importance among them.

His mind reverted to another thing.

"But the dead man back there," said he. "We haven't buried him, you know!"

"What would we bury him with?" asked the other harshly. "Our bare hands? Our hunting knives?"

He shrugged his shoulders.

"There's them on the prairie that will bury him right quick!" he concluded.

Johnnie Tanner followed the glance of the other, and his eyes went up with a shudder to certain black specks which circled in the air above him.

He drew in a great breath. It seemed to chill his heart. Two hours before, the Pawnee had been a great chief, in the pride of his strength, his wealth, his cunning, his fame.

To-morrow?

He dared not even pursue the thought.

It was now the afterglow of the sunset, which was slowly fading away in bronze and greenish copper lights along the west.

"Then why did big Broken Knife stay back there with the dead man so long?" he asked.

Raney interrupted him, rather than answered his question.

"Questions," said he, "is things that can sometimes be answered with eyes. Use your eyes, and you'll find out. He's coming up now."

And up came the Cheyenne chief, his horse galloping rapidly with a pounding stride that was audible far and wide across the plains.

He raised a hand to greet them and swung into place on the right-hand side of the boy.

The latter, at first, hardly dared to look askance at the

formidable warrior, but, by degrees, he began to steal glances. And it was then that he saw, from the bridle of the Cheyenne's horse, something dangling, something that looked like a bit of rag—an obscure thing.

He puzzled his mind about it, for he felt that this might be a partial answer to the puzzle of why the Cheyenne had remained behind with the dead man.

But he was not sure. He could not conceive what the thing might be, and hazily his mind went back over the pictures which he had seen in books, or descriptions done in detail in print. At last, through the course of his thoughts, came a pen sketch which showed a warrior returning triumphant from battle, with two such ragged things hanging from his bridle.

He remembered now. It struck him numb in the brain. This was the wet scalp of Talking Wolf!

29 · ON WITH THE DANCE

THEY made a dry camp that night. And when they turned in, the boy said to his friend in English: "Did you hear him say that Long Arrow was the man who carried the message? Could that mean Harry, the thief?"

"Why, it's Pawnee Harry, of course."

"But how could the Cheyennes let him go back and forth through their camp when he's known to be a Pawnee, or almost a Pawnee?"

"Because he's a trader and has a white skin."

"But he could be a spy on them."

"Aye, likely he is, and likely they know it. But if he brings 'em what they want, they're likely to let him use his eyes and go to. That's the Cheyenne way. They put their trust in their braves and their Sky People and let the enemy go hang."

Johnnie Tanner went to sleep, slowly digesting this information. When he wakened in the morning, he found that he was alone with Hank Raney once more; the Cheyenne had disappeared!

Hank, however, showed not the slightest concern because of this desertion. Broken Knife, he was sure, had

147

departed merely for the sake of preparing a better reception when his white friends reached the Cheyenne encampment.

So they breakfasted on a mouthful of jerked venison, and then started on across the prairie.

To Johnnie Tanner, it was a delightful day, not so much because of what he expected at the end of the ride, but because he had the bay stallion at hand to watch. He was on the gray mustang again, and, keeping the stallion on a short lead, he spent hours petting and stroking and talking broken Pawnee to the horse. This caressing, it was plain, was a novelty to the animal. At first, he winced, under the hand of the boy, and his frightened eyes grew as bright as the eyes of a startled deer. But he soon grew accustomed to the soothing voice and the touch of his new master.

Raney looked on with approval.

"Injuns," he said, "even the Cheyennes, they take uncommon strong to a good hoss, but the way they show how they like him, is to rig him up with a painted hide and a lot of bells and things hanging from his bridle. And they'll spend a half day braiding feathers into the tail of their favorite hoss, but they won't spend any time at all in talkin' to it. They're wild folk, and they keep their hosses wild. You take Midnight, here, that follers me around like a dog now. Why, when I got hold of him, he'd jump a mile if you looked cross-eyed at him. He was that kind of a hoss! But a hoss that loves you is two times your hoss."

They made a long march, that day, clinging to a direction which Raney seemed to be perfectly sure of. The day died; the twilight came, deepened, departed, and finally it was full night, with the stars blinking and then shining in clear white hosts above them.

Yet Raney pushed on, and presently the boy could make out a glow before them in the far heart of the night. This illumination grew and grew.

"Is it the Cheyennes?" asked Johnnie Tanner.

"It's the Cheyennes," said Raney. "It's sure enough the Cheyennes, and they're gunna make a night of it."

"How can you tell that?"

"By the way that they've lit up their fires. See them tepees shining like lanterns in the dark!"

148

In fact, as they came closer and John Tanner could see the individual lodges, they seemed to be glowing white from the strength of the fires inside. Perhaps it was not that the fires actually struck through the leather sides of the lodges, but each was illumined by the shafts that poured out from the open tepee entrances. A strange little white, burning city, it seemed to the boy, and more beautiful than anything he ever had seen before.

They came to the edge of a broad, shallow ravine. On the farther side stood the village, and in the center of the ravine they saw, dimly flashing under the starlight, a quietly meandering stream. At the same time, they heard the full voice of the wakened town. And what a voice it was!

It seemed to Johnnie Tanner like one prolonged scream from many voices, at first, but by degrees he could pick out the elements. Above all was the yipping and yelling of the dogs, a sound that ran in waves from one side of the town to the other, mingled with howls and frantic snarlings, as now one section of the wave became entangled in a fight, and now another. Under the regular uproar of the dogs, Johnnie next heard the voices of crying infants, needle sharp, piercing the brain. And there was a shrill chorusing of children, as well, leading up to the resonant shouts of grown men, all deep-throated.

"It's like a madhouse, to listen to it," said Johnnie Tanner.

"Aye! To listen, it's a madhouse," said Raney. "But that's nothing to what it will be when we get inside."

They rode into the ravine, crossed the stream, and had come to the farther verge when they were stopped by a sudden voice that seemed to boom at them from the very deeps of the ground. Hank Raney hardly checked Midnight—he had made Johnnie mount the bay stallion for the entry into the town—and, giving his name and that of the boy, he rode on.

A shout followed him. The sentinel sprang to his feet and sprinted for the shimmering mass of tepees.

"No hurry," said Raney to the boy. "Let 'em have a chance to work off steam, or they're likely to blow up, and carry you and me along with 'em."

He laughed as he said it, but what followed was hardly a laughing matter for the boy. The sentry who had gone before was hardly out of sight before the Cheyennes came pouring out, very much as the hive stirs and then throws out a humming, tumultuous cloud of avengers when the outlook wasp returns with tidings of danger.

Exactly so did those Cheyennes rush out from their camp and come streaming over the level land to get at the two night-bound riders. And, as they came, they shrieked. They bounded high. Some of them stopped to dance a few steps, overcome with the rhythm of the emotion inside their hearts; they looked as though they had been stopped and started prancing by a fit of colic.

Some came with empty hands. Others carried many weapons but, as the mob came closer, Johnnie Tanner forgot to wonder at anything except the sheer physical bulk of these people. He had thought that Talking Wolf was a man big enough for any one. But he was hardly large enough to strike the lowest average among the Cheyennes in sheer height. As they ran, the robes blew back from around the almost naked bodies of the braves, and John saw that they were painted hideously, in long stripes and bars and some more formal designs, or attempts to reproduce a natural object.

With a rush like the rushing of the sea, they swept about him. Terror gripped him. They seemed more like bounding devils than like human beings. But they did not tear him from his horse. They leaped around him. They brandished weapons close to his head and his body. They seemed to be shouting, whole armies together, in his very ear.

But the bay stallion took this demonstration without the slightest confusion or nervousness. It seemed entirely accustomed to such receptions as this for, arching its neck, it went forward with a proud and quiet air. The boy was amazed by the steadiness of the wild stallion. And when he glanced across at his companion, he saw that Hank Raney, also, seemed perfectly at ease.

To be sure, the human sea was not raging so wildly about him.

They were now inside the lines of the tepees, and here the din, as it seemed, shut a sudden wall around him. The yells of the warriors had shocked him outside the lodges. Now he was intimately among the caterwauling of dogs, neighing of horses, screeching of children.

He was more bewildered. His brain began to spin, and constantly he cast his look toward Raney, only to find that Hank Raney seemed to be having the time of his life!

But it was too much for the boy.

Thereafter he could only remember bits and moments of the wild night. He remembered, among the rest, how the chief, Broken Knife, sat loftily upon his best war pony, painted hideously for the celebration, but smiling on Johnnie Tanner and holding out his hand in welcome.

He remembered a moment when a band of a score of youths, who must have been barely initiated on the warpath, for they were no older than himself, came whooping about him, admiring the bay stallion, admiring Johnnie Tanner's rifle, his clothes, and all about him.

Through the white sheen of the clustering lodges they passed. A lofty bonfire began to throw up its arms into the black of the sky, putting out the stars. Around it the painted devils danced, and their more grotesque shadows leaped and lengthened beside them. Medicine men went up and down in a hideous, undulating dance. One had the semblance of a great bird, with the head of an owl, and huge, fiery eyes, now red, now black as the firelight struck upon them. And another seemed a monstrous wolf, a true wolf's head set upon a human body. But the jaws of the wolf moved. It seemed to snarl and gnash its teeth at the owl.

Broken Knife burst into the circle and through it. He stood in the center, with the rosy firelight shining and dancing upon his powerful body. He began to chant. He began to dance. The people listened, as if enchanted. Here and there the rhythm of the chant overcame one of the warriors, who would arise and begin to dance, in turn, in a little circle, very like a rooster making love to an indifferent hen, thought the boy. And, in the end, the dance of Broken Knife showed how he had taken the scalp of Talking Wolf.

The scalp itself was produced on the end of a lance. Johnnie Tanner grew very sick, indeed!

A score of hands dragged Hank Raney into the center of the arena. He did not dance. But he strode up and down. He shouted. Johnnie could understand his Cheyenne fairly well, and he understood that Hank was telling

151

the Cheyennes a most prodigious lie which had to do with certain spirits of the air who lived far among the eastern clouds, where the sun stands up in the morning. And these spirits loved the Cheyennes, and they had breathed into the mind of a white man, and they had sent this young man across the land, a hundred marches, and they had sent him that he might be a friend to the Cheyennes!

Gradually he came to realize that this story had to do with himself, and he was horrified. He wanted to shout out that the thing was false. He sweated with shame and with indignation and waited for the Cheyennes to break into peals of derisive laughter.

But they did not laugh. They merely swayed their shoulders from side to side and nodded their heads and every now and again the train of the narrative was broken by a terrific war whoop.

The story came to the battle with Talking Wolf. But how altered it was!

It appeared that when he, Johnnie Tanner, learned that Talking Wolf was an enemy of his beloved people, the Cheyennes, then the boy had made medicine and the medicine was so potent that Talking Wolf was drawn across the prairie from a great distance, like a leaf in a storm wind. And the boy sent his two friends away, because he did not want them to be injured by chance in the battle.

And when they were gone, he made the Pawnee rise up out of the grass. So the Pawnee arose and fired a shot with his rifle stretched out, so that the muzzle of it almost touched the breast of the boy, but the boy breathed, and the bullet glanced aside from his magic breath. He fired a pistol bullet into the body of Talking Wolf and stopped his charge. Then he struck him through the body with his knife. Like an eagle swooping out of the air, he had leaped at Talking Wolf. Like a striking eagle he had thrust his knife into the heart of the Pawnee.

Suddenly a voice yelled: "Striking Eagle! Striking Eagle! That is his name!"

And a dozen others picked up the chorus. The mass shouted until it seemed to the boy that the stars shook. And Striking Eagle was the name they yelled. He knew that he was now christened forever among these people until some great new deed rubbed out the old name.

Yet he remained hot and ill at ease as the narrator unblushingly told that the name was the true name, and that the Eastern Sky Spirits called the boy Striking Eagle. He proceeded to tell how Striking Eagle had given the scalp and the three coups to be counted upon Talking Wolf to the Cheyenne people and to Broken Knife. For himself, he only kept the horse of the Pawnee, as a proof that he was the enemy of the Pawnees forever!

Amazed and dumbfounded by this wild fiction, or mass of fictions, rather, poor Johnnie Tanner knew not which way to turn. And suddenly motion on his part became impossible. A dozen of the greatest warriors, each a huge and war-scarred man, seized the bridle of his horse, formed in a cordon around him, and led him within the circle of the watchers.

They forced the horse to walk slowly around the fire, and at this every brave bounded to his feet and began the war dance. The medicine men were there, half a dozen, each more grotesque than the other. And beyond the prancing, spinning, bowing braves, the boy could see the children leaping up and down in order to get a better view of the white hero, even though only in glimpses.

Beyond them, still, he could see the women, many of them holding up tiny, naked children that they, too, might fill their eyes with the spectacle and become warriors in their time. The bodies of the little ones were not nearly so dusky a red as the complexions of the matured Indians. In the ruddy glare of the firelight, they shone like gold against the dark background of the night.

And every face was smiling; all were shouting with joy or in a mad frenzy.

Suddenly he was parted from all of this. He hardly knew how, but at last he found himself in the lodge of Broken Knife, himself. Yonder was Hank Raney, helping himself to the buffalo meat which stewed in the big pot over the central fire. On the walls were odd-shaped designs in blue, crimson, yellow, and green, the forms of the buffalo, the bear, the deer, and the rising sun, and narrative picture strips of the exploits of the great hunters. Broken Knife, himself, sat against a back rest, smoking, his eyes never stirring from the scalp which hung in the smoke of the fire. And the stately squaw was laying a bed, deep and soft, for the stranger, while a seven-year-old girl stood between Johnnie and the fire, gazing entranced at him.

There was only one note of sorrow.

It came from the older daughter. She was fourteen. She seemed older. She was as slender as a deer, as wild and as graceful; like a frightened deer, she had stared at the boy when he entered the lodge; then, slinking away, she dropped inert on her own bed and began to weep.

Even Johnnie Tanner did not need to ask why she cried. He knew it was because of her brother, Hawk-that-rises; and now the pulse of her stifled sobbing was in his ear continually.

Otherwise, now that the swirling confusion of that reception was ended, a certain warm complacence was mounting in the breast of Johnnie. He began to feel quite the man of the moment, conscious of a new dignity in which he had been dressed.

But the sobbing of the girl took all the glory from him and made him remember many unpleasant things, chief of which was that now he was as far from the stolen revolver and the Daughter of the Moon as he had ever been during all the journey from New York.

Then, in the midst of his worry, with the thought of his father and of poor Aunt Maggie in his mind, he felt again what he had felt more than once before during his long journey—that Fate had charge of him and was pushing him he knew not whither, at its own imperial pleasure.

Big Hank Raney, having finished eating, with a spoon made of buffalo horn, now came and squatted on his heels beside him. Like an Indian, he seemed able to keep that position indefinitely, without fatigue.

"What're you thinkin', son?" he asked the boy. "Are you homesick? Are you worryin' about Long Arrow? Is it the lyin' powers of Hank Raney that's upset you? Or are you only thinkin' about the pretty black eyes of the girl over yonder? Think of anything that you want to, son, but don't you look twice at that girl, because if you do, you'll find out that you've tumbled over the brink of a well, and the fall that you'll get will sink you here into the green of the plains for the rest of your days!"

30 · THE BLACKBIRD

It amazed the boy to see that Hank Raney had hit not upon one of his themes of trouble, but had been able to touch on them all in turn. It increased his respect for him; therefore, he touched upon the nearest theme.

"Look here, Hank," he said softly, "tell me why it is that you strung together all those yarns when you were talking about me? Think, when they find out the truth, which they'll do the minute that they sit down and think things over, how they'll despise us both! I hated it, besides. I wished that you hadn't done it!"

He flushed hotly as he spoke, and Hank Raney looked upon him with a mildly twinkling eye.

"Well, lad," said he, "I know that you're true blue and as honest as the day. But just look at things like this. You got to give people what they want. Look at the junk that the traders bring out onto the plains. Plain steel would be better than the stuff they bring, half tin and what not. But the Injuns want a lot of decoration, and so decoration they get. Besides, you got to give them what they can understand."

"But can't they understand the truth?" asked the boy fiercely.

He glared at Hank Raney, but Hank merely smiled again.

"Could you understand the truth about a lot of the things that the Injuns do, from your side of it? Could you understand why they torture their boys before they make 'em warriors? No, you couldn't understand it, and I can't hardly. No more could they understand the truth about you. The truth about you is a lot better than all the stuff I talked.

"But suppose that I sat down and told them that your father had lost a gun on the other side of the world, and that you didn't even wait to say good-by to him, but just disappeared on the trail and left him back there in his tepee bitin' his nails and thinkin' that you're dead, and maybe orderin' up the death feast, with your womenfolk

155

cutting off their hair and slashing their bodies by way of mourning for you.

"Suppose that I told them the truth of your leaving and said how you'd done all of this trailing, and nearly got starved, and nearly got killed a dozen or so times. Why, they wouldn't hardly believe it. No, they'd likely begin to smile behind their hands. They'd think I was a liar, and that you was a bigger liar, maybe, of the two of us."

Young Johnnie Tanner frowned and strove to consider this. But finally he broke out: "At least, you didn't have to bring in all of the stuff about magic, when I had the fight with Talking Wolf."

"You don't think I had to, of course. And I didn't. But the truth was a lot more wonderful than what I told 'em. The truth about a half-baked kid, which is all you are, that has barely learned how to ride and shoot and handle a knife; the truth about him getting taken from behind, and then putting up such a fight that he came off without a scratch and killed the big chief and hard-handed fightin' man, Talkin' Wolf. Why, son, that was pretty wonderful. It was a lot more wonderful than all of the talk about magic that I gave 'em. I wanted them to appreciate you. That was all."

Johnnie Tanner still shook his head.

"Oh, Hank," said he, "as long as we're with them, they'll expect me to do magic tricks to surprise them!"

"No," said Hank Raney. "These old frauds, the medicine men, they don't do their tricks every day, but only when nobody's looking, and they see a slick chance. They start to making their rain when there's a promising-looking big thunderhead standing up on the rim of the sky. But the people never see through 'em. They don't want to see through 'em. They want to believe that the world's a wonderful place, filled with good spirits and bad spirits, and some that will listen to what men say, and some that won't. That's the way of 'em.

"They're like children, only that they're better than children. You made medicine once; likely you'll make it again; but if you do, they'll always be mighty surprised and grateful, the way that they are when the regular medicine frauds do their tricks a few times a year. Now, you go to bed. You've heard and seen enough to make you

156

pretty well dizzy for one day. Sleep is the trick for you, Johnnie. Good night!"

So Johnnie Tanner turned in, as he was bidden.

His bed was fenced in like a stall with blankets on either side, so that he had sufficient privacy. Only at the foot it was open, between the two posts which supported the saddle, the weapons, the belt, and all of his possessions except his pistol which he kept under his head.

The fire had been allowed to die down. If he lifted his head, he could see the red coals. Now and again, a little tongue of flame jumped up and set the inside of the tepee awash with dancing shadows. And at such times he could see the smoke which had gathered thickly in the top of the lodge, slowly rising through the vent above.

It was a strange bedroom, the strangest that he ever had seen, but the comfort of it washed out all other senses. After so many weeks of sleeping on the hard ground, the supple willow rods of the well-stretched bed, and the heaped skins covering them were to Johnnie better than a feather bed. He seemed to be sinking deeper and deeper into delicious comfort, whereas, he really was sinking only into profounder weariness and sleep.

So he slept, at last.

It seemed to him that he had hardly closed his eyes when the hand of Hank Raney shook him by the shoulder. He sat up with a groan and with a yawn, and rubbed his eyes, gaping, as he stared about him.

"What's the matter, Hank?" he said. "I've barely fallen asleep."

"It's been a mighty short night, then," said the hunter, grinning. "Because there's the sunrise!"

And behold! there it was, streaming through the open flap of the tent with the promise of a glorious, clear day.

"Come on, come on!" exclaimed Raney. "Now's the time for a plunge, and then we'll eat a meal enough for ten men!"

So the boy staggered to his feet unwillingly, and out into the open. Blear-eyed, drunk with fatigue, his hair tousled and on end, he saw the elder girl of the family, who had wept at the sight of him, the night before.

She did not weep now. Instead, she gave him the most friendly, the most straight-eyed of smiles. And, all in a flash, he was recovered from his drowsiness. He was totally himself again and found the world a place of extraordinary beauty.

She was bringing up a jug of water from the river, and she walked under the weight as straight as a young sapling. There was a flowing grace in her step, and the deep, rosy olive of her skin was flushed like the morning sky.

She gave him the morning greeting. It was like a faint, sweet breath of music. And he went on, dazzled, staring before him. The whole of the bustling camp was before his eyes. Children were already out playing. The braves were hurrying down for the morning plunge. The old men were stepping out for a slow promenade. The dogs were up and about, playing tag, having their first fights, sitting down with stretching grins of pleasure while they scratched fleas.

But Johnnie Tanner saw very little of this multitude of interests. His mind's eye was employed in recalling the dimpled elbow of the girl, her smile, the snowy flash of her teeth, and the deep, luminous eyes.

"Hank, what's her name?" he asked dreamily.

The other stopped short and glared at him. Then he said solemnly: "Her name is a long tangle of Cheyenne that means something like the Blackbird-that-comes-first-in-the-warm-spring-days. You could call her the Blackbird, for short. But the best way for you is to make it shorter still, and forget all about her!"

31 · THE HUNT

"Why, Hank, you talk as though I would try to marry her!" said the boy. "And I wouldn't. You know that!"

"Do I?" said Hank Raney. "How do I know that?"

"Why, I wouldn't be marrying for ten or fifteen years."

"And a dog-gone good thing if you didn't," said Hank Raney. "But this is the way of it: Injun girls will marry from twelve years up. They're marriageable before the whites. And a good many bucks have wives when they're your age. Now, look me in the eye. You're gunna be around these Cheyennes for quite a spell, likely. And while you're here, every one of these here girls—and some

158

of them as pretty as you'll find, whether white skins or no —will all of them be ready to see Striking Eagle. Yes, sir, they'll turn around to see him. They'll even go a long ways for a look at the dust that he's raised. Now, are you gunna keep your head and forget that they's such a thing as a female woman, or are you gunna be a dog-gone young fool?"

"I won't be a fool," said the boy. "I'll try not to be a fool, only—"

"Only, the Blackbird is a little different, eh?"

Johnnie Tanner sighed.

"I don't mean anything," he said meekly.

"You see to it that you don't!" said the other sternly. And he led the way down to the swimming place, stepping out with great strides.

They stripped off their clothing and dived in. Other men were already there, flashing through the water, as agile as sleek fishes. Johnnie watched them with envy and with admiration. They seemed as much at home under the surface of the water as on top of it.

"They'll see that I'm not good at swimming," he said dolefully.

"They'll blame the Sky People for not teaching you more," said Hank Raney, with his sardonic grin. "Besides, now is the time for you to begin learning."

So, into the water headed young Tanner, making a great splashing as he hit the surface. When he came up again, and struck out with a churning of arms and legs, he expected to see mocking grins on the faces of the Indians who were bobbing here and there on the pool. But he was pleasantly disappointed.

They regarded him with grave and respectful eyes and, when he climbed out onto the bank again, he knew that there was no laughter behind his back. Deep, gruff voices gave him greeting, but they all were serious.

Hank Raney took notice of it all.

"You can't do any harm in the eyes of these people. You're a sort of a sacred proposition, right now, son!"

They dried their bodies by whipping off the water with the edge of the palm. Then they ran up and down in the wind and, when they were merely damp, they dressed again and started back for the town.

By this time, the fires for the day were started and

smoke was rising from the top of every lodge. Water and wood had been brought in. And when the rim of the sun made a little arc of fire in the level eastern sky, the day was well started and a hunting party was forming.

Raney and the boy swallowed, hastily, some of the eternal buffalo meat that never failed to be stewing in the lodge of Broken Knife. It had no salt in it and no flavoring of any kind; and though Johnnie Tanner was, by this time, accustomed to saltless meat, still he thought that he never had tasted a more unsavory mess.

"How can you eat it?" he murmured to Hank Raney.

"Well," said Raney, "it is dressed up with a sauce that is always right in my mind."

"A sauce?" echoed the boy.

"I mean, there was a time when I nearly begged out on the plains. Lost a hoss—broke its leg in a dog-hole. Missed a water hole afterward. Nigh starved, nigh thirsted to death. And then I come to a Kiowa village and first food that I put my teeth into was stewed buffalo meat, and ever since that time the taste of it is sort of good to me. Maybe the same time'll come for you, the same as it has for most of the rest of 'em out here. They're hunting. Do we go along?"

"We haven't been invited," said the boy.

"Invited?" cried the other. "Son, there ain't a man in that gang that ain't hankering to have us along—you mostly. They know that they can't match Midnight, but they's a lot of aspirin' youngsters that would like to race their pa's best hosses agin' that bay of yours. Don't you suppose they'd've been off on the trail long ago, if they hadn't been dangling around the camp here, wishin' and hopin', but not wantin' to disturb the great young white chief that dropped out of the sky and come all this ways west to help the Cheyennes?"

Young Tanner looked at his friend with a flush of anger. Then he laughed.

"Will you go along?" he asked.

"I reckon that I'll manage to try a hand," said he. "Come along with me. And, mind you, if you miss a single shot at a buffalo, some of the power of your magic is sure gone away from you!"

"Bother the magic!" exclaimed Tanner impatiently.

"I'm sick of the Sky People, too. I want to be just a boy, the way that I really am."

"Aye, you'll like it, well enough," replied his friend. "But lemme tell you something. It's easy for a young boy to grow, but it's mighty hard to shrink him after he's got big!"

Some of this last remark remained in the mind of Johnnie Tanner as they went out and mounted their horses. He had been foisted into the position of a man, and, would he or would he not, in that place he would have to remain or else be disgraced.

They took ordinary ponies, and led Midnight and the fine bay in reserve for the actual charge on the buffalo, if any should be found. It was a ride which Johnnie Tanner would never forget. By this time, he had been fairly well schooled as a rider, and the interminable days on the back of the wily gray mustang had made him a very fair horseman. As big Raney said: "One bad horse was better than ten riding masters."

Raney himself was a fine performer on horseback.

Nevertheless, it seemed to Johnnie that he was seeing horses ridden for the first time, when he watched the Indian youths racing their ponies over the green grass. Most of them were clad only in loin strap and moccasins, and their naked bodies flashed like burnished copper which had been polished over again, as they darted here and there, playing games as they rode and using the horses like sets of four legs which had been grown onto their own human bodies.

They could all do a certain number of very difficult tricks. They could hang by heels and toe, streaming down toward the ground. They could climb under the horse and up the other side by means of swinging swiftly under the neck of the galloping animal. They could flatten themselves on either side of the racing animal and then shoot with bow or gun under the neck at an imaginary enemy. They could do these and other things but, more than any one feat or series of feats, there was a sense that every one of those youngsters was a complete master of the horse.

The sight of their skill made him very self-conscious. He felt that he was jolting heavily up and down, almost

161

breaking the back of the animal he rode. But though the Indians were always laughing and chattering together, they never appeared to be mocking him. They kept at a little distance. Only, now and again, he would feel shy eyes looking toward him out of the savage faces. They were the boys and young men, who plainly wanted to join him and enjoy the society of the Pawnee killer!

At this, he could not help laughing a little. He felt as helpless as a child in the cradle, in the presence of these hardy young warriors; and yet he could see the respect with which they watched him.

Broken Knife, the leader of the hunt, came up beside Raney and the boy and repeated to them the details of the report which had been brought to the camp. The scout had come close to the great herd, and from the advantage of a low knoll he had looked over the living sea. Not only was it a great herd but, above all, there was in the midst of the animated ocean a white buffalo. That is, the head and the back and the sides of the bull, so far as could be seen, were the purest white!

Broken Knife rode on again, and the boy was surprised to find that even Raney was excited by the last tidings. He asked what the peculiar use or advantage of a white buffalo might be, and Raney replied that a white buffalo skin was far more potent and precious than a scalp, even. He who possessed such a thing not only had a great personal treasure, but he had added something to the status of the whole tribe to which he belonged.

For the white skin was the visible sign of the great Creator. He did not actually appear in the white buffalo as in the divine Apis of Egypt, but the white was his sign, and the degree of nearness to divinity was instantly discernible in the purity and completeness of the coloring. Sometimes a marked leg, a head, even a whole side was cut off, if the remaining portion of the hide was flawlessly snowy. Usually even the best had a black mark—as between the eyes, or above the rim of one of the hoofs.

But now and again appeared that rarity, the buffalo which was as snow from head to foot. Lucky the man who possessed such a thing! Lucky the whole tribe when such a treasure was vouchsafed to it! For it was considered, in the light of a pledge from the great ruler of the world of the spirits, the driver of the clouds, the rain maker, that he would always give his best gifts to his chosen people.

"You talk," said Johnnie Tanner, "as though you almost believed it all, you're so excited."

"Of course, I'm excited," said big Raney. "This hunt will mean more to 'em than a big victory over the Sioux or the Pawnees. I dunno how many scalps would have to be taken to make up a thing as good as the bringing in of a white buffalo skin. Even if it ain't perfect, it's a good deal! Talk about the killing of Talking Wolf? That was nothing compared to the show the Cheyennes will put on if they see a white hide brought in. You better go out and kill that buffalo, my lad, if you want to make yourself really famous with this tribe."

"All right," said Johnnie Tanner, grinning. "I'll go and kill the white buffalo, if you want me to."

They had hardly finished speaking in this manner when the whole train of the hunters was hushed by a few signs, transmitted back from the leading scouts. The herd had been sighted. At once, those who possessed fresh horses mounted them. The discarded animals were rounded into a close herd, which was held by a few of the youngest boys who would gradually drift it in the direction of the hunt, after the charge had been sent home. And now, Johnnie Tanner, on the bay, set off at the side of Raney and approached the scene of what was to be a famous hunt, indeed.

32 · THE WHITE BUFFALO

It was not a dead level, this section of the prairie. It flowed in softly smoothed hummocks, like those low waves which the wind raises on the ocean long before the storm comes near. And, as the stream of the hunters poured across the hills of green, dipping up and down, sometimes the head of the procession was lost to the sight of the rearmost hunters.

In the same way, the buffalo herd was completely out of sight until the hunt was very close to it, indeed. Then

Johnnie Tanner had a glimpse of it, the flankers of the herd being not more than two hundred yards away. He could not see all of the living mass. He could only look across a few ripples and waves of the whole, in fact. But an extra sense told him immediately that it was a far vaster spectacle than the big drove into the rear of which he and Raney had fired not many days before.

Spread out on the low prairie hills in a widening wedge, as far as he could see from the narrow angle between the two hummocks before him, Johnnie Tanner watched the bison flowing slowly forward. And then a low moan of excitement came from half a dozen of the Indian hunters who were near him.

He saw their arms stretched out and the next moment he saw the cause. It was a very odd thing. No doubt it was simply due to a confirmation of the ground, one bit of it projecting well above the backs of the crowding bison, a great bull, visible almost to its feet and shining purest white in the strong sunshine. The very horns, the beard, the enormous and shaggy mane were all white; and like white satin the flanks of the vast beast were glimmering.

It no longer seemed strange to the boy that the Indians looked with reverence on such an animal. This spectacle was more marvelous, to him, than had been the sight of the Daughter of the Moon, even when he held the gleaming beauty of it cupped in the hollow of his palm. The dusky, dingy color of the rest of the herd was like smoke. This was a form of divinest fire, and it seemed to have been uplifted by a magic hand from the midst of the throng to tempt and mock the eager hunters.

That sight was enough. There was no waiting for the signal from Broken Knife. The whole stream of the young horsemen rushed like arrows off the string and headed straight into the masses and diverse currents of the buffalo.

So sudden was that attack, so close did the hills and the tall grass allow the riders to come, that the herd was not alarmed until the riders were almost among them. Then they set off in a single huge wave, and the roar of their beating feet made a dull thunder in the ears of the boy.

He was slow to get into action. Raney was far ahead of him by this time. The last of the Indians was already entered into the herd, yelling, whooping, firing guns and rifles. Yet all of these sounds of human manufacture, even the explosions of the rifles, were little, half-heard whispers lost in the flood of the thundering stampede.

Just before Johnnie Tanner struck the herd itself, the bay carried him over the back of a low hill, and from the crest of this he looked over a great panorama. The wind blew in his face across the rippling hillocks, and on those low hills the prairie grass was tall, bending and flashing in the sun, except where the forefront of the fleeing herd had reached it. There it was beaten flat in a trice. And what a forefront, what a body that herd possessed! The little glimpse he had at first had been a mere wedge, a thin entering wedge of the whole. It poured darkly across the prairie. He could not tell where the prospect ended; to the west, far off, where were the humped, galloping backs and the lowered, massive heads, a sort of mist went up from the buffalo, composed, perhaps of bits of shredded vegetation flung upward by the clipping feet of the monsters; and perhaps their hot breaths were in it; and undoubtedly, here and there in bald spots, the surface of the ground was beaten to thinnest dust, which quickly puffed upward in the nostrils of the wind.

Through that mist, and among all the masses of the buffalo, Johnnie Tanner still could see the white bull, gleaming like a star. Even from a distance, it was patent that he stood forth not only on account of his color, but because he was a giant of his breed!

Another thing was clear, also. Every hunter who charged into the host was aiming his course directly for the sacred bull! As they rode, they fired right and left, loading and reloading, into the flanks of the animals nearest; but they opened small triangular passages in the great herd. Some of those channels remained open; others were closed almost at once by some cross-current of movement within the mass. But still each hunter was driving toward a rather definite point within the herd, and the direction of the converging lines pointed toward the white buffalo.

However, his relative position was likely to change. It was not likely that he would again be held up like a flag, as it were, to arouse the hunters and give them direction. He would be lost in the mist above the stampeders, in the ebb and flow of the surging herd.

Johnnie Tanner saw all these things in the second or so during which the bay was striding across the hilltop. Then down into the madness of the hunt the stallion carried him.

The heart of the boy came up into his mouth as he saw those lumbering, formidable behemoths of the land, heard the clattering of their hoofs, the pounding of their feet, saw the little, wicked red eyes of the bulls, and the threatening horns, shaken from side to side.

But the stallion had no fear. Plainly he was well trained for this work, and he leaped straight in between two mighty bulls.

Johnnie took aim, fired, and the bull ran on beside him, but swerved off to the side. So did the animal to his right. And the ones in front parted to let him through. He found himself in just such a triangular channel as he had seen formed by the other riders.

Incidentally, he had not dropped his first bull.

He reloaded, taking three times as long as a more expert hand would have done. Then he tried again on another, a cow. And again the beast ran on, merely shaking its head!

He hoped that his failures would not be noted. But he was wrong! Two Indian youths now raced up beside him. One, with a ponderous old rifle, dropped an animal with a single shot. The second, swaying well out from his horse with a bow ready strained for the shot, drove a hunting arrow into the side of a bull until only the feathered butt of the shaft was left sticking out.

That arrow would be, to the hunter, a token. He could reclaim his kill by it at the end of the day. Now he dashed on, digging his heels into the flanks of his pony. Another arrow was whipped onto the string. Again he swayed to the side. The naked shoulder muscles of that mighty archer tensed into knots and sliding rolls. Again Johnnie Tanner heard the twang of the string like the brief hum of a wasp driven past his ear down the wind, and another buffalo was smitten. It ran on only a few strides, then lurched to its knees, with the blood coughing in a great stream from its lips.

By this time, Johnnie's rifle was reloaded, and he picked out the biggest bull at hand. He took his aim. He offered up a prayer that he might not be shamed in the eyes of

166

these youngsters. Already they had seen him fail twice. So, half aiming and half praying, he fired again.

And again he failed to strike a vital spot!

Miserably he saw that bull merely shake its head and bound forward all the faster.

He glanced aside. The eyes of the youths were fixed upon him. They had noted. He saw them shake their heads, as he thought. And crimson shame burned the face of the white boy.

They would not be able to avoid smiling, those keen and brave and expert young hunters. That day, they would pass the word among their fellows, and the Cheyennes would shrug their powerful shoulders. They would attribute the slaying of Talking Wolf to a blind chance. And had it really been any more?

The heart of the boy became wretchedly small and cold as a stone in his breast.

The two young Cheyennes had disappeared, driving their bloody traffic in some other part of the herd. And Johnnie Tanner gloomily reloaded.

They had entered a district where there was little grass for a stretch, and as a result a dense dust cloud arose, blinding him, stinging his eyes with alkali, which explained the absence of any grass.

Before him was an obscure mass of laboring backs. He looked behind and saw that the channel, which he had driven into the herd, had closed behind him. A sea of threatening waves all around him, and the beat of a single one of them might be death to him. Compared to the bulk of some of these brutes, the bay stallion seemed a mere plaything, a toy.

He had reloaded, now. But he hesitated to fire. Already the day was ruined for him. And the hunt would soon be over.

A wedge opened through the dust cloud that blew against him. Looking back through it, he could see half a dozen of the hunters already dismounting beside their kills.

He set his teeth and stared about him through the blowing dust. Should he turn back now and confess his failure, no matter with what bitterness?

Something flashed like silver, to the right and before him.

A gun, he thought, at first.

Then the sheen of it gleamed more clearly. Upon his amazed eyes loomed the white buffalo itself! What a monster it was, what an incredible and beautiful monster! It seemed to run shoulder-high among its mates. He saw it strike against an ordinary bull, and the latter was flung aside like water from the prow of a great, swift ship.

Then the red madness of the hunt mounted to the brain of Johnnie Tanner. He pointed the head of the bay stallion toward the shining goal. He rode straight at the target, and before him the buffalo divided. His throat was aching. He became aware that it was torn by his own shrieking war cry of frantic delight.

Doubt departed from him, now that he was arrived at the great goal. Fate was in it! Fate had caused him to fail thrice. Fate had brought him, of all those powerful and seasoned hunters, to the side of the great white bull.

Yes, doubt was gone. He raised the rifle with the surety of the angle of death. He looked for a moment at the unbelievable bulk of the great beast. He saw the shivering of its mane in the wind. He marked its striding, twice as long as the normal stride of a bull. Then he fired.

Onward strode the bull, as swift as ever; but still there was no doubt in the mind of young Johnnie Tanner. He merely looked on with a puzzled frown and then nodded, his surety confirmed, when the monster staggered.

It staggered. The sway of its ponderous body knocked aside the lesser beasts near by. It stopped. The stampeding buffalo parted on either hand, and there was Johnnie Tanner left alone beside his prey.

33 · STRIKING EAGLE

THERE is a wild rushing of thought, a frantic outgoing of the senses when one wakens from a busy dream into the stillness of the cold and quiet morning. For a few moments, the uproar and the dust of the nightmare or the unearthly beauty of the dream remain, fading out like a ghost in the daylight.

So it was with Johnnie Tanner, as he sat on the back

of the panting stallion and watched the enormous buffalo. Far away fled the thunder of the herd. The dust cloud gathered over them; they were lost to the eye and remained only a dying muttering of hoofs. All the plain behind them was dotted with the fallen. They seemed far off and insignificant to Johnnie Tanner. It was as though he looked down upon them from a lofty cloud and with impersonal curiosity stared at the petty, trifling, antlike actions of those fellow human creatures.

They were moiling and cutting and pulling at the toughly fastened hides, or they were cutting up carcasses. There in the distance, melting out of its particular dust cloud into full view, came the boys, hurrying on the extra horses at a rushing gallop. Shortly, they would be loaded with the heaped meat and with the blood-dripping robes which had been torn from the buffalo.

It was a day of great rejoicing for the Cheyennes. This single hunt would fill their meat pots for half a season. On account of this great kill, the women, the children, the aged, and even some of the warriors would surely be at work frantically, for days and days, building racks, keeping up the fires all night to dry the meat while the sun continued the cure in the day. It was a day of festival for the whole tribe, but all of these things and the great red slaughter spread over the prairie behind him mattered little to young Johnnie Tanner; whatever else he saw was only from the corner of the eye, so fully did the monster bull possess his mind.

Everything about it was different. Its shining wet muzzle and nose were pink; its polished hoofs were pink, also; and never was there seen hair of such length upon a buffalo or of such silken texture, curling and waving in masses over the hump and smoothing out at the flanks, but everywhere dense, soft and lustrous. The horns upon its head looked small compared with the bulk which they crowned, but, considered separately, each of those horns could hold deep potations for twenty men around a campfire.

He seemed, to the boy, like a pure-white cloud, fallen out of the sky to the ground. Even the feathery plume of his tail, which literally dragged upon the ground, was totally untainted and unstained by the prairie green; and his eye was an angry red star, watching Johnnie Tanner, but with a reserved and inward burning wrath, as though the great bull knew of punishment which would surely overtake the rash and impudent hands for the blow they had struck at the Indian god, this day!

Johnnie moved on his horse until he was exactly confronting the beast. Eye to eye, they considered one another, the young human turned wild beast for the moment, and the wild thing struck patient by death, enduring man because it could not flee from him.

The exultation quite went out of Johnnie's heart. That sense of a guiding fate which controlled him, which had thrust him out here in the heart of the plains, which had driven him on, which had allowed him to miss when he fired at two ordinary targets, and then had brought him to this tremendous goal, that sense of being a tool in the hand of some obscure and all-reaching power still bewildered the boy. He was both exalted and humbled. He would have been very glad to be some thousands of miles away, and at home.

But he would never again be a "play Indian." His friend, Raney, was right. He had grown too far; he never could shrink back into his old self.

In the mystery of this moment, as he stood confronting the bull, he tried to understand something of life; he strained his mind after it; but it was like peering at a fleet-footed antelope. The very idea which he was struggling to attain, grew dim and went out.

The buffalo bull began to waver at the knees; his head drooped lower.

Then Johnnie Tanner, looking up from his dream, saw that he was not alone. A great circle had gathered around the bull. The whisper had gone out, and those who turned in this direction could see the giant like a white hill on the prairie. So they came rushing. Each man made a circle around the monster to make sure that there was no single spot of brown or black on the hide. Then the hunters, young and old, became silent and each took his place.

They were bloodstained from head to foot. There was blood on the moccasins, on the leggings, on the naked arms and shoulders, blood in the very hair and in the crowning feathers; even the horses were stained and streaked as though they had rushed fetlock-deep through the carnage of a battle. But now the red-handed hunters became as so many stones. There were both expectancy and fear clearly shown in their eyes.

For a white buffalo was accepted as a sacred thing, but this giant, in all his bearing and appointments, was trebly sacred. The same thought which had flashed through the mind of the boy, as a mere fantasy, came seriously home to every one of the Cheyennes. For they lifted their heads, man after man, and stared for an instant at the luminous white clouds which wandered across the blue prairies of heaven. Then they dropped their glances to the standing bull.

Suddenly the giant dropped to his knees. The impact seemed to shake the ground; there was a sighing sound, not from the dying bull, but from the hunters gathered around him.

Now he leaned forward. His head sank until his muzzle was pressed against the ground. It was a strange spectacle. He seemed to be making obeisance not to the hand which had slain him, but to some almighty power. Leaning still farther, he slumped slowly, gently to the earth and lay still. The fire departed from the red eyes. He was dead.

"Now, what?" asked the quiet voice of Raney at the shoulder of the boy.

Johnnie started. He saw that every eye was fixed not upon the bull, now, but on his own face. Broken Knife stood by him with something of reverence and something of awe in the glance he gave to the white lad. Yonder, also, was that same powerful young brave whom he had seen burying arrows to the feathers in the bodies of the buffalo. That grand hunter had seen the white man fail once and again, but there was no mockery in his eyes now. He was agape, bewildered, reverent.

So were they all.

"What now?" repeated Raney.

Johnnie Tanner felt abashed. For how could he put hand to that shining mountain of white?

Then a new idea suddenly came to him.

He dismounted from the back of the bay stallion. It rewarded him for those long hours of careful kindness by following at his heels, doglike. And the braves murmured softly to one another.

It occurred to the boy that what he was about to do

171

was perhaps foolishly spectacular; but nothing was more patent than that all the crowd yearned for some pictorial action to be remembered and written down securely in all minds.

So he clung to his purpose.

He went to Broken Knife and held out his hand.

"My friend," said he, "will you lend me an arrow?"

Broken Knife, frowning a little in surprise, without a word drew an arrow from the quiver which was slung across his shoulders, and presented it, butt first, to Johnnie.

The boy took it and, walking up to the fallen giant, he parted the long hair above the spot where his rifle bullet had entered. A gust of wind stirred the hair. It seemed to him that the entire dead body quivered at his touch.

But he overcame the little chill of unearthly horror that passed through him, and drove the arrow point into the wound. Then he turned back to Broken Knife. The bay stallion turned beside him, but with its watchful eye cast back toward the great buffalo.

"This is a present from me to you, Broken Knife," said Johnnie Tanner. "It is to you and all the Cheyennes, because they are all my friends."

There was a single, deep, muttering sound. Every Indian, in the age-old gesture of astonishment, clapped a hand over his mouth and stared. Then that spell snapped. Johnnie Tanner swung up into his saddle, and at that signal the whole body of the braves swarmed in from the magic circle and crowded about the dead bull to touch, fondle, stroke the curling hair, lift the ponderous hoofs, take reverently in both hands the great plume of the tail, which glistened like white fire.

A babbling sound arose. There was happy laughter and one phrase repeated over and over, a sound with which the ear of the boy had but newly grown familiar. It was his new, his Indian name, Striking Eagle! That was the burden of the song of praise which went up from the mob.

Of those many warriors, who had swept in on the kill, big Broken Knife himself was the exception. He, when he heard the announcement of the gift to him, and through him to the tribe, had folded his brawny arms across his chest. His eyes flashed. His ugly face grew terrible. One would have thought that he was enraged to the soul and

172

controlling himself, to keep from leaping at his enemy. He stared at the boy with a fire in his eyes for a long moment, until Johnnie Tanner, half frightened, smiled a little, and looked aside. Then the chief, in turn, went up to the dead bull, striding past the boy without a word.

34 · RANEY PHILOSOPHIZES

TANNER and Hank Raney separated from the rest. They had no real concern with the kill. What Raney's accurate rifle had brought down would be turned over to the host who was entertaining him, Broken Knife. That followed as a matter of course. He had simply put a mark upon each one, the sign of Broken Knife.

Raney looked thoughtful, frowning down at the ground as the two went off, side by side.

"He's angry," said the boy to Raney.

"Who is?"

"Broken Knife."

"What makes you think so?"

"Why, didn't you see the look that he gave me? I thought he was about to cut my throat. I never had such a look from any man!"

"Didn't you?" said the other.

And then Raney lifted his head for the first time and looked with the same frown at his companion.

"Don't you know," said he, "that Broken Knife was so heated up that he was on the edge of jumping into a war dance and a song that would have sounded like eagles screamin'? Angry? Why, lad, if you asked Broken Knife for an arm, he'd want to give you a leg, too. So would the whole tribe. Maybe some of the medicine men don't feel so good about you, just now. Their dog-gone parlor magic don't look so strong, compared to a dead Talking Wolf and a dead white buffalo such as I never seen before, and dog-gone me if I think ary a one of the rest of that red lot ever seen the like, either!"

"What have I to do with the medicine men?" asked the boy. "I didn't use any magic. What sort of stuff do you want me to think, Hank?"

Raney shook his head in mock despair.

173

"You're never gunna understand, even though I've already explained it to you before, word by word. Tell me what you think you've done, to-day?"

"Why, I've had a grand time. I've seen a great hunt. And I've shot at three buffaloes. I've missed dropping two of 'em, and the third one I managed to bag. That's all."

"You missed two, eh?" said the other sharply.

"I didn't say that I missed 'em. I mean that I didn't get the bullet into the heart."

"Did anybody see you fail to drop 'em?"

"Yes. A couple of young braves. One of them is a wonderful archer. He put his arrows in up to the feathers."

"Two of 'em saw you miss, eh? Well, that makes it perfect, I should say."

"Why does it?"

"Well, you ought to be able to see, son, that these here Injuns ain't fools."

"I think they're not. They may be a little superstitious, but they're real men, it seems to me."

"You can lay your money on that point. They're men, all right," said the hunter. "You can guess that when they take a look at you, you don't make 'em dizzy by being big and strong?"

"Of course not," said the boy. "I look like nothing at all, compared to them. They're regular Hercules."

"You ain't so very much at home swimming, either?"

"No, I'm not. And they're like fish."

"At riding, you don't particularly grow into your saddle?"

"Why, I don't ride at all, compared with them. What are you trying to do, Hank? Do you think I'm proud of the way I do any of those things?"

"No," said Hank Raney. "But just to go on for a minute. Are you one of the best rifle shots in these parts?"

"Certainly not. I'm just sort of average, maybe."

"You're average, all right," said Raney, with conviction. "And you're better than that. Deer fever is never gunna upset you, son! I've seen that with my own eyes. But now, you add up what those Injuns know about you, and what's the result?"

"You tell me, Hank. I don't know."

"Well, the result is this. They see that you're just a kid—but you've killed Talking Wolf, and I've told you before what that means to them. I've told you that they're sure to write that down as sheer magic and big medicine. And then you come out hunting. You ride pretty bad, compared with them. They see you shoot, and you miss a couple of easy shots. That's straight, ain't it?"

"Yes, that's just what happened. I've only finished telling you so."

"Well, then, Johnnie, and now you foller this! What is every man of the lot of them trying to do? To get at the white buffalo, of course. And every brave of the lot has bought medicine from the medicine men to give them luck; and those that think they're gifted, they've gone and made medicine themselves. And every one of 'em had purified himself by burnin' sweet grass, and such kind of rot."

"As though it were a religious ceremony?"

"That's just what it is. Buffalo is buffalo. But a white buffalo is religion."

"Well, they seem to feel that way about it."

"If it's religion," went on the hunter, "then it means that their Great Spirit is running the show and directing who will kill that buffalo. D'you follow me, now?"

"Ah," said the boy. "I understand now. It was only chance that brought me to the white bull. But the Cheyennes will think it was 'medicine' that gave me the shot!"

"Think it? They don't think at all. They know, now, that you've got medicine that's as strong or stronger than the medicine of the regular doctors of the tribe."

The boy sighed.

"I don't deserve much credit," he said, "but still, I'd like to get a little more respect as a man."

"Bah! You ain't a man. You're a priest to 'em now," said Hank Raney. "You're such an important man—well, you'll see the signs of it, pretty soon. Wait till we're back in the village, and you'll see how they carry on! And dog-gone me, if you don't sort of give me a chill up the spine, myself! How come you to give that buffalo to the chief? Didn't you know that that white robe is worth a pile?"

"I'd heard that. But he's been pretty kind to us, Hank. And I'm not out here to make money, particularly!"

"No," said Hank dryly. "I can see that. You'd rather make your money tapping thugs over the head and swip-

175

ing their pocketbooks, eh? Well, every man to his own taste!"

He laughed. Then he went on:

"It was a fine thing that you done, there. Style is a great thing everywhere, but it's particularly a great thing out here among the Injuns. You got no idea how important it is, old son! And the picture of you stabbing the chief's arrow into the bull and then making a present of the bull to the whole tribe—why, you know what will happen?"

"They seemed glad, all right," decided the boy.

"They're gunna cut up that meat and dry it. Every tepee in the Cheyenne tribe will have a strip of it. Not for eating. No, sir! But for a sacrifice. A bit of that meat, burned, would be as good as the burning of a scalp, say. It would be able to accomplish pretty nigh anything for the brave that made the sacrifice. Yes, sir! That white buffalo you could've sold for about everything that the Cheyennes have got."

"It's a strange thing!" muttered the boy.

"Aye," said the hunter. "It's strange. And that big silky robe will be cured by every woman in the village doing a bit of work, here and there on it. Every woman will give her eyeteeth to have a chance to do some of that work. God's work, d'you see? And then that robe will be hung up in the big medicine lodge, and every Cheyenne in the pack will feel that Broken Knife is about the greatest chief that they ever had, because through him the great present came to the whole Cheyenne outfit. You foller my drift, son?"

"I begin to see. You make it pretty important, Hank."

"That's what it is to them. You're a magician. You were certainly sent down from the Sky People. They parted that crowd of buffaloes. You shot at a couple. You missed. Of course, you missed. The Sky People were not interested in common buffalo. They had sent you in to get the big white boy. Don't you see what a perfectly logical yarn it makes, from their viewpoint?"

"It gives me chills up the spine," said Johnnie. "I don't want to be a fool or a wizard. I won't be either. I'll go and tell Broken Knife that it's all rot. I'm just a boy like any other boy in the tribe, and I won't have them thinking that—"

"Hold on!" interrupted Raney.

"Well?"

"You tell me a little something. What would Broken Knife do if you went to him with a yarn like that?"

"Why, he'd listen, of course."

"You bet he'd listen, and then he'd be a mighty sad Injun, I tell you," said Raney. "And he'd say that he knew he wasn't good enough to eat the dust you'd walked on, but it makes him pretty sad when you feel that you have to come and tell him a thing that ain't so, because you don't want to let him know the real truth about you."

"But I'd be telling him the real truth about me, Hank! That's what I want to do, and nothing but that."

"Bah," said the hunter. "If you tell him that you're only an ordinary kid, like other boys, he's got two proofs ag'in' you. He's got Talking Wolf, and he's got the white buffalo. Look here, lad, he would only have to look back to the way you stood up there—pretty slick and proud you looked, I gotta say myself—and stuck his arrow into the bull and made the present to the tribe. He would only have to remember that, to make himself sure that the Sky People were working in you, and that they're right at your shoulder all the time. You try to tell him anything different, and you'll make him mighty sad."

"It rather beats me," said the boy, with a sigh.

"What Broken Knife is really hoping," said the other, chuckling, "is that one day you'll just feel pretty friendly with him, and that you'll smoke a pipe and tell him, through the smoke, about your life at home."

"Dishwashing, and chopping kindling, and sweeping floors—do you mean that he'd be interested in that?"

"That? No, of course he wouldn't. I mean, he wants to hear about your real home. Up there in the blue. He wants to know how you rode your favorite eagles down and fished the small birds out of the sky and flew up again, plucking the little birds as you went, until you got close enough to the sun to roast 'em. He wants to hear a lot of little details like that, and about how soft a cloud is to sleep on, and all kinds of things."

He struck his hands together, while the boy listened, agape.

"And why don't you do it, son?" said the hunter.

"Tell them such whopping lies as that, Hank? Oh, you're only laughing at me!"

"Laughing? Not a dog-gone bit. These here Cheyennes won't be upset by anything that you can contrive. Only, if I was you, I'd take some hints from me. I got some ideas about the furniture of an Injun heaven that'll make their eyes pop right out of their heads. That's what I'll make 'em do. You trust to me, and let me give you an idea or two!"

"Hank! Hank!" cried Johnnie Tanner, alarmed. "Don't you talk that way. I wouldn't tell them lies like that for anything in the world."

Raney shook his head in disapproval.

"You're missing a lot of tricks, then," said he. "Fact is that their tongues is hangin' out, waitin' for you to talk miracles to 'em."

"Then they can just start in and disbelieve in me, because I'll never tell 'em lies!"

"All right, then, and the longer that you're silent, the more they'll be sure that you won't talk because you don't trust 'em." The boy merely sighed.

"I'm all in a puzzle, Hank," he confessed.

"You'll come out of it one day," said his friend. "But you've got to remember one thing. The other day you got a new name. To-day, you confirmed your right to it. They'll call you White Buffalo, besides Striking Eagle, from now on. But, sooner or later, you're gunna see that while you're with the Cheyennes, Johnnie Tanner is dead, and in Johnnie's skin there's a new spirit, and it talks Cheyenne, and it played thunder with the Pawnees, and the name of that spirit is Striking Eagle. Why d'you mind a lie or two, if it makes a whole tribe feel comfortable, and honored, and happy?"

35 · THE PAPOOSE

THEY passed back to the village ahead of most of the hunters, who were still cutting up meat, stripping off buffalo robes; but the word of all that had happened had gone before him. The boy knew it when he went riding among the tepees to get back to the lodge of Broken Knife. A rumor and a voice went before him and Raney. People came running, but they did not shout when they saw him. They stood still and gasped.

Then a squaw came, panting and sweating with haste. Perhaps she was forty, but she looked older. She possessed that peculiarly repulsive ugliness which is both fat and wrinkled. In her arms she carried a two-year-old boy baby, which cried in a harsh, hoarse voice, the voice of a child which has learned to complain with every breath. The naked body was like that of a brown frog. The stomach was a fat paunch, and the limbs were scrawny, fleshless things.

In front of the riders, the squaw halted. She held up the baby at arm's length above her head, as though she were going to cast it in the face of poor Johnnie Tanner.

Out came a rush of lament. He could not understand all the words. They poured forth in a certain rhythm, such as a great emotion always imposes upon speech. He, baffled, embarrassed, frightened also, could make out that the child never had thriven since birth. Some wicked spell had been cast upon it. And what had it lacked? Good, fat buffalo meat, upon which the entire tribe had flourished, that was its constant diet. All the meat that it wished to cram it could have. And it had fed from the first with a hearty diet.

But the food seemed to do it no good. It put no strength in the limbs. It only gave a frog paunch and wizened limbs. Now she stood before a great man who would know how to cast out the evil spirit. Let him tell her what to do. She would do it, and so would her husband. He would sacrifice the two scalps which were his pride, and his three best horses. Yes, he would give away his entire horse herd, if that would bring health to his son, his only child!

When that frantic oration ended, the child was screaming louder than ever.

"What in the world can I do?" said the boy to big Raney.

But Raney was swallowing a grin.

"How do I know?" said he. "I never was a medicine man in my life. I don't know anything about it. But if

179

you're both a prophet and a doctor, you're gunna be a great man among the Cheyennes, son."

"Tell her that I can't help her. I don't know anything about it," pleaded Johnnie.

"Tell her yourself," answered the other. "I won't talk for you, or I'll get myself a bad name all through the tribe. Say 'no' yourself and see how she takes it!"

So Johnnie braced himself to say "no," and, as he gathered his courage and summoned a scowl, he looked down into the ugly face of the squaw and saw the frightful misery which was printed in it. He stared at the body of the squalling child, a shrill, wretched moan throbbing in every breath it expelled.

And yet it had been raised on good, fat buffalo meat, all it could eat, day or night!

He remembered, when he thought of that continual abundance, the miserable famine of his imprisonment in the railroad car. After that starvation, food had forever a new significance for him. To see a well-provided board was like hearing an audible blessing.

The squaw clutched the baby forcibly to her breast.

"Oh, my father," she cried. "I see the wisdom rising in your face and in your eyes!"

The stifled baby screamed louder than ever. She regarded it not. With a pitiful and intent hope she continued to stare into the face of the white boy.

Johnnie Tanner half closed his eyes. But there was no voice in his conscience to tell him what to do. To remain silent would do no good. Any experiment would be better than nothing at all. How, after all, could he phrase his words with a sufficient piquancy and clearness to give them meaning for the squaw?

He gathered a little air of authority. He pointed to the paunch of the yelling child.

And that instant the child was still. It stared at Johnnie Tanner with wet, reddened eyes. The lids were puffed by continual weeping. Its mouth hung weakly open.

"I hear you, master," said the squaw, almost whispering. "He hears you, also, and the bad spirit, too. Most wonderful!"

"The bad spirit," said Johnnie Tanner, "is in the belly of your son. The bad spirit eats the food you give your boy. Starve that stomach and the bad spirit will die.

180

For two whole days give your son no morsel to eat, but plenty of good clean water. At the end of two days—"

He paused. Then, blushing a little at his own duplicity, he added: "At the end of two days, take the smoke of sweet grass to purify the boy and the lodge. With the smoking grass in your hand, walk three times around your lodge. When you go inside, the spirit will have fled."

They rode past the squaw. Stupefied with new hope and joy, she could not even speak. But she followed them with worshiping eyes. Other women and children had gathered. And the voice of one of them said, as Johnnie and Raney rode on: "You see, the bad spirit knew the great medicine man. The moment Striking Eagle speaks, his medicine begins to work. See, the child no longer cries!"

It was true. Perhaps the novel sight of the pale skin of Johnnie Tanner had been enough to enthrall the youngster's attention for the moment and make it forget its own troubles.

But Johnnie had chills working and twisting up his spinal marrow.

"I couldn't help it," he confided dolorously to Raney. "I had to say something. I hope—I hope that the baby won't die, Hank. What do you think? Shall I go back and tell her—"

"Don't you do it," said Raney. "It may be a good thing. You can't tell. A good starving is the best thing for every man's belly, now and then. And you shake up that Injun boy's digestion a little and he may turn out all right. I don't think you could've thought of a better thing."

They got to the tepee of Broken Knife. By this time, the swift-winged rumor had gone before them. A group had gathered by the entrance to that lodge. One figure stood out above the rest. It was a tall, gaunt old man, with the carriage of a Roman senator and the emaciated body of a saint. His arms were folded across his breast. His face was covered with thunderous gloom.

"That's Tree Bender, the great medicine man," muttered Raney to the boy. "I told you so. It ain't the medicine men that are glad to have you with the tribe, son! He's come down here to look a curse at you!"

Tree Bender did not have much chance of seeing or being seen, however, for every one in that waiting group fell into a commotion as the two riders came up. When

181

they dismounted, a full half dozen of the boys and young-er braves leaped to do honor to the benefactor of the tribe. Big Raney they paid no attention to.

But they struggled together to be the first to unsaddle the bay horse and to carry the equipment into the lodge of Broken Knife and hang it duly upon the poles at the foot of the boy's assigned bed. They led off the bay to hobble and pasture him, and an excited youngster—he must have been fully as old as young Johnnie Tanner—eagerly pleaded for the right of herding the horse, of watching over it day and night until it should be needed, of answering for its safety with his life!

And he showed a half-headed old hatchet with which apparently, he proposed to fight for his trust!

Then he hurried inside the tent to escape from the bustling officiousness of the others. But it was not much better inside the tent.

The Blackbird had smiled at him most radiantly that very morning when he left the lodge. But now she stood up from her work of beading and remained solemnly with bent head and eyes on her feet, without speaking. The squaw, her mother, was putting the finishing touches to the arrangement of folded robes with which she had heaped and padded the back rest of the young guest. Even she hardly dared to smile. She backed away and glanced about her with a hunted look, as though guiltily trying to remember something.

Johnnie Tanner was wretched, but Raney said to him quietly: "Say something to them, won't you? They'll stand around like lumps of wood and never sit down in your presence, if you don't make 'em easy!"

Johnnie Tanner searched his brain in vain for a moment. Then he cast himself headlong down on the robes, exclaiming in his best Cheyenne:

"Hah! This is softer than a saddle! Who was the wise chief who said that the lodge of a friend was always a happy home?"

The compliment worked like a new stroke of magic upon the women. He saw them lift lighted faces and ex-change happy glances. The ice was in that instant broken.

Perhaps he was hungry and would eat? He certainly would eat. Some of that venison, broiled over the coals of the fire? It was an agreeable thought, to Johnnie Tanner. And then a little of the buffalo stew, in the first place, to quiet the appetite? That was also to his pleasure.

Lordly he felt, albeit guilty in his lordliness. He looked at Raney, with a shamed smile in his eye, but Raney merely said: "You're going to give me a comfortable stay here with these Cheyennes, son. Any man'll be able to get fat on the leavings from your table, seems to me!"

So they were served by the two women, who went about their work shyly and happily, as though in the service of superior beings.

"It's like new clothes," said Raney, later. "You'll get used to it, but it kind of cramps you at first."

And the boy could not help inwardly agreeing. Everything of his past began to seem dim compared with a light-headed sense of pleasure which was mastering him.

The hunters began to drift back, loaded with meat and hides. And around each of them a cluster of the curious gathered. All had the same great central story to tell of the slaying and the giving of the magic buffalo, but no listeners ever tired of hearing the yarn grow, more marvelous at each repetition.

It was not until the late evening, however, that the last of the hunters came in, and then there was enacted a strange spectacle.

Four noble warriors came to the lodge of Broken Knife and asked Raney and young Johnnie Tanner forth to view the scene. The Cheyennes could not have selected four braves more eminent for bloody deeds and courage. The stained feathers of their long, flowing headdresses proclaimed their quality. They carried medicine pipes and staves. They were brilliant and hideous with paint.

"Something's in the air," said Raney. "Something's in the air that'll be worth seeing and hearing. Look at them four bucks. They're as proud as pallbearers. Stick up your chin and walk proud, son!"

In fact, it was impossible for Johnnie Tanner to walk without a certain dignity, now. The four conducted him to the central open space of the village, and there the entire population was massed. A sigh and a murmur went through them, and they melted to either side before the coming of the six.

But it was the boy on whom they fastened their eyes. He was the cause of their excitement.

Presently out of the distance came a wavering brilliance of torches. Another rustling whisper went through the crowd. The lights approached, and now something lofty and white could be seen. It drew still nearer. And now Johnnie saw a close-ordered body of braves in full regalia, a-sweep with feathers, frightful with unique designs in the most brilliant paint, around that lofty form of white which, in a moment, he recognized as the great white buffalo bull!

The hide had been stripped off it, the skin cunningly had been drawn from the head, even, and the horns left to crown all most realistically.

Men walked inside the heavy pall of that skin, which must have been cunningly framed out with withes, so that the natural form was kept amazingly well. The braves who carried the burden raised it on the butts of lances so that it appeared even loftier than in real life. It bulked incredibly large. It dominated the eye that looked upon it.

And Johnnie hardly wondered when he saw the Cheyennes prostrating themselves on either hand before the monster. As it approached, he made out Broken Knife walking in front of the trophy with the step of a conqueror.

Ah, a great day, a glorious day for Broken Knife, even though he shone only in the reflected light that issued from another!

Now the four braves took Johnnie Tanner by the arms and urged him forward. He was forced, reluctantly, into the flare of the many torches. The marchers halted. The boy stood before them, and suddenly he was alone. His four escorts had disappeared. Even Hank Raney was nowhere near.

Fear swept over Johnnie Tanner. He cast one frantic glance around him to find succor.

Then big Broken Knife stepped forward once more. He drew the boy to his side. They walked together toward the ample entrance of the medicine lodge, and before them, behind, to either side, passed the ghostly muttering and sighing of the awe-stricken crowd.

And all of those whispers seemed to be forming over and over again one phrase, as though it had an infinite variety of crowded meanings: "Striking Eagle! Striking Eagle! Striking Eagle!"

Why was the step of Broken Knife so slow, so deliberate, so instinct with pride? Because of the trophy that followed behind them, but chiefly because of this young lad who honored him by walking at his side.

The wide panels of the entrance to the medicine lodge opened suddenly. Within, Johnnie Tanner saw the hideously masked forms of many chosen dancers. Other throngs were scattered on the outer edge of the lodge. He felt that he was entering into a sanctum, though a savage and half childish one, perhaps. Shame filled him and pride greater and more thrilling than his shame, for he knew that his entrance would, in all their eyes, make the lodge still more revered.

At the very verge he paused an instant. Broken Knife paused with him. The procession of the guards behind him halted. The huge white buffalo was stayed, also, and all its bearers.

"If I go in," the boy was saying to himself, while his heart trembled, "what am I doing to myself? If I go in, shall I come out the same Johnnie Tanner or something new, a new soul; I don't know what?"

Then, in the midst of his thought, just beside the entrance where the torchlight flamed most brightly, he saw Blackbird, the daughter of the chief, her hands pressed together at her breast, fear, joy, and admiration in her eyes, and her parted lips murmuring something which he could read from afar: "Striking Eagle! Striking Eagle!"

To her he was a very king of the air, to them all a sacred and a lordly power. To himself, he was young Johnnie Tanner, victim of odd freaks of fortune and of chance.

Should he pass through the wide opening into that pseudo-holy place, or should he remain honestly outside, with the truth which he knew about himself?

He looked again at the girl.

Her bronze beauty flowed upon his mind with music and delight. He stepped forward.

The big chief moved with him reverently, measuring his own pace by that of the messenger from the Sky People, the symbol of the other world, the slayer of the white bull.

And behind them came the chosen guard and the towering, majestic form of the buffalo, which with its hump brushed the top of the entrance.

The chosen worshipers marched on. The flaps were drawn slowly together.

All others were excluded. Hank Raney remained with braced legs and folded arms among the outer throng. And he heard the slow rhythm of a drum begin inside the lodge. His heart jumped.

He could guess what was happening inside. That was not what mattered. But what was happening inside the heart and the soul of Johnnie Tanner?

36 · BIG CHIEF JOHNNIE

WHAT happened inside that great medicine lodge, even Johnnie Tanner could hardly have told. The clouds of sacrificial smoke, made all dreamlike, with the nightmare forms of the masked dancers, springing up and down, and a hideous din of horns, of drums, of rattles, of whooping and yelling braves.

In the center of the lodge the lofty outlines of the white buffalo dominated the scene, but just what was taking place he could not declare. Only he knew that everything appeared to turn on himself and the presence of the hunting trophy. He could understand Cheyenne quite well, until the speakers grew excited, and when man after man approached him and made a frantic speech, it was plain that they were all making some connection between themselves, the buffalo and the white boy. Just what the connection was he could not tell, but every brave, in turn, placed something at his feet until he had a pile of trinkets lying before him.

Broken Knife gave the most mighty token—a great necklace of the claws of a grizzly bear which in the eyes of his tribe was equivalent to several coups in battle against a human enemy. Besides, there were ornamented tomahawks, a number of knives, some in beautiful white leather cases, eagle feathers, a magnificent painted buffalo robe, a two-barreled rifle of an excellent new make and, altogether, a whole heap of prizes which made his boyish heart swell with joy.

Suddenly the ceremony was ended.

He thought, in a way, that the tribe was repaying him in part for the slaying of the white buffalo and the donation of the magic pelt. But there was something more intended. As they broke up, half a dozen of the younger braves loaded themselves with the gifts which had been showered on Johnnie and accompanied him on his way to the lodge of Broken Knife.

The night was in an uproar. There was not only the barking of the dogs and the screeching of wakeful children, but, here and there, out sprang strange bursts of noise, where the Indian youth were serenading their loves.

"Do you hear?" said Broken Knife. "This is a night of happiness for our people!"

There was just a shade of emphasis placed upon "our" and the boy, with a catch of his breath, realized that he was now considered a member of the Cheyenne tribe!

When he got into the lodge, he was in a fever to talk with Hank Raney, but the latter was soundly asleep and snoring, so that Johnnie could not confide in his friend until the morning.

As they came up from the morning swim, he told him all that he could remember. When he finished, "You left something out," said Raney.

"What?"

"You stopped, there, outside of the medicine lodge. Well, then, what was it that made you go ahead again?"

The boy considered. Then he flushed.

"I can't tell you that," said he.

Raney whistled.

"All right," said he. "You're flying too high for me to see where you're going. But I hope you'll land on your feet, son."

From that moment, a slight estrangement set in between them. But it was not greatly noticed by the boy. For his part, he was constantly employed in attending feasts and listening to the warriors count their coups, telling their endless stories of war and great deeds of hunting. He was taken into the council of the head chiefs and the old men, also, the third day after, where he heard them

187

consult on the policy of sending forth an expedition against the Crows.

His own advice was asked. He counseled peace; and the weight of his young voice seemed to break down all opposition. Those who were in favor of the measure in the first place merely hung down their heads; they remained sullenly silent and the expedition was not voted. He was amazed that his casual opinion should have such weight!

They were coming out of this meeting, when Johnnie saw before him the huge and ugly form of the squaw of Spotted Bull, she who had lifted up her child for him to bless and cure. Now her face shone. There were tears in her eyes, and she told him that the boy was well! For two days, rigorously, she had watched his lips, so that not a morsel of food should pass them. On the third day, she gave him a light diet. For two days he had screamed in a continual rage. His heart began to flutter. But afterward, he ate, and his starved stomach received the food eagerly. Then he slept. He awakened cheerful. His eyes were bright. He lay on his bed without making a sound and smiled happily at his mother and his father.

"The bad spirit is gone. It heard your voice and flew away," said the squaw. "You have given another warrior to the Cheyennes, and you have brought happiness into our lodge. Spotted Bull is your friend. He loves you. He wishes well to you!"

Such thanks were not enough to express the mind of Spotted Bull, it appeared, for when the boy got to the lodge of Broken Knife, he found there a string of five horses waiting. They were a present from the brave to the healer!

"I shouldn't take 'em. I can't take 'em," said the boy to Raney.

The latter was just in from a short hunting excursion. He sat in front of the lodge, cleaning his rifle.

"You do what you please," said he. "You know these folks a lot better than I ever will!"

Was there contempt in his voice?

"What's the matter, Hank?" asked Johnnie.

Hank Raney suddenly lifted his hand and pointed sternly at his friend.

"The matter's you," he said. "The trouble is inside of

188

you. But you're gunna get in deep, pretty soon. You can't feed buffalo bones to a puppy. He ain't got the teeth to crack 'em."

"What do you mean?" asked the boy.

But Hank Raney went stalking off, apparently sunk rather in gloom than in anger.

It left young Johnnie Tanner greatly upset. He was about to rush after his friend and demand a further explanation, but somehow he knew that all of his asking would bring no response. Perhaps there was something that Raney himself could not explain; it was merely a vague sense of coming disaster. At least, that vague expression about puppies and buffalo bones probably indicated that a young boy could not live very long in the full rôle of a man.

A cold feeling of disaster impending grew in Johnnie. He went slowly into the tepee and there he found Broken Knife's daughter, the Blackbird, alone.

His premeditation made his approach so soundless that she was not aware of him at once. She was engaged in painting a design on the white leather of a quiver-case, a work usually reserved for the older men who had a special talent, but in the case of the Blackbird she possessed a real power to draw, and she put in the paint with a swift surety.

As she worked, she sang, her head canted critically a little to one side. Happiness kept her smiling. Out of that happiness the song flowed also, and though it was like other Indian chants, the pure, soft thread of her voice took away the harshness, the lack of any harmonic design, and made the thing like one of those faraway hymns such as the wind sings among the lonely mountains.

When she saw Johnnie Tanner, she looked up with a start, and hastily turned the face of her work away from him. Then she jumped to her feet and stood in the attitude of one awaiting orders.

Johnnie ordinarily would have been embarrassed by the sight of such subservience; now his trouble was too deep for such a reaction. He stared at her with thoughtful eyes.

"Blackbird," said he, "why do you act like this? You're not my slave, or my daughter, or my squaw, and——"

He stopped. The last word had tipped up her head

189

and flooded her face with color. The red throbbed and glowed in her skin. And Johnnie felt as though a light were shining on him, through deepest darkness.

"I am only the daughter of your friend," said the girl. "What have I done to make you angry? My father will turn his face away from me; my mother will beat me if she knows that I have made you angry! What do I do that is wrong?"

He sighed. She was so extremely lovely, in this moment of distress, that he found it hard to keep on thinking; his mind was entangled as he looked at her. All mental processes stopped short.

"Listen, Blackbird," said he.

"What Cheyenne woman does not listen when a chief speaks to her?" asked the girl, wondering at him. "Tell me what I must do, and I shall do it."

"Do this," he said. "Remember that you're nearly as old as I am, that you know just as much, you can ride a lot better than I can, you could follow a trail better, you could probably run faster." He considered the slender grace of her body, and nodded. "And I'm not a chief, either. I know very little. All the men who act as though I were somebody important, they're wrong. I'm only a boy. I want to tell you that, and make you remember."

"I shall remember," she said gravely.

He sighed with relief.

"I knew I could explain to you," he said. "I don't want you to look at me as if I were any one superior to you. I'm not! Even of the boys of my own age in the village, there are hundreds stronger and cleverer than I am. I happen to have done a couple of things since I reached your people. Well, all the Cheyennes think I did those things with a great medicine, that I'm very brave and powerful when I want to be, but I tell you it's only chance, and not power, and—"

He paused to take breath, and in the pause he saw her smiling faintly.

"Now I understand," she said.

"Well," said Johnnie, blushing a little, "even if you despise me after you know the truth about me, I think I'd rather have you despise me than have a wrong idea of me. I'm not a great man: I'm nothing important at all; I haven't the power that they are always speaking about."

"Ah, no," said the girl. "Of course, it is not in you. It lives there above us, and it only comes down to you from the spirits who live there, and who love you!"

He stared at her. Her face was illumined with a great conviction and he saw that he had done all of his explaining in vain. He sighed, and his sigh was almost a groan, as he went on, desperately: "Blackbird, don't you think I should know what I am?"

Her smile broadened. Her attitude had changed so that in her eye there was something of pity, of wonder, of admiration all commingled, as when a mother looks at a child. She was lovelier then than he ever had seen her before; her beauty pulled at his heart-strings.

"Striking Eagle," she said, "perhaps you don't know all about yourself. The torch which burns doesn't know that it is casting a great light, but it dazzles eyes far away."

He saw that it was a hopeless matter to strive to convince her. He merely shook his head and made a gesture of surrender. "Ah, well," said he, "I won't try to argue any longer. But my friend is not with me, now, and your father is away. So I am going to ask you for advice. Spotted Bull has sent horses and tied them for me outside this lodge."

"I know," said she. "But that is not all he would give. If you knew the heart of the brave, he would give his own blood! Why should he not? His son was dying. Now his son will live."

"But don't you see?" said the boy, breaking into a sweat. "It wasn't anything. I only happened to think of something that just by a chance helped the little boy. He may get sick again and—"

The girl was still smiling, still shaking her head with a perfect complacence.

"How can the boy become sick again," she asked, "after you have blessed him?"

Her eyes shone more brightly; the smile disappeared; she looked upward like one inspired, and then back at Johnnie Tanner.

"You do not know the power that is in you, but we Cheyennes know it and we feel it. We have seen great medicine men. Some of them have done very wonderful

191

things. They have worked with medicine, mixed powders, burned strange smokes, danced and sung to the spirits, sacrificed, laid on hands; but you only speak, and the good spirits listen to you at once and send down power to you; and you only speak, and the evil spirits run away before you and dissolve like smoke in a strong wind.

"Now you wish to tell me that you are only like other young men. Well, I say that you carry fire and don't even know that it is in your hand! Is not that more wonderful to us? I am only a girl. I must stay in the lodge and work, and I have not seen you when the power came down on you from the sky. But my father saw you strike Talking Wolf dead, and he said that the flash of your knife was like the gleam of lightning. It dazzled him. And the hunters who saw you standing beside the medicine bull, the great white buffalo, did they not all see that a sort of mist of light surrounded both you and the bull?"

"Oh, Blackbird," said the despairing boy, "are you going to believe all those things?"

Her breast heaved.

"Shall I call the squaw of Spotted Bull a liar? Did she not stand there in front of this very lodge? Did she not bless the lodge and all in it, because you live with us? Did she not swear to me that, when you told her how to cure the baby, there was a terrible gleam in your eyes, and her heart trembled, and her bones became light, like the bones of a bird? There is no understanding in a little papoose. But the baby was silent, also, when you spoke. It began to smile. Ha! I have heard all these things from an honest woman. All the tribe knows her!"

Johnnie mopped his forehead. Then he held up his hand.

"Well, we won't talk about it any longer," he said, gloomily, submitting to this gigantic misconception of a childlike people. Perhaps when the stories were repeated a few months longer they would become yet more marvelous.

"You are angry," said the girl, sadly. "But I must speak the truth. When my eyes are dazzled, I know that there has been a light; but what am I to pretend that I understand? I am a woman, and a chief speaks to me!"

She bowed her head.

"Stop it, Blackbird!" he commanded. "Look up at me and don't go carrying on like that. Well, I give it up.

But let me have some advice. Wise as you want to make me out, I don't know what to do. Those horses from Spotted Bull. It's too much. I don't want them at all. They can't belong to me!"

The girl frowned, with a sudden look of pain.

"Is Spotted Bull an evil man?" she asked. "Are his hands wicked, and can you take nothing from him?"

He groaned. His brain began to spin.

"I'm the most bewildered boy in the world. That's all I know," said he. "Well, I'll keep the horses, then. What shall I do with them?"

"I shall speak the word and send some of the men or the boys to take the horses out to the pasture to put with the rest of yours."

"Hold on, Blackbird!" he exclaimed. "I'll do it myself. You wouldn't be sending men out to do work for me, and wait on me when I can—"

She straightened. She stamped a little.

"What man among the Cheyennes," she said, "is not proud to win a word, a breath, a single glance from the Striking Eagle by a far greater service than such a foolish little thing as this?"

She stepped to the lodge flap and threw it wide open. She called and the thing she said was: "Who has ears to hear the want of Striking Eagle?"

There came a clamor. The shrill voices of boys predominated. But men were speaking, also. When she told what must be done with the horses, Johnnie Tanner, standing frozen-faced within the lodge, could hear the rush in answer. Goose flesh formed prickling all over the boy's body. But he made a gesture of surrender. Turning, his glance fell upon the half-painted quiver-case. The design was fairly complete. It showed a great white buffalo and a mounted warrior who pointed at it, and from the tip of the warrior's finger to the buffalo's side leaped a streak of jagged lightning!

So that was how they thought he had killed the bull!

HE did not leave the lodge again until evening. He spent the rest of that time sitting or lying in a sort of stupor, trying to puzzle out what he should do next. Plainly, Raney was right. He was becoming too deeply involved in this affair.

Big Broken Knife came in at dusk. He had been out hunting all day, and he reported that not a single head of game had been killed by all the hunters of the village. It was an unprecedented thing, for this season of the year.

"But did you ask before you started?" asked the squaw of the chief.

And she gestured toward the boy.

"No," muttered Broken Knife. "I did not think. I was a fool!"

Johnnie felt a new surge of panic. Was he to be the provider of game, as well? Was everything to be blamed upon his head?

The chief turned to him. It was not to speak of the poor hunting, however.

He said, with an air of greatest respect and reverence, that an old companion of his upon the warpath and in the hunt was that moment standing before the lodge. It was his hope that Striking Eagle might be induced to heal him. His left hand was struck off at the wrist, ten years before, by a Pawnee hatchet. Would the great messenger from the sky kindly let him have a new hand, either by sudden miracle or by a process of growth, no matter how painful?

Johnnie moistened his dry lips. He looked straight across the lodge and there his glance fell upon the face of Raney, at once amused and compassionate. But what could the answer be? The faith of these children was infinite. He could not return a mere, blank no.

"Tell your friend," said Johnnie to Broken Knife, "that no power ever was given me to make new limbs grow. I am sorry. I shall speak to the spirits and ask them if there is any hope for his missing hand. But I'm afraid that nothing can be done."

Broken Knife hesitated, as though he wished to press the point, then, reluctantly, he stepped from the lodge to give the message. Johnnie Tanner, miserably, could hear the soothing voice with which the chieftain spoke.

Then, through the dusk of the day, Johnnie Tanner hurried out from the lodge. Wrapped in a light blanket, he managed to get through the village without attracting attention, and he spent three hours in wandering up and down under the stars.

There was only one event in his promenade. As he walked, he was turning the matter back and forth in his mind. All logical good sense called him swiftly from the Cheyennes. His place was in the world of white men. His mission was still unaccomplished and the treasure of his father was in the hands of the thief; above all, the Cheyennes themselves were now beginning to demand of him the totally impossible.

In the midst of these thoughts, two swift horsemen careened up to him and halted, demanding harshly who he was. They were outposts set to guard the camp. He saw the starlight glittering on spear points which were held steadily a scant foot from his breast.

He threw back the blanket which veiled him.

"Do you know me, friends?" he asked.

"It is Striking Eagle!" gasped one of the men in a frightened voice.

They had known him by the mere sound of his words! "Forgive us, father," said the second warrior. "We should have known if it had not pleased you to wrap yourself in darkness thicker than the rest of the night!"

They withdrew hastily. But the boy remained standing still. "Father," to a fifteen-year-old youngster! And then, he had wrapped himself in darker night.

Suddenly he began to laugh.

It was absurd, but there was something delightful in his position. Considering the number of his subjects, what king had such power over the minds and hearts of his people?

He must leave them. Yes, of course. Yet, when he thought of it, one face and the remembered sound of one voice held him like a song that was never out of his ear. What was the girl to him, Cheyenne as she was? What could she ever be? And he, mere child, why should he be weighing and pondering such a thing as a woman, old or young?

He went back toward the village with his mind made up. Whatever else he did, he would leave the tribe!

But he walked more and more slowly as he approached the lodge of Broken Knife. And, when he came to it, he heard the sounds of hearty laughter. He stopped and listened, and there was the voice of the Blackbird, bubbling with mirth.

"He said that he was only a boy; he tried to tell me that he was less important than I am!" she cried.

"Ah, traitor," said he to himself. "She repeats things. She hasn't a still tongue. Well, that's the end of her with me."

More laughter had followed this remark from the girl. The boy gritted his teeth. Then the drawling voice of Hank Raney broke in: "You can see how it is. He's used to wonderful things. You know the way the boys like to slide down snowbanks in the winter? Well, he was used to sliding down cloud banks, the same way. Sometimes he'd roll off the white, shining part and get into the muddy rain clouds. When he came home after that, his mother used to scold him. She used to make him pretty unhappy, especially when he took to jumping from cloud to cloud, because sometimes he fell through and—"

At this stream of nonsense, the boy waited to hear a ringing burst of derisive laughter, but there was only a general gasp, and then the voice of Broken Knife exclaiming: "But how could he live, if he fell from the clouds to the earth?"

"Why, he never fell all the way," said that fluent liar, Hank Raney. "They always have some eagles around handy, according to what he told me. And when they saw a boy drop from the clouds, they'd fly down, half a dozen of them, like arrows, and take him in their beaks and claws and carry him up home again, safe and sound, except that the talons would give him a good scratching on the way. But you can see, used to what he's been through, nothing that happens to him down here seems very important. He doesn't set any stock in the way the spirits have talked to him. He's simply used to them. He knows them all by name. That's the way that it is with him! He's different!"

There was an amazed murmur from the Indians. Johnnie Tanner wanted to rush in and call his friend Raney the greatest liar in the entire world. But he restrained himself. He made his entrance with appropriate slowness. He felt the eyes of every one upon him, but he went silently, gloomily, to his bed and sat down on the end of it.

Raney spoke to him in Cheyenne. He resented that. Why couldn't the man speak to him in English?

"My friend, Striking Eagle," said Raney, "we have had terrible news this evening, since you left us. Broken Knife wants to talk to you about it."

Johnnie looked up at the chief.

Broken Knife stood up. He said, quietly: "My son, Hawk-that-rises, is to be sacrificed by the Pawnees. They have heard of the death of Talking Wolf. His brothers want to sacrifice my son to the soul of Talking Wolf. They have sent out messengers to all their hunting and war parties. Very soon, Hawk-that-rises will be dead, unless some one makes a great medicine and saves him."

He paused and looked at the white boy significantly. Johnnie Tanner understood. He looked in agony toward Hank Raney, but Raney was stubbornly scowling at his pipe bowl, which he was cleaning. He refused to answer the glance which, he must have known, was falling upon him. The heart of Johnnie Tanner sank into his boots. If he refused, they would simply detest him as a liar and an ingrate and an unfriendly spirit. They thought that he could melt mountains, apparently, if he had a will to do such a thing.

He looked aside. The eyes of the girl were on him, too. Her lips were parted. Her eyes were great dark wells of despair, dimly lighted with a flicker of hope. There was no doubt about what she would think and feel if he refused. Perhaps she would not hate him. She would merely wonder at the hard heart of the magician who refused to use his magic, so easily in his hand!

A sort of madness swept over poor young Johnnie Tanner, bewildered as he was.

He jumped to his feet. His eyes were fiery as he looked around him.

"Then we start this minute and ride to the Pawnees to save Hawk-that-rises," he said. "Begin! You, Broken

Knife! You, Raney." The latter lifted his head, blinked, gaped, and then slowly stood up.

"If that's what the magician says," said he, "then we'd better go along."

The people in the tent were fairly quivering with excitement. Johnnie could hear the beating of his own heart.

"If I send out the call," said Broken Knife, "all the warriors will come. Every man will be happy to ride at the rear when Striking Eagle leads the way."

Johnnie shook his head, mournfully, savagely. Of what use were numbers? Led by him, uninformed lad as he was, what could they do? At the best, challenge danger, and then trust to the glorious speed of their horses to escape!

"We go alone, we three!" said he determinedly.

And alone they went.

In ten minutes they were on their horses and heading through the camp, with Broken Knife in the lead. They had merely picked up weapons, a little food, water bags, and off they went, suddenly. The girl and her mother had helped them prepare, with hands that fumbled and with frightened eyes.

Only, as Johnnie Tanner was going through the flap of the lodge, the Blackbird caught hold of his hand with both of hers. How strong was the grip of her slender fingers! No white girl had such strength. No white girl, he told himself, ever had such woe and beauty in dark eyes.

"You three!" she said. "And the whole Pawnee camp—for my brother will surely be in the center of them all. And if—"

She stopped herself. She stood back and made herself smile at him.

"I am only a woman. I am only a fool," said she. "I should know that you do only what the happy and strong spirits tell you to do, and all will be well!"

Yes, she was smiling, when he looked his last upon her.

Then he went hastily out into the night, for tears were beginning to sting his eyes from angry self-pity.

He had plunged into a sea of danger. What would ever come of it all?

They were passing through the shimmering, white rows of the Cheyenne lodges. Then they were out in the darkness of the plain. Broken Knife led the way, his shoulders great and square against the stars. He knew the direction of the Pawnee tribesmen, surely.

Raney fell back to his young friend.

"Now, son," said he, "you'd better get a new inspiration from the spirits and tell Broken Knife to turn back. Otherwise, you're gunna bump your head against a stone wall."

Savage resentment stung the very soul of the boy.

"You go back, then, by yourself," he gasped. "I don't want anything to do—with cowards—and traitors!"

38 · TO THE RESCUE

THEY went forward across the great green sea of the prairie for days and days. They went like children, blindly.

Sometimes it seemed to Johnnie that he no longer could hold back the maniacal laughter which was forcing itself up, swelling in his throat, pressing against his very teeth. The chief, Broken Knife, was the naturally accepted leader. He started the marches. He selected the halting places. He called the day's work ended. They drew closer to the enemy's country and, on the day that Hank Raney picked a Pawnee moccasin out of the grass, the chief divided the night into three watches. Johnnie Tanner slept through his, his head upon his knees.

The chief was utterly complacent. They were riding into a tigers' den, but he was happy. He trusted in what? In Johnnie Tanner, falsely known as the Striking Eagle, medicine man and magician!

And what, then, held the big, gaunt, powerful, sardonic white man, Raney?

Why, he had been called a coward and a traitor by a mere boy, that same Johnnie Tanner. Therefore, he was riding on silently to meet his death. He never spoke to Johnnie. He never looked at him, but held straightforward on the trail.

And Johnnie himself?

Every day, as the sun came up, he swore to himself that he would tell the chief that this was madness, and every day he failed to find the words. He remembered his talk with the Blackbird. There was no hope of making one Cheyenne, of that division of the tribe, believe that he, Striking Eagle, could not accomplish practically anything that he desired. No, their minds were fixed, as toward a north star. And he was the star—he, fifteen-year-old Johnnie Tanner!

They sat close together one night, eating the sun-dried venison, chewing hard on the tough stuff. It was like wood. They had no fire this night. Even Hank Raney began to turn his head and peer into the darkness. And the boy knew that they were near the end of the march.

"To-morrow, before the sun goes down, we shall find them," said the chief, at last. "Do you make no medicine, Striking Eagle?"

"Our medicine is made," answered the boy, grimly.

"It is well," said the chief.

There was not a shade of doubt in his voice. He was as trusting as a child. And, even through the darkness, Johnnie Tanner could feel the bitter smile of Hank Raney.

He, himself, when rolled in his blanket, lay for a long time looking up to the blazing stars and the white powder of the Milky Way and he could not sleep. It was Raney at whom he chiefly wondered. He was only a boy, but Raney acted as though he had been insulted by a peer equal in years and wisdom. Otherwise, why should he nurse the bitter grudge so long?

And Johnnie himself could not understand what moved him—not the thought of Hawk-that-rises, surely. Rather, it was the knowledge that in the Pawnee camp was Harry, the thief, and, above all, that singular and recurring sense of a directing fate, against which it was foolish for him to rebel.

At last the stars blurred, he slept, and in the morning he wakened, realizing that he had not been roused to keep his share of the night watch. No matter how great a belief the chief had in him as a medicine man, it was plain that he also believed that boys need sleep. And Johnnie was touched.

They had started from the Cheyenne encampment with three horses apiece. They went on with the whole lot until shortly after noon when the chief had them hobble out six of the mounts. There were left, for the boy, the bright bay stallion; for Raney, Midnight, of course; and for the chief himself there was a chubby brute with thick, hairy legs, a gross cartoon of a horse. For all its looks, however, its speed of foot and endurance had been proved.

After the final selection of horses, they halted a full hour. Raney and the boy ate and had a pull at the water bags. But the chief squatted on his heels and employed that hour in painting himself carefully.

The last time, no doubt, that he ever would make himself terrible to look upon! Johnnie Tanner, watching the ceremonial process, thought of arrows in level flight, of the clanging explosion of rifles, of the slash and tear of knife blades ripping through the flesh, of naked humanity lashed to a post and the fire kindled around it, and dancing fiends among the shadows, red-copper highlights being struck from their shoulders and muscular arms by the fire. He thought of those things, and his courage sank into his moccasins.

But then they mounted and went silently forward. The other two did not look behind, but Johnnie could not avoid giving a final glance to the six horses which had been left behind them. They were grazing contentedly, all except the gray mustang, which was making frantic, foolish, hobbled efforts to follow after them.

This made the heart of Johnnie ache more than ever. They crossed some swales of uneven land. The sight of the six horses was cut off from them, but the eager, lonely neighing of the gray mustang pursued them.

"He's my best friend," said Johnnie faintly to himself. "He's my best friend, and I'll never see his ugly head again!"

His mouth began to twitch at the corners. He had a tremendous desire to burst into tears, but he savagely fought back the weeping and scowled down at the bright fields of grass.

In the late afternoon, the chief halted them and arranged them in a longer file, thirty yards between him and Raney, and the boy an equal distance to the rear. It was a strange procedure, but plainly Broken Knife expected that danger was soon to be met.

Then they went on.

A little later, Johnnie saw a big buffalo wolf come to the head of a soft swale of grass land. It looked at them for a time. It sat down, and with the calm impudence of the wolves, which seem to know exactly the range of a rifle, it deliberately scratched itself behind the ear.

It looked at them again, then standing up, it went over the ridge of the swale and disappeared.

The moment that it was out of sight, the chief put spurs to his horse, and sprinted furiously in the direction of the beast which had disappeared. Raney followed suit. Johnnie, filled with wonder, imitated their example. He could not imagine why the two seemed bent on riding down a prairie wolf. It seemed the sheer madness of the hunting instinct.

But, when the bay brought him over the top of the swale, he saw a good reason enough.

The buffalo wolf had disappeared. Instead of this, there was a half-naked Indian racing through the prairie grass toward a horse in the near distance. By the cut of his hair, plainly this was a Pawnee. An outlayer, then, a spy who had been recognized as such by the keen eye of Broken Knife. Old tales of the Pawnee skill in assuming the pelts and the manners of wolves flashed back upon the mind of Johnnie Tanner. But still he could hardly believe that the beast he had seen on the hill was human under the skin.

The Pawnee, in the meantime, had reached his horse and mounted it.

Big Broken Knife rushed on, drawing his rifle. He fired but the Pawnee rushed along, unharmed.

Then Hank Raney jerked Midnight to a halt, lifted his own rifle and sat for a long moment. Johnnie Tanner was rushing up on the bay. He shouted at Raney to shoot! But still Raney held his aim. It seemed that the Pawnee had traveled an impossible distance, when at last the rifle spoke.

And the Pawnee rode on!

Johnnie Tanner drove the bright bay stallion hard in pursuit. He was in the lead now. Would they both let him ride on alone to the encounter?

Then, quite suddenly, he saw the warrior before him slump to the side and spill out, his hands flung far from his head.

He struck the ground. He rolled, head over heels, and disappeared into the grass. The Pawnee pony, veering to the side, went off with long, stiff-legged jumps and finally halted and looked back toward the spot where its master lay.

That master would never rise again. He would never again wield whip or club on the tender flanks of a horse.

For Johnnie Tanner found him lying face downward with a red, purple-rimmed spot in the center of his back. Poor Indian! He was done for the instant the bullet struck, but he had kept to the horse in the vain hope, it seemed, of getting to help, of saving his scalp.

Raney and the chief came up at the same moment. They dismounted and turned the warrior on his back. He was powerfully made, but hardly out of his teens, though the savage strain of his race was imprinted on his face.

"A long shot!" said Broken Knife. "I never saw a longer or a better shot. The spirits of Striking Eagle must have helped the bullet on its way, my friend."

Raney said nothing in return. But he looked at the boy with a silent sneer.

39 · IN PAWNEE CAMP

UNSCALPED, unplundered, they left the Pawnee, face upward in the grass. They must not risk having about them the fresh smell of blood, for that would have a meaning for the sharp noses of the Pawnee dogs.

So they went on, and rode into the deep evening until they came in sight of the shining lodges of the enemy. They were well placed between a dark strip of woods that grew along the site of a slough, and the faintly gleaming waters of a little stream. But the lodges themselves fascinated the boy. In every one of them must be at least one warrior, fierce, well trained, ready instantly to leap upon a horse and rush out to battle. It seemed to Johnnie that the bright city must contain a whole multitude!

Broken Knife led them around by way of the woods. Through these they went on foot, leading the horses, until through the trunks of the trees they saw the glimmering of the lodges, close at hand. Then the horses were tethered.

"Mark the place well, each man," said Broken Knife,

softly. "Here we may come back one at a time, or only one of all the three. But each man, when the thing is done, flees for himself. Unless you will it otherwise, Striking Eagle?"

Young Johnnie Tanner started. It seemed amazing that his advice should be asked at that moment; but then he remembered that he was a man of vast importance, a dreadful warrior!

He could have laughed, but he knew that the least sound might betray them. He simply whispered in reply that the plan was good. But what should they do now?

Go straight forward upon the camp!

Behold, Hank Raney strode grimly out from the woods, with the chief beside him, and Johnnie Tanner felt his knees shake as he followed. He began to feel that he was in a dream. It was not credible that a sound-minded man like Raney would march up toward an enemy camp in this manner.

Once, as a wave of chanting from many strong voices came loudly from the camp, Broken Knife halted his party.

"Listen," said he. "They are, indeed, very happy. Perhaps they will sing another song to-morrow at this time."

The boy clutched the arm of his friend, Raney.

"Hank," he said, "you don't mean that you're really going straight on with this?"

Raney shook off his hand. He muttered in return:

"Turn back, then, if you're a coward and a traitor!"

Johnnie Tanner walked on with them. He hardly knew whether he was more frightened or sad. He had lost the friendship of Raney forever. That seemed clear. And he was sure that they were walking into the throat of a cannon. But, all three wrapped in their blankets, with Broken Knife in the lead, they kept straight on.

Suddenly half a dozen big wolfish dogs rose out of the dark of the ground before them and set up a yapping, shrill chorus. It was to Johnnie Tanner as though a powerful searchlight had been flashed upon them. And trouble quickly followed. A shadowy horseman came swaying across the plain toward them. He halted. "Who is this?" he demanded.

"You know my voice," said Raney suddenly, in excellent Pawnee.

"No," said the other.

"Bah!" said Raney, turning to his two companions. "He does not know my voice. You see what I said is true—the Pawnees use children for soldiers in these unlucky days!"

And he led the way, walking straight forward. Johnnie Tanner thought for a moment that the guard would rush at him, but the young brave, as he saw the dignified striding of Raney and the Cheyenne, apparently decided that he had best make no trouble, so he pulled his horse about and went on with his rounds of watch.

And straight into that wasp nest of enemies went the trio, with the glint of the lights twinkling on them. They walked slowly, Raney still in the lead. At the moment of contact with the enemy, he had stepped forward as though it were his right. Last came the boy, stretching his legs to make his stride seem more manly.

Every time they passed a tepee, the light shining out through the entrance, his heart shrank in his breast. But they walked straight through the encampment without being once hailed. They were near to the opposite rim when Raney halted them again.

"Well," he said, "I guess that we're used to the camp now. They don't seem to have eyes to-night, Broken Knife."

"No," said the other. "There is some great excitement in the air. Perhaps they already are drunk on the blood of my son? Who knows? And what shall we do now?"

"We can't ask where your son is lodged," said Raney. "Every Pawnee is supposed to know that."

"They will know his place as well as the fire knows the center of the tepee," said the Cheyenne.

"Brother," he added, turning to the boy. "Will you look for us through these leather walls and tell us where my son may be?"

"Aye," said Raney grimly. "Now your medicine can be a help to us."

Johnnie Tanner did not laugh. He did not even feel an irritation. Dread thoroughly had paralyzed all the faculties of his mind except the senses.

A tall, spare warrior, noticeably slender even under the big robe which enveloped him, went by with long strides. A friend encountered him and they halted.

205

"Where do you go?"

"I have been at the lodge of the widow of Talking Wolf. I have talked to her."

"What does she say?"

"Go and talk to her yourself, Long Arrow. Go and talk and persuade her. Now is the time when the boy should be sacrificed. Talking Wolf is dead. What use is it to her to wait so long?"

"She wants to marry Hawk-that-rises, perhaps, if he'll become a Pawnee."

"He won't become that. He'd far rather die."

"Well, I'll go and talk to her, then. Who is guarding the boy?"

"Two braves who have just come in from the hunt to the south. They both are young."

"Young men make sleepy watchers," said Long Arrow.

"That is true. Speak to the dead man's wife, Long Arrow."

At last the name went home, suddenly, into the brain of the boy. Long Arrow! Was not that the Pawnee name of Harry, the thief, Pawnee Harry of the traders?

Long Arrow strode away. The other Pawnee went past the three watchers without noticing them, and the boy heard the Cheyenne chief murmur: "Wonderful! Wonderful! The spirits put down that man to guide us the moment Striking Eagle asks for their help!"

And he started off in pursuit of Long Arrow.

The coincidence seemed rather strange to the boy also. But in a camp where the chief object of curiosity must still be the captive, it was not so strange that the name of Hawk-that-rises should be on every tongue.

In single file they went, the Cheyenne leading, the hunter next, Johnnie Tanner last of all. And now he found that terror no longer made him cold and his hands and knees weak. Instead, he was tingling with excitement.

Hawk-that-rises was not in his mind now. Instead, he was seeing again before his mind's eye the narrow, lean face of the thief, as he had sat like a crow on the backyard fence, and again on the deck of the steamer, and again in the street at St. Louis. It was not altogether chance that had made him see Harry on each occasion after the first. It was not chance now, in a sense. And yet that ghostly sense of fate was near the boy now. So his fear was struck from him; he became clear of eye and brain.

They turned in toward the center of the encampment, following Long Arrow. That was sure to make their difficulties greater, no matter what they attempted to do. But it could be taken for granted that the lodge of such a chief as Talking Wolf would be in the heart of the village.

So they saw the tall man reach the entrance of a lodge and pause there an instant. The entrance flap was put back by the bare, brawny arm of a warrior, and Long Arrow entered.

The Cheyenne, without a moment's hesitation, led the way to the shadowy rear of the lodge and there they dropped to the ground, all three. Each began to move to obtain some peep hole through which the interior of the lodge could be seen and the speakers more readily overheard.

As for young Johnnie Tanner, he found a ragged rent which looked at though it had been made by the teeth of a mischievous dog. Through that he stared, and the first object his eyes fell upon was the narrow, evil face of Harry, the thief!

Suddenly he felt that he had come to the end of the long trail!

40 · HARRY, THE PAWNEE

HARRY sat at sprawling ease, filling the bowl of a long-stemmed pipe from his tobacco pouch.

"Where is the woman?" he was asking.

"She has gone out. She will come back at once," said one of the Pawnee guards.

Bringing his eye closer to the tear in the leather, Johnnie Tanner could see almost all of the rounded interior of the lodge. The place was almost naked. No doubt it had been furnished as well as the best during the lifetime of Talking Wolf, but after his death the widow, in the frenzy of her first grief, must have given away everything. There was not even a cooking pot over the fire that smoldered in the center of the tepee.

But the furnishings of the lodge were of the least interest to Johnnie Tanner; only he shuddered a little to realize what after effects had been in the knife stroke that took the life of Talking Wolf! But now he scanned the other inhabitants of the lodge. Pawnee Harry, complete in deerskin, loaded with beadwork, with a fine robe flung back from his shoulders, looked a man of much greater importance than when he had sat on the fence in New York. A walking staff was beside him. At his hip there was a holstered weapon, the Colt revolver, beyond a doubt.

The two guards, as had been said, were young, but almost their full strength had come upon them. They looked to the boy like a pair of huge, dangerous cats. Each carried the inevitable knife. One had a war club; the other was armed with a double-barreled pistol which he was continually taking out and fondling. Undoubtedly his choicest possession.

But all these three, even to the boy who stared into the lodge, were of less importance than the prisoner.

He sat against a back rest to the right of the entrance. He seemed at first in an attitude of easy, free repose; then the eye of Johnnie Tanner saw the thongs that held him, a double twist of strong rawhide around the wrists and another around the ankles. A narrow band held back his long hair so that it might not fall forward over his face. And that face was the most noble that Johnnie Tanner ever had seen among the Indians. The features were bold enough, but finely chiseled. The eyes were big and set under a spacious forehead. Above all, the expression was cheerful and patient. His skin was not dark. It had the same ruddy olive tint as that of his sister, the Blackbird.

How could Broken Knife be the father of such a pair?

A hand touched Johnnie. He got up with haste and found his two friends already standing.

"I come again, after a while," Harry was saying, inside the lodge. "Tell the woman that I was here and that I shall come again. If she has good wits, she will let the sacrifice take place to-morrow. The ghost of her husband won't wait forever."

208

"Well, women are fools," said one of the guards. "Maybe Hawk-that-rises has put a spell on her."

A cheerful voice, which Johnnie guessed was that of the prisoner, replied, "I have put no spell on her. I have hardly looked into her face. Do you think that I wish to wait longer? Is it a pleasure to me to have the eyes of the Pawnees looking at me every day? I am ready, my friends!"

"Hai!" said the voice of Harry, the thief. "They will yell and howl when the word comes to the Cheyennes! Well, I wish that I could be both there and here."

"You hate me because I understand you," said the boy, calmly as before. "That is all!"

"Well," said Harry, "I'll see you turn into a woman when the fire begins to bite. A slow fire, Hawk-that-rises, that will rot away your feet, first of all."

He laughed.

"When the fire is burning," said the young Cheyenne, "we shall see. Perhaps I shall laugh also."

"I'm going," said Pawnee Harry. "Tell the woman when she returns."

"We shall tell her."

Johnnie Tanner moved suddenly to the side. The chief laid a hand on his shoulder, as though deprecating any early move, but Johnnie Tanner merely whispered: "Wait here!"

And he stepped around the tent cords which were pegged out to stakes and circled swiftly around the horses which were tied near the entrance to the lodge, such horses as a great Pawnee chief might be expected to own, sleek, glimmering in the starlight, with small heads and fierce, bright eyes. The widow had not disposed of that portion of her wealth, it appeared.

He arrived in full face of the lodge as the entrance flap was thrown back and the lofty form of Pawnee Harry stepped out. Half a dozen other Indians were prowling slowly by, dignified, wrapped in their robes. But Johnnie Tanner did not hesitate. He stepped close up to the tall, spare form and pushed the muzzle of the pistol very firmly into the man's stomach.

"Don't speak, don't whisper, Harry!" said he. "If you do, I'll kill you on the spot."

A faint, groaning sound came from the lips of Harry the thief.

"The kid!" he muttered.

With his left hand, Johnnie Tanner reached for the holster at the hip of his enemy. He drew out a revolver, sure enough, and, feeling eagerly on the handles of it, he felt the familiar design that identified it as his father's gun. It was loaded. The weight of the weapon told him that.

"Now walk back around the lodge," he commanded. "Walk slowly, don't you dare to speak. I'll be behind you, and I shoot straight, Harry!"

Harry, hesitating only one instant, looked up and down over the numbers of Indians who were in speaking distance. Any one of them could bring him help, and would do so at a word. But the help could not come before a bullet had crashed through his body.

So he obeyed, and walked slowly around behind the lodge. There was a dim twilight here, the faint glow of reflected fires making the air seem to smoke.

And, as the two came up, Johnnie Tanner said to Raney: "Here's the man, Hank. This is Harry the thief. And I've got the gun back, too. It's in my hand! Will you help me tie him?"

"Tie?" whispered Raney. "Cut his throat. That'll be the best way to gag the cur."

"Raney, is it you?" whispered Harry. "For God's sake, have mercy on me. I'll lie like a stone, if you tie me. I won't try to raise an alarm. Raney, why should a man like you want to murder me?"

"It ain't murder," said Raney, in the same whisper. "It's more like sticking of pigs when the slaughter time comes. Here, friend," he added aside to the Cheyenne and in that tongue. "Help me tie this one!"

"A Cheyenne!" breathed Harry the thief. "And the kid together with him. I'm gunna turn religious. I'm gunna get religion. There's too many queer things happen in this dog-gone world."

And then the gag closed his sacrilegious mouth and the hard binding cords of rawhide were whipped rapidly home, fastening the man hand and foot. They left him lying like a log on the ground.

"Now?" said Raney to the chief. "Here's our best

chance. There's only two guards in the lodge and no visitors. We'll never have a more likely chance than this. How'll we start it?"

"What does it matter!" murmured the chief, half panting with savage expectation and pleasure. "The magic of the Striking Eagle makes all easy for us. But we will cut the tethers of the horses as we go. Then at the entrance to the lodge you will call, and when one of the guards comes, you will speak to him, while the Eagle and I pass inside the tepee. I shall attack the second guard. The Eagle will set free my son. And while we are doing this inside the lodge, you can strike down the other guard outside. Is that well?"

"Well enough," said Raney. "Come on then."

But he himself paused. He touched the shoulder of the boy, and then took his hand in a good, hard grasp.

"The meanness is rubbed out of me, son," said he. "What was wrong with me, I dunno. But you're a man. You've done your job. You've caught your thief. It staggers me, but I've seen the thing done, and maybe there's magic in the air after all!"

"Oh, Hank," said the boy. "I've been pretty miserable. But I've got my father's gun in my hand now. And that means that we're going to win through with Hawk-that-rises. I feel it in my bones. You and me together, Hank— we've got to win!"

"Aye," said the big man. "We've got to and we will!"

They rounded to the front of the lodge. As they went, stealthily they cut the tethering thongs of the horses. One of the half wild beasts reared straight up. A passer-by loudly called out. But the horse settled down again, and no alarm was given.

They stood before the entrance flap, and Raney gave the summons. The guard, however, shook his head.

"If you wish to speak to me, come inside."

"Not before others, friend," said Raney.

"Then wait till to-morrow. I cannot leave the tepee!" said the guard.

41 · UPSET

THE simple plan of attack was instantly changed by this refusal. But Raney replied: "Very well. I'll speak to you now, inside the lodge. This is on your own head!"

The guard stepped back, Raney strode in after him and loudly exclaimed: "You are Gray Antelope, the son of—"

What Gray Antelope was the son of, Johnnie could not tell. For his own part, he had pressed in rapidly, at the heels of Raney, and the Cheyenne chief was immediately behind him, when the first guard, catching sight of the face of the white man, only partly enveloped by the buffalo robe, raised a shout which died in the midst of the cry. It went out in the sound of a crushing, sickening blow, followed by the fall of a heavy body.

The skull of the first Pawnee guard had been shattered, doubtless, by the stroke. But Johnnie Tanner did not pause to look at what had taken place.

Instead, the instant he was inside the lodge entrance-flap, he bounded to the place where the prisoner sat, his knife in his hand, and two quick slashes made Hawk-that-rises a free man!

At the same time, Johnnie placed the knife in his hands and gave his arm a jerk that helped him to his feet.

He whirled, pulling out the revolver of his father, and found that the entire scene about him was, to him, one of utmost horror and dread.

Both of the young Pawnee guards had seemed to him brawny, powerful fellows when he glimpsed them through the rent at the back of the lodge. But the second man was more than merely strong. He was brave and swift as a panther.

He saw his fellow fall, head beaten in by a powerful stroke from the war club which was dangling in his hand. The same instant, the young Pawnee sprang forward. Before him was Raney, who had felled the first guard and not yet turned after the stroke. Just behind Raney, rushing forward, came the great Cheyenne war chief, Broken Knife. And the Pawnee, pulling out his double-barreled pistol, snapped down both the hammers. And they both failed!

He did not hesitate. He swung the long-barreled weapon like a club and felled Raney with the force of his stroke. Broken Knife, leaping in at that very moment, collided with the falling, senseless body of Raney and toppled headlong.

All in a trice, the attacking party had lost its victorious odds. Against the Pawnee, who had scooped up Raney's own pistol, there remained only two half-grown boys. And the yell of the warrior would soon bring a host about him.

In the hands of the Cheyenne lad there was only the hunting knife. But his blood was pure and true in the great crisis. Instead of holding back, he went straight in, like a tiger. Swiftly he ran, crouching low, and the Pawnee swung the aim of his gun steadily toward the young fighter.

But Johnnie Tanner was the real danger.

He had been half staggered, when he saw the confusion that had befallen his friends. But the revolver was now in his hands. He raised it. He saw down the sights the heaving, glistening breast of the big young Pawnee, and he unflinchingly pulled the trigger.

The young warrior toppled backward, dead or dying. At the same instant, Broken Knife lurched upward from the floor of the lodge, furious for the fight. Then he saw his son freed before his eyes, and even in the midst of the confusion, Johnnie Tanner watched the two confront one another for one split part of a second of blinding love and devotion.

Fools could call the Indians barbarians, after that moment, but never Johnnie Tanner. He had seen too much in that broken breathing space.

"My friend, my friend who has fallen. He is not dead!" cried Johnnie in a gasp, as he dropped to his knees beside poor Hank Raney.

"Bring him out, my son; bring him out while I clear the way. The Pawnee dogs are here. I make the way, and you follow!"

The yell of the second guard had gathered a number of Pawnees, in fact, in front of the tepee, and as the two youngsters leaned and picked up the bulk of Raney, Broken Knife cast a blanket over him and stepping through

213

the entrance flap, he shouted to the bewildered and suspicious braves outside:

"Horse! Horse! They have stolen Hawk-that-rises! The Cheyenne demons have carried him away. Treason! Treason! To horse and follow!"

A screech answered that shout, a screech from many throats. They did not pause to consider that the words had been spoken in an accent very unlike that of a true Pawnee. Perhaps they attributed the difference to the emotion of the man who shouted.

But instantly, as they yelled out their rage and hate, they scattered to get the horses and to pursue the enemy.

In the same moment, the boys got the hurt man through the entrance. And Raney, groaning, straightened, struggled, slipped from their hands and stood erect.

"What's happening? Why're we marching in the middle of the night?" he asked, half out of his head.

"Hank!" whispered Johnnie Tanner. "The Pawnees!"

That word cleared the brain of the hurt man.

A woman was before them, shouting something, and then her shout turned into a frightful scream: "Cheyennes! Cheyennes! They are here!"

The chief, Broken Knife, was already on the back of a horse, and his newly liberated son followed, with a leap like the spring of a wildcat. Raney followed. Johnnie Tanner was last of all and, last of all, he galloped the wild mustang through the Indian camp at the heels of his friends.

It was like the writhing of a supple, powerful snake, so strong and quick were the movements of the rounded barrel of the horse, so wild and uncontrolled were its leapings. But he had this advantage: behind him the pursuit was not yet organized and, before him, the other three riders were cleaving a way, scattering the throng that rushed out of lodges to stare and wonder at the alarm of galloping horses. They leaped out, expecting horse thieves, and they found the galloping enemy right upon them. Several men the lad saw topple backward, as though struck down by amazement.

One he saw lift a war bow, which he had brought from his lodge with the arrow ready on the string. The ready revolver of Johnnie Tanner dropped him writhing to the ground. He was hurt, but not dead. The bullet had flown too low for that.

He looked back as they reached the outer verge of the camp. Behind him, he could see, in the dim, uncertain light of the lodge fires, many warriors mounting their horses, women and children who were throwing up their arms into the air, dogs leaping, and on his ear was a tumultuous howling that screeched and died off as the racing horses broke out from the last rim of the camp and drove into the outer dark.

Where were the guards who rode on watch?

Ah, there they were, good riders coming in from either side—men who flattened themselves along the necks of their horses; but Raney fired, and the first rider swerved his horse to the side and fled, apparently badly hurt. And Broken Knife fired, and the second man went down, horse and rider spinning head over heels.

The woods loomed before them. The underbrush crackled as they burst through it. Down they leaped. And into the saddles of the waiting three horses they bounded.

Only young Hawk-that-rises remained on the bare back of the Pawnee mustang he was bestriding.

What difference was that to him? He was at home.

So off they went, racing, and behind them they heard the pattering and drumming of hundreds of hoofs.

A hundred yards is not much by the daylight. But a hundred yards is much at night in rolling ground, when the flying goal disappears, and the sounds of the pursued come dimly back, from one point or from another, seeming now to be in front and now to be on one side, now another.

In half an hour of frantic riding, the four found themselves drawn away from the noises of whooping, the sounds of galloping. Broken Knife drew down to a dogtrot, and the others followed his example.

First one and then another took the lead, the others streaming out behind in single file, and so they went on, hour after weary hour, until the very soul of the boy ached with weariness.

Surely they must stop. They could not go on forever. There were ten thousand words that must pass between the father and his son.

But no. They held on their way.

Water was reached about midnight. They made a brief halt to water the stock. But no words were exchanged even here. A little later, they picked up the hobbled stock which they had left behind that afternoon, and the gray mustang whinnied joyously when it scented its master.

Then on and on they went, and the stars grew dim, and the morning came gray and still around the wide girdle of the world.

They were safe, but they were making doubly sure.

42 · THE LOST PEARL

ON the back of the bay stallion, Johnnie Tanner was nodding, swaying first to this side and then to that, half asleep as he rode, shivering with misery and exhaustion. But the others went on with straight backs, unwearying.

And the Cheyenne boy?

His long imprisonment did not seem to have softened his thews and sinews. He was tough and hardy as either of the other two. Johnnie Tanner admired and envied the upright grace of the lad and wondered how he could last so well. But then, as the morning light quickened and the sun arose, he remembered a thing which made him half forget his own fatigue.

The Daughter of the Moon! Was it still there in the hollowed handles of the gun?

He turned and slipped back the catch, he turned the gun over—and nothing fell into his hand!

He turned it up again. His eyes were dim with horror and with fear, but when he looked down into the cavity, there was nothing to shine back at him.

The pearl was gone!

Raney saw his face at that moment.

The big man, at the water course, had washed the blood from his face, and now he showed no sight of the blow which he had received in the Pawnee tent.

He was smiling as he drew up his horse beside the bay stallion which kept on, with a stride, silken-smooth.

"You look upset, son," said he.

"I've lost!" said Johnnie Tanner hoarsely. "I've lost the

thing that I came for all of this distance. Harry the thief, he found what I was after. He found it in the handles of the gun, and I—"

He became silent. Suddenly he could see his father's face, the gray, keen, resistless eyes that went through a man to the soul.

"I'll never be able to go back to him. I'll never be able to go home to my father!" said Johnnie.

"You've lost it, have you?" said Raney. "Well, I don't blame you for not going back. Nobody'd want to return home and have the folks think that he'd been a thief. You better stay out here with the Cheyennes; give 'em hunting luck—they're sure to have it, anyway. Make rain for 'em, too. That's the life for you. As for your old man, why, if he's lost something valuable, he might as well lose his son, too. What's the difference in a son, more or less!"

Johnnie, at that moment, looked before him, and he saw the two Cheyennes riding side by side, their heads straight forward; only now they turned suddenly and looked at one another, and Johnnie saw them smile.

It was enough to fill his eyes with stinging tears.

"I don't care what you say, Hank," said he. "I can't go back. I'm ashamed and afraid to go back!"

"Are you going to the Cheyenne camp again?" asked Hank Raney, curtly.

"Why, of course!" He looked at Raney with wonder. "Where else should I go?"

"Home!" said Raney.

He added, severely: "Oh, I've seen you looking at the girl, at the Blackbird, like a sick puppy at the moon. I've seen you about to break out howling to her. If you go back and face her again, with all her pretty looks and ways, how long'll you keep yourself from marryin'? You said once that you was ten or fifteen years from marryin'. Rightly, so you should be. But how d'you feel about it now? You been among the Injuns. You're a Cheyenne brave, now. D'you figger that you wouldn't take on the Cheyenne way of marryin' young?"

Johnnie Tanner looked before him, aghast. And his heart ached in his breast.

He could not answer.

And Raney went on: "Well, it's a good life enough. You marry your squaw. She does the work. You lay around and work at magic, and the tribe kowtows to you. That's a pretty good life. You eat boiled buffalo meat. You wear beaded deerskins. After a while you have some kids, half-breeds. Some of the half-breed kids are kind of fetching, my way of thinkin'. Yeah, you better ride on to the Cheyenne camp and fix yourself for life with 'em. You'll be chief. You'll be the grand chief and medicine man of the tribe one of these days!"

Now, as the other spoke, Johnnie Tanner saw the truth rise up and look him in the face. Bitterly he recognized the facts. And the call of his race, the inevitable call of blood, sounded a trumpet in his ear. It was hard. It was bitterly hard to do, but he saw his duty with a stern and calm recognition.

In that moment, he became a man. All the dangers and the troubles through which he had passed had not done so much to him. The iron went into his soul, and through it.

So he turned to Hank Raney.

"Thanks," said he, simply. "You've shown me what I've got to do, and I'm going home!"

Raney nodded, but said not a word in answer.

A little later, they camped. The others squatted and chewed their dried meat. But Johnnie Tanner, rolled in one turn of his blanket, was instantly asleep, groaning his weariness at every breath as soon as he was unconscious.

When he wakened, the sun had traveled across a great arch of the sky and was westering halfway from the zenith to the far horizon. He sat up with a start. Some of the horses were grazing near by. Big Broken Knife and Raney were out of sight, but the boy, young Hawk-that-rises, was sitting patiently beside the white lad, so placed that his shadow had been keeping the sun from the face of the other. These things Johnnie realized as he rubbed the sleep from his eyes. Then he jumped to his feet.

"Have I been stopping the march?" he asked, excitedly. "I've been weak. The rest of you were able to go on long ago!"

The Indian boy smiled at him. No, he was not merely a boy. Manhood had come to him much earlier than to a white youngster, and the deeds he had done on the trail, his dangerous captivity, had matured him. There was gravity on his brow, gentleness in his eyes.

"Do you think that we wish to hurry on," said he, "when we have you with us? Would not the spirits tell you, if danger were coming?"

"Ah," said Johnnie, gloomily, "have they been telling you, too, that I have a great medicine?"

"Say nothing of it, brother," said the Indian. "I ask no questions. You have taken the life of the treacherous man who captured me. You have given me my own life, afterward. Why should I wish to ask you foolish questions? I have waited here to offer you what I can offer. My blood, and my brothership!"

Johnnie Tanner stared. He did not understand. Then, like a flash of light, he remembered what he had read, somewhere, of the ceremonial of the blood-brotherhood.

The other went on: "There are two trails before you, Striking Eagle. A man already waits for you on each one. There to the north and east is the way to friend who brought you to us. There to the south my father is waiting. Each of them knows that to-day you choose your people. They have agreed that they will not persuade. Which trail do you take?"

Johnnie Tanner could hardly answer for a moment. And then, again, the gray, keen, piercing eyes of his father seemed to pierce his soul. He lifted his hand and pointed to the north and east.

It seemed to him that Hawk-that-rises bowed a little before him in submission; it was merely the falling head of a disappointed man. But the Indian lad made no argument.

He only said: "Life is long, and the years take us into strange valleys. You may come to us again?"

The voice of Johnnie Tanner broke out from his very heart. "I'll come again," he said. "If I live, I swear that I'll come again!"

"Then," said the Cheyenne boy, "if it is pleasing to you, let me take back your token to my people to keep them from mourning. Let us change blood: Then, some other day, you will feel the prairie fever and the call of the Cheyennes, and when you return to us you find a brother waiting, and the door of his lodge is open!"

"Let it be as you will," said Johnnie. And he waited.

But his answer flushed the other with joy. Instantly he acted. He drew the knife from his girdle. He held it toward the earth, toward the four corners of the sky, toward the golden flaming sun.

"Under-earth Spirits," he said solemnly, "Sky People, Father Sun, hear us, give us your blessing!"

Then with a bold stroke he slashed open his forearm, so that the blood spurted. He took the hand of Johnnie Tanner, and the latter set his teeth, but the cut he received was hardly more than a scratch. Then Hawk-that-rises placed the two wounds carefully together. Blood dripped down from his finger tips to the ground and splashed the green of the grass with red, as the young Cheyenne bound the arms together.

And he said, while Johnnie Tanner grew a little dizzy:

"Now all spirits, good and evil, know that my heart gives blood to the body of Striking Eagle, and the heart of Striking Eagle gives blood to mine. We are united; we are one, as two branches that spring from a single tree. Half of my spirit I give to him; half of his spirit he gives to me!"

He unbound the arms; still his wound bled a little as he grasped the hand of Johnnie Tanner, and the blood ran down and covered their grasping fingers.

"Now you will come back, surely," said Hawk-that-rises. "The Cheyennes wait for you. They offer sacrifices to bring you back. You will not forget. My blood will speak inside you for all of our people."

They said no more.. They merely smiled on one another and then, almost as though ashamed of the emotion they had shown, they became busy in preparing for the white boy's departure. His bay stallion was saddled. His other horses were put on the lead. He mounted.

He said to Hawk-that-rises: "What is mine in the lodge of your father is yours. My horses that run with his herd are your horses. Farewell, brother!"

"Farewell, brother!" said the Cheyenne.

But, for all of his courage, his voice trembled. And the stinging in his own eyes made Johnnie Tanner swing his horse about and ride desperately, blindly, toward the northeast, where Raney waited for him in the rich green of the prairie.

43 · GOING HOME

THEY came on their first tidings of importance at Fort Leavenworth—strange and unexpected tidings, as they stood in the compound and listened to the competitive bidding for their horses. Only the bright bay stallion and Midnight were not offered under the hammer. And at this time a grizzled trader, lounging near them, said: "Strangers, if that coat of tan was peeled off the young feller's face, a mite, I'd write him down for the lad that the man in Liberty's askin' so many questions about, and nobody to give him much satisfaction."

"What man?" asked Johnnie Tanner, suddenly.

"Why, a feller all the ways from New York, by his tellin' of it. A feller that had a son up and run away from him, and he's trailed him along a mighty misty trail all this ways, and here the trail plumb goes out."

They got to Liberty as fast as horses would carry them; they galloped into that town as though on a charge against an enemy, and five minutes later, in the hotel, Johnnie Tanner was standing before his father while Hank Raney lounged in the near distance.

And those bright, gray-green eyes probed the very soul of the boy.

"What made you do it, Johnnie?"

"The gun was stolen. I started. It was kind of half accident that I kept on the way—and that my way was the way the thief took. It was almost—it was almost spooky, in a way! And then—I can't tell you everything. But here's the gun. I found the thief, and I found the gun, but—"

He drew himself upright. His eyes started a little.

"You may think that I'm telling you long lies, that I sold the pearl, and gambled the money, or did something like that. But the truth is that the thief had found the catch. The hole was empty."

He paused, miserably.

There was no change whatsoever in the keen, probing expression of his father.

221

"Why didn't you turn the thug over to the authorities, then, Johnnie?" asked the quiet voice of his father. .

"Because I found him in a Pawnee camp, and our own scalps would have been mighty welcome to the Pawnees, I can tell you. Hank Raney was there with me and—"

"Johnnie," said the father, "we're going to need a lot of time to talk this over, man to man. And that's what it will be. I saw you a boy, the last time we met. You've become a man since then.

"But now about the pearl. Do you really think that I would leave such a thing as the Daughter of the Moon lying in a gun in an unguarded room? No, no, Johnnie! There were other men who knew that hiding place, that hollow in the handles of the weapon. The reason that I went downtown that morning was to give the pearl to a reputable jeweler, and the price he paid for it was thirty per cent more than my highest hopes. What I left in the gun was an imitation, a bad imitation, the worst kind of a thing, my poor lad, and that trick of mine, which was intended to catch a crook, caught you, poor Johnnie!"

Then he said, slowly: "It's been a hard time for your poor Aunt Maggie. She's been half distracted. It hasn't been an easy time for me, either. And as for you, well, I think that you've been condensing years into days. Now go up and wash and come down to eat with me. I want to talk with your friend, Raney."

Thunderbolts of happiness had fallen upon the head of Johnnie Tanner. But still, as he went up to wash himself for the meal, his wits were spinning. If only he had done the cautious, cowardly thing, it would have been very well with him. No one could have blamed him greatly, except for an act of childish folly. The mere loss of a revolver, certainly, would not have been sufficient to condemn him.

But he, rushing headlong forward, had fallen, as from the height of a cliff, into the wildest of dreams. And was he entirely glad that he had wakened from it? There was his father, there would be Aunt Maggie. But did they entirely compensate for the wild red men who had loved and believed in him?

He came downstairs to find his father in the closest talk with Hank Raney, and still, during the dinner, the older men talked, and the boy was left to his dreams, half sad and half delightful.

Two days later they started down the river on the long journey home. The horses went with them. And Hank Raney had been persuaded to make the journey clear to the city of New York. "What could I do there?" he asked,

"I don't know what," said the elder Tanner. "But there's always a place for a man, Raney!"

So they stood on the deck of the ship, saw the mooring lines cast off, heard the shouting of the crew, the barking of rapid orders, when down to the edge of the dock rode a strange figure on a piebald horse, liberally streaked with Indian paint, the man in the saddle wearing the feathered headdress of an important Cheyenne chief.

He faced Johnnie Tanner. He raised his war lance above his head in a grasp so strong that the long spear trembled from end to end, and there he remained while the river boat slid off down the stream.

Said one of the passengers: "Who's that Cheyenne?"

"That's old Red Feather," said another, "and he's an uncle of that famous fellow, Broken Knife."

"But who's he saluting on the boat?" asked the first speaker.

"I dunno," said the second man. "It looks like he was praying to the sun god!"

The older Tanner looked at Raney, and both of them at the boy, but Johnnie Tanner did not heed their glances. He was looking back up the river at the noble figure of the Indian, and unforgettable sorrow was in his eyes.